ALLEN PARK PUBLIC LIBRARY #4
8100 Allen Road
Allen Park, MI 48101-1708
313-381-2425

D1398506

DISCARD

EMILY'S CHANCE

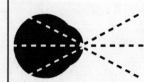

This Large Print Book carries the
Seal of Approval of N.A.V.H.

THE CALLAHANS OF TEXAS, BOOK 2

EMILY'S CHANCE

SHARON GILLENWATER

THORNDIKE PRESS
A part of Gale, Cengage Learning

GALE
CENGAGE Learning™

Detroit • New York • San Francisco • New Haven, Conn • Waterville, Maine • London

GALE
CENGAGE Learning™

© 2010 by Sharon Gillenwater.
Thorndike Press, a part of Gale, Cengage Learning.

ALL RIGHTS RESERVED
This book is a work of fiction. Names, characters, places, and incidents are the product of the author's imagination or are used fictitiously. Any resemblance to actual events, locales, or persons, living or dead, is coincidental.

Thorndike Press® Large Print Christian Romance.
The text of this Large Print edition is unabridged.
Other aspects of the book may vary from the original edition.
Set in 16 pt. Plantin.

LIBRARY OF CONGRESS CATALOGING-IN-PUBLICATION DATA

Gillenwater, Sharon.
  Emily's chance / by Sharon Gillenwater.
    p. cm. — (Thorndike Press large print Christian romance)
  (The Callahans of Texas ; bk. 2)
  ISBN-13: 978-1-4104-3536-1 (hardcover)
  ISBN-10: 1-4104-3536-9 (hardcover)
  1. Large type books. I. Title.
PS3557.I3758E65 2011
813'.54—dc22   2010051770

Published in 2011 by arrangement with Revell Books, a division of Baker Publishing Group.

Printed in the United States of America
1 2 3 4 5 6 7 15 14 13 12 11

ALLEN PARK PUBLIC LIBRARY #4
8100 Allen Road
Allen Park, MI 48101-1708
313-381-2425

To our precious granddaughter, Kylie Elizabeth Gillenwater. May the Lord hold you close to his heart and always keep you in his care.

To our first grand-daughter, Kyla Elizabeth Ollsdale. May the Lord hold you close to his heart and always keep you in his care.

"For I know the plans I have for you," declares the LORD, "plans to prosper you and not to harm you, plans to give you hope and a future. Then you will call upon me and come and pray to me, and I will listen to you. You will seek me and find me when you seek me with all your heart."

Jeremiah 29:11–13 NIV

1

Man meets woman. Man loves woman. Man marries woman.

Chance Callahan looked down at the three cartoon scenes he'd drawn on some scratch paper a few days earlier. A scruffy cowboy and pretty lady running from an old building, a raging fire behind them. Pretty lady smiles at tired, dirty cowboy, and his heart pounds out of his chest, stars in his eyes. Beautiful bride and love-struck groom standing before the preacher.

If only it were that simple.

It was only the second of February, and he already had spring fever.

Shaking his head, he turned his attention back to the notes he'd made that afternoon while he and the insurance claims adjuster inspected the old museum. As a building contractor, Chance had figured out before the man arrived that the structure couldn't be saved.

Which meant the Callahan Crossing Historical Society meeting tonight was going to be about as cheerful as a coroner's inquest. He wished he could tell them — and his pretty lady — that the building could be repaired at a reasonable expense. But it couldn't. It had suffered too much damage from the fire that had ravaged their small town a week earlier.

The building was almost a hundred years old, and most of it had been affected in some way by the fire. The whole thing would have to be brought up to current fire and health codes. It would cost far more than what the insurance would cover.

In many ways, worrying about a museum when a third of the town had been destroyed seemed just plain wrong. So many families had lost everything; some both their homes and businesses. Ranchers and farmers had lost livestock, pastures, and miles of fencing.

The only blessing was that no one had been killed or seriously injured. Though badly shaken by the experience, folks would pick up and get on with their lives. Most planned to stay in Callahan Crossing. But a few had no way — or no heart — to rebuild and had already moved away.

His mom felt that opening the museum

again after a decade-long closure would lift folks' spirits. She thought it might even bring in a little money from tourism and give the town a boost. Particularly if it was done right this time, with good displays and organization instead of a bunch of odds and ends thrown together in a jumble.

He didn't see how that little ol' museum could do much for the town, but setting it up would keep Emily Rose Denny around for a while. And that was something he wanted. Badly.

Satisfied that he'd included everything in the report, he clicked the print icon on the computer screen and waited as the laser printer zipped out thirty copies. He didn't know how many people would be at the meeting tonight, but he believed in being prepared.

He couldn't think of any suitable options for the museum right off the top of his head, though surely there must be some. He owned a building downtown that he'd been fixing up, but it was four times the size of the one they'd planned on using. His mom had been concerned because they'd barely had enough items to put in the old one. They had less after the fire. Even if he offered to donate his building, it wouldn't be suitable. Two big rooms with a handful of odds and ends would look dumb. And it sure wouldn't draw tourists.

For now, Emily was busy trying to salvage what she could, but he didn't know how long that would last. Though only part of the building had burned, there was extensive smoke and water damage to the contents. He doubted there was much worth keeping. They might have to abandon the whole project, and she'd skedaddle back home fast as greased lightning.

He'd find a way to stop her from heading back to San Antonio, even if he had to propose marriage to do it. Courting her first would be better, of course, but sometimes a man had to charge out of the chute to win the prize.

And hope he didn't land in the dirt instead.

Leaning his head against the back of the chair, he closed his eyes and pictured the pretty blonde who had been hired to reorganize and redesign the museum.

Chance had first met Emily during the fire. The chief had ordered the Callahans and a few other volunteer firefighters to canvas the town and make sure everyone had evacuated. At that point, it was impossible to control the wind-whipped grass fire that had become a mile-wide inferno. They could only try to save lives.

The smoke had been so thick that he almost didn't see her van outside the museum. When he told her to leave, she promptly ordered him to carry out some boxes she hadn't gotten to. She hadn't been exactly bossy, just determined to save precious local history, old pictures, and historical documents that had been gathering dust for decades. Foolhardy, he supposed. Especially when it wasn't her town's history she was trying to save. But if they hadn't done it, everything would have gone up in flames. That whole section of the museum had been completely destroyed.

He'd sent her to his parents' house at Callahan Ranch, only to see her again late that night with his mom and sister helping at the shelter their church had set up.

At twenty-nine years old, he was ready to settle down. Unfortunately, the eligible females in the area — at least the type he might want for a wife — were few and far between. Over the years, he'd dated almost every single woman in the county who seemed the least bit interesting. And almost as many from the neighboring counties. But he never took anyone out more than a few times. Better to hurt their feelings early than to let them get their hopes up and hurt them worse.

He'd quickly learned that many women were more attracted by the Callahan wealth and name than they were by him. He wanted what his parents had; what his sister, Jenna, and her new husband, Nate, had — a deep and lasting love that would weather the ups and downs, the good and the bad.

He'd never experienced more than a passing fascination with a woman until he met Emily Rose. With her, it had been love at first sight. Well, maybe at second sight, since it was so dark from all the smoke the first time that he hadn't gotten a real good look at her.

When he walked into the church shelter about 1:00 the next morning, he'd been filthy from fighting the fire, exhausted, hungry, and heartbroken by the devastation he'd seen. She glanced up and gave him a smile that almost knocked him over. He looked into her gentle, deep blue eyes and thought, *She's the one.*

He didn't know if the Lord had been speaking to him, or if he'd heard the whisper of his own heart. It didn't much matter. He intended to ride his pony down this trail and see where it led. Lord willin', it wouldn't be off a cliff.

Besides working at the museum, Emily

had spent numerous hours helping at the shelter. She was a total stranger who'd only arrived in town a couple of days before the fire, but she cheerfully served meals and helped distribute donated food and clothing. Both yesterday and today when he'd taken a break from the cleanup efforts and gone to the shelter for lunch, he'd spotted her holding someone's hand, giving another a shoulder to cry on, or praying with people.

Other than when he met the insurance man at the museum, he'd spent the past two days piling up debris and ashes with his bulldozer and loading them into his company dump truck to be hauled away to the new landfill.

He and Emily both had been putting in such long hours that he hadn't had a chance to talk to her alone for more than a few minutes. How was a man supposed to get to know the woman he wanted to marry if they couldn't spend time together without everybody and their uncle listening to the conversation?

"Lord, I sure would appreciate it if you could make a way for Emily to stay here a while. I can't shake the feeling that you sent her here for me, that there's going to be something good between us. But we'll never find out if she hightails it back to San

15

Antonio."

Stacking up the copies of the report, he slipped them into a blue manila folder and set it on top of the big U-shaped oak desk. If he hustled, he could take a shower before walking across the yard to the ranch house for the meeting. Stinking like diesel fumes, soot, and sweat wasn't the way to make a good impression on a woman, particularly a city gal who was probably used to men in expensive suits and smellin' purty from fancy cologne.

Scooping ground coffee into the coffeemaker, Emily spotted Chance through the window as he walked toward the ranch house. She straightened the hem of her light orange sweater and brushed a piece of lint from the matching slacks. Then she silently told herself to quit primping.

He opened the back door, stepped into the kitchen, and flashed her a smile. "Hi, darlin'. Am I late?"

"Right on time." If any other man called her *darlin'*, she'd punch him. Somehow it didn't sound disrespectful coming from Chance; it seemed sweet and sincere.

Slightly over six feet tall, with the physique of a construction worker, the handsome builder and cowboy had an easygoing charm

16

that spoke more of confidence than pride. He was a man comfortable with himself and his place in life. He was also one of the most kindhearted, godly men she had ever met.

A drop of water glistened in his dark brown hair, and she caught a light, refreshing hint of aftershave as he leaned against the cabinet next to her. His bright turquoise shirt emphasized his dark tan. He laid a blue manila folder on the counter. "Did Mom get my message?"

"She didn't mention it." Emily put the coffee scoop back into the can, snapped on the lid, and moved it toward the back of the counter in case they needed to make more later. She removed a package of yellow and green striped paper napkins from a paper grocery sack, then folded it up and laid it on the counter, revealing the answering machine. A red *1* blinked up at her, so she pushed the play button. At the sound of his voice saying, "Hi, Mom," Chance reached over and deleted the message.

"I don't have good news."

Emily flipped the switch on the coffee-maker, turned to face him, and looked up into clear, green eyes filled with concern. Her heartbeat quickened. "How bad is it?"

Before he could answer, his mother swept into the kitchen, wearing her usual Wrangler jeans and cowboy boots with a light green silk blouse, strand of pearls, and pearl earrings. Her strawberry blonde hair curled softly about her face. Sue Callahan smiled when she saw her youngest son. "Oh, good. You made it." She stopped in front of him and studied his face. "What's wrong?" she asked quietly.

"There was a lot more damage than we first thought." He spoke softly, so no one in the next room would overhear them. "The insurance company only covers what it costs to restore the building to the way it was before the fire. It won't pay for bringing it up to code. And that's going to cost a lot."

He tapped his finger on the folder. "I wrote up a detailed report and made copies for everybody."

Frowning, Sue opened the refrigerator and removed a pint of half-and-half, pouring it into a yellow pottery pitcher. She set it beside the matching sugar bowl and containers of French vanilla and hickory nut powdered creamers near the coffeemaker. "Can we use the insurance money to buy another building?"

"You should be able to since you didn't have a mortgage. Though you may need to use some of the money to demolish the current building. It's going to be an eyesore."

18

He glanced at Emily, then focused on his mom again. "I'm sorry to spring this on you right before the meeting. I left you a message, but you hadn't checked the answering machine."

"We were late getting home from town, and I didn't think to look at it. Ramona left early to get her hair fixed, so she missed your call. I doubt I'd have solved the problem even if I'd known about it sooner." Sue took a deep breath, releasing it slowly. "We'll just have to pray about this. At least some of us will. If we're supposed to do this thing, God will provide a way."

She looked at Chance again and tipped her head. "You look beat."

"I am. But I'll be fine after a good night's sleep." He glanced at the two Texas sheet cakes sitting on the counter. "And if I get some of that cake."

"You're putting in too many long hours. You should have taken a few more days to rest between fighting the fire and starting on the cleanup."

"The sooner we get done, the quicker folks can start rebuilding. I'm only pitching in for a little while. Yesterday and today, the only ones working were the county road crews and me and my driver. But the state is sending in several teams with bulldozers and trucks. They're supposed to arrive tomorrow. Work crews from the prisons at Colorado City and Abilene will come in daily to remove dead trees and pick up what the bulldozers can't.

"Despite all the help, with a hundred houses burned, counting those two in the country, plus the gin and the businesses we lost, it's going to take months to clear all the debris."

"After you finish with that, you'll be working just as hard helping people rebuild. You're pushing yourself too much, son."

"I'll be busy, but it will be fun and not nearly as tiring. I've already gotten several calls from folks who had insurance. I have a meeting scheduled in the morning with one family. I anticipate more soon, so I won't be running full throttle on the cleanup."

Sue shook her head and looked at Emily. "I'm glad my boys have a good work ethic, but sometimes they take it a little too far. Like their father." She focused on her son again. "I'll move you up to the beginning of the meeting so you can go home and get some sleep."

"Thanks, Mom. I appreciate it." Chance waited until his mother walked out of the room, then turned to Emily. He rested his hands lightly on her shoulders. "Don't start

20

packing your suitcase yet. We'll think of something to get this project off the ground."

"Only if you can work miracles. I've seen the Historical Society's budget and treasurer's report. They don't have any money to add to what they'll get from the insurance."

"Have faith," he said softly. "I don't think God brought you here just to make you go back home again so fast."

"I hope you're right." When he dropped his hands to his sides, she was surprised by a sudden intense feeling of loss. A hug would be nice right about then. But she wasn't about to tell him that.

2

Her thoughts spinning, Emily followed Sue into the living room and sat down on one of the wooden folding chairs they'd set up for the meeting. She was going to lose her job. It was certain now, not merely the possibility she'd considered for several days. Despite Chance's optimism, Emily didn't see how the Historical Society could continue with their plans to reopen the museum.

She didn't need the job or the money. Her grandfather had provided a large trust fund that enabled her to live quite comfortably. Even lavishly if she wished. Theoretically, she could set up the Callahan Crossing Museum for free, but that wouldn't look as good on her resume. Internships and volunteer positions already took up too much space in that document. She needed to add to the three other paid positions she'd had organizing and designing small museums.

Emily had known when she chose her

career that competition for positions in large historical museums was stiff. But she was willing to start out as an assistant curator and work her way up the ladder.

Who was she kidding? She'd give her eyeteeth for an assistant curator position in a prestigious big city museum. Unfortunately, usually only the largest museums hired people full-time. The others relied on part-time help or volunteers — with the emphasis on the latter.

Still, the opportunity to reorganize the Callahan Crossing Museum had been a blessing and a challenge she would have enjoyed. She had looked forward to turning it into something the town, and she, could be proud of.

Her parents would once again have a grand time pointing out the futility of her chosen profession. They had wanted her to go into medicine so she could join her father in his plastic surgery clinic, until they had finally realized science wasn't her strength. Business or political science had been their preferred options.

When she had chosen a bachelor's degree in history, they'd grumbled, then decided that if she went on to earn her PhD, she could land a prestigious job at a university or perhaps with the government.

After learning she intended to earn a double master's in history and museum science, her mother had investigated the opportunities in the field and had thrown a fit. It would take Emily forever to achieve what they considered an acceptable level of success — head curator or director of a major museum where she would earn at least eighty thousand dollars a year. There simply weren't that many positions available.

Emily was determined to prove them wrong, though she concluded it might be a slower process than she liked.

Glancing around the living room of Dub and Sue Callahan's large ranch house, she paused to watch Chance. He had taken a seat in a big red leather chair, listening as Ed White, who was in his sixties, spun a yarn about hunting javelina in South Texas. Chance smiled at appropriate moments and appeared relaxed.

But she knew differently. He cared for these people, and he hated to disappoint them. He hated to disappoint her, which was amazing. There hadn't been many people in her life who'd worried about her feelings.

Chance shifted in the chair, looking in her direction. His expression softened minutely, warmth filling his eyes when he met her gaze. His mom walked past him to join a couple of people on one of the two big red leather sofas. Though he nodded as Ed wrapped up his story, he suddenly seemed a bit uneasy.

She was surprised by how well she could read his expressions. But she liked it. She smiled, trying to encourage him, hoping to lessen his concern about both the museum and her. He responded with a whisper of a smile.

And Emily got a big lump in her throat. She was going to miss him. Not that they'd seen each other much, except in the evenings when he ate supper with his parents and visited with them and her for a while.

Sue was right. He looked tired, and no wonder. During the fire, he'd started building the fire line with his bulldozer before the Texas Forest Service dozers arrived. And he'd kept at it even when those drivers switched out hours later.

He'd been totally exhausted when he'd come to the shelter with his father and brother early Wednesday morning to eat and rest. They'd gone back to the fire a few hours later and finally called it a day when fresh teams of firefighters came in that afternoon.

But he'd been back out there Thursday

and Friday to assist with hot spots. He'd taken off Saturday for his sister's wedding and Sunday to rest, but he'd hit it hard Monday morning. Dealing with such destruction — especially when he probably knew most of those affected — had to take a toll.

From the first time they met, it had been plain that he was a caring man. During the fire, when he learned she didn't have any place to go, he'd sent her out to his parents' house. She'd been there ever since.

The original arrangement with the Historical Society had been for her to stay in Maybelle Huff's cute little rental house. But it hadn't survived the blaze. Thankfully, Emily had been able to throw her own things into her van before she'd raced to the museum. So she hadn't lost any of her belongings.

As Sue tried to get folks' attention and start the meeting, memories of the fire flashed through Emily's mind. In hindsight, she supposed she'd bordered on lunacy to stay in town and save things from the museum. But the old city council minutes and pictures that told the town's history from the late 1800s were irreplaceable. She didn't regret her actions one bit. She just wished she could see the project through.

26

"All right, y'all, we need to get this meeting going. Ramona made chocolate cake for us, and the quicker we get finished, the sooner we can eat it." The group quieted down. "Maybelle, are you ready to take notes?"

"Yes. I already passed out the copies of the minutes from the last meeting."

"Good. We're going to skip reading them out loud for now." Sue glanced around the room at the twenty people present. Not everyone in the Historical Society had come out to the ranch. Several were dealing with personal losses, and the museum was the last thing on their minds. "I'll give y'all a chance to bring up questions in a little while. But first, Chance has a report on the condition of the building."

Ed cleared his throat. "According to the rules, we need to read the minutes."

"I think we can bend the rules a little this evening." Sue looked at Chance.

Ed frowned. "You aren't following the proper procedure. We need to hear the treasurer's report."

"It's right there in front of you, along with the minutes. Read them silently if you think you have to do it right now."

Chance glanced at Emily and rolled his eyes. She smiled back, though she was worried that the meeting might get out of hand even before Chance gave his report. That it would afterward was a given.

"When I was head of this society, we followed Robert's Rules of Order." Ed tapped his finger on the minutes to emphasize his point.

"And it was a big pain sometimes." Jim Johnson grinned at Ed. "Bridle your tongue, you grumpy ol' galoot. We got more important things to cuss and discuss. Let Chance speak his piece."

"Thank you, Jim." Sue smiled sweetly at the middle-aged farmer and pointedly ignored Ed's scowl. "Chance, go ahead."

"Yes, ma'am." He sat up a bit straighter and scanned the group. "I met the insurance claims adjuster at the museum this afternoon, and we went through the building thoroughly. There is extensive damage in addition to the part that actually burned. As I expect you know, the windows blew out from the heat. We checked several places and found the wiring melted inside the walls, including at the opposite end from the part that burned. So all of the wiring will have to be replaced. There is also a lot of water damage to the Sheetrock. What wasn't ruined by the water was affected by the heat, so even that Sheetrock will have to be replaced since it won't be as fire resistant."

"The insurance will pay for all of that," Ed muttered with a bored expression.

"It will to a certain extent."

"Certain extent, hogwash," Ed blustered. "We have replacement coverage. Have had ever since we bought the building."

"Yes, sir, you do. But replacement coverage means the insurance will only pay to restore the building to its condition before the fire. It won't cover bringing it up to current fire and building codes. With it being so old, that will mean a great deal of additional expense — higher grade wiring, better roofing, a sprinkler system, insulation, more expensive windows, improved plumbing, floor, et cetera. There are also some major structural problems with the foundation, roof, and one wall that weren't caused by the fire and won't be covered by insurance."

"What kind of problems?" Jim asked.

"One side of the building has sunk lower than the rest of it. I think the foundation can be raised, but it's not easy and won't be cheap. The top of the wall has broken away from the roof and is leaning outward. There is a four-inch crack between the roof and the wall that runs almost the length of the building."

"Oh, my! Is it about to fall down?" Sue glanced at Emily. "Emily has been working in there all week."

"I think it's safe enough to get the rest of the things out of there as long as we do it quickly."

"I didn't see a crack." Emily squirmed a little as almost everyone glanced in her direction. "I would have told you about it if I had."

"With all the smoke that's been hanging in the air, I'm not surprised. Since the wind finally cleared it out this afternoon, the sunshine coming in at the back of the building warned us of the trouble before we even checked back there."

"What's the bottom line, Chance?" Ed asked quietly. His expression reflected everyone else's concern.

"A quick preliminary estimate of materials puts the repairs above what the insurance will pay at a minimum of thirty thousand dollars." Several of the members gasped. "A ballpark range on the labor cost is another twenty-five to fifty thousand, depending on how much volunteers can do." Chance handed Ed the reports that he'd printed off, listing the damages and the estimated cost of repairs. The older man took a copy and gave the stack to the person next to him. The only sound in the stunned silence was the shuffling of papers as folks passed them around.

Chance waited a few minutes, giving them an opportunity to peruse the information. He'd added the options suggested by the insurance adjuster.

"So the insurance man thinks we should just tear it down and start over?" Maybelle frowned at the sheet of paper before she looked up at Chance.

"He doesn't think the building is worth repairing, and neither do I. You'd definitely be better off with something else, though I don't believe starting from scratch would be the most economical. There must be other suitable vacant buildings in town that you could buy for less than you could build. It might even be better to lease something than go to the expense of buying one. That's something y'all will have to sort out. There is also the possibility the city will want you to demolish the current building, which will take some of your money."

"Not if someone volunteered to do it." Ed's eyes narrowed as he turned toward Chance. "Like you."

"Sorry, I can't. My equipment isn't big enough to handle the job. I might be able to help haul the debris away, but I can't guarantee it. As soon as the insurance and FEMA checks start coming in, I'll be swamped building houses." Chance relaxed against the back of his chair, and the commotion started. So many people began talking at once, Emily didn't know who said what.

"What are we going to do now?"

"We can't fix it, that's for sure."

"Got to tear it down. Can't leave an eyesore like that if we want to attract people to town."

"We might as well give up."

"What are we doing even trying to start the museum now? Maybe we ought to just donate the insurance money to the Fire Victims Fund."

The room fell silent with that comment, and everyone focused on Sue.

She gave them an encouraging smile. "Don't give up yet. I still think opening the museum will benefit the town. We have some wonderful history that a lot of people who live here don't even know about. People benefit from being connected to their past. That's more important than ever now. If people know their heritage, it gives them another link to the town and to each other."

"Somehow it seems wrong to spend so much money — even the insurance money — when so many folks are hurting." Maybelle rested her notepad on her lap. "The little house we lost was a rental and covered by insurance, but we still feel bad about it. I can't imagine how others who lost their homes feel."

Several people murmured their agreement.

Emily knew she had to speak up. She'd wrestled all day with whether or not to say anything because she didn't want to give up on the museum. But these people needed to know what they were up against. "We have another problem."

That got everyone's attention.

"At least half of the museum's contents can't be restored. Most of what can be saved are small things that were in the display cases. There is one buffet that cleaned up okay and a couple of chairs. All the other furniture either blistered from the heat, actually burned, or was ruined by the water."

"But you saved all the documents and pictures, right?" a soft-spoken lady asked. Emily couldn't remember her name. In fact, it was the first time she'd heard the tiny, white-haired woman say anything other

ALLEN PARK PUBLIC LIBRARY

than a greeting.

"Yes, we did. I know some of you have furniture or other things at home that you're willing to donate, but will it be enough to fill a museum?"

"Depends on how big a place we wind up with." Ed lightly scratched his jaw. "Between what we had already and what folks here were willing to donate, we figured we had almost enough for the old building. But we hadn't put out the word yet that we could use donations."

"I have an idea," the quiet, shy lady said.

"Go ahead, Frannie." Sue gave the elderly woman her complete attention, as did the others.

"I think we should look for a building that would hold our museum and also have a meeting room. We might have to partition it off, but throwing up a wall wouldn't be too hard. My Henry did that in a couple places we lived so each of the kids could have a room of their own. There's not a good place in Callahan Crossing for meetings, luncheons, or teas and such. At least not anything beyond church fellowship halls, and sometimes they're hard to reserve."

"The meeting room is a great idea, but it wouldn't be good to have a full kitchen in the same building as the antiques." Emily

hated to squash the idea. "The main problem would be cooking. Even the best vent and exhaust system won't get rid of all the cooking odors, smoke, and grease, which would damage the things on display."

"We'd have to have a special permit for that too." Maybelle chewed on the end of her pencil. "But if we had the food catered so it arrived hot, or only had cold things, we wouldn't need a stove. Just a big refrigerator."

"If that would work for you, then it's a wonderful idea." For the first time all day, Emily felt encouraged, even excited. "You could charge enough rent to cover your expenses and add some money to the Historical Society's treasury. You could be responsible for the food and charge extra, or let others bring it in for their events. I've seen similar things done several places, some with better success than others. It's crucial to have people responsible for the meeting space and the catering who are dependable and organized."

"We could manage that." Sue beamed at Frannie. "It's a terrific idea. We'll have a couple of major things to do first. Ed, would you look for someone to demolish the old building and find out what it will cost?"

Ed nodded and wrote himself a note.

"Now, who wants to be on the committee to look for a new building?"

"I'll be on it," Jim said. "We ought to look into where the Ben Franklin store used to be. That building has been vacant for about three years since the furniture store moved out."

"But it's almost as old as the one we had," another man said. Emily really needed to learn who all these people were if she was going to work with them. She noticed Chance scribbling something on the back of one of the extra reports, his forehead wrinkled thoughtfully.

"Yes, but I think it's in better condition." Jim twisted around to look at the other gentleman. "The last folks who rented it did some remodeling seven years ago before they moved in. It's a shame they couldn't make a go of the business, but we'd benefit from their improvements. It might not cost nearly as much to bring it up to snuff. From what I've seen, good historical museums — at least the ones that have the best ambiance — are in historical buildings."

"Ambiance?" Ed snickered. "Tryin' to sound all citified on us, Jim?"

"Naw, I just like the word." Jim grinned and crossed one leg over his other knee. "Atmosphere and mood say the same thing but don't sound as good."

"It's true that a museum in a historic building does better, especially in smaller towns." Emily sensed Chance's gaze and glanced at him. His small-dog-with-a-big-bone grin jumbled her thoughts for a second. "Uh . . ." She looked back at Jim. "It helps make visitors feel as if they've stepped back in time. Was the store on Main Street?"

"Yes." Sue nodded. "Frannie, would you like to help Jim check on it?"

"I'd be delighted to."

"Excuse me, Mom." Chance waited until Sue looked at him. He glanced around the room, eventually focusing on Emily. "I bought the old Morse Building a year ago and have been fixing it up in my spare time, restoring what I could but still bringing everything up to code. I finished it the week before the fire. I didn't mention it earlier because it's so much bigger than the one you had that I didn't think you'd be interested. But with your new plan, it might be perfect. It's already basically divided in half by a central brick wall, with a large opening in the wall that connects both sides."

"Isn't that where Hampton's used to be?" Maybelle asked.

"Yes, ma'am. Originally, there were two separate buildings that shared a wall. After

Mr. Hampton bought them, he opened up part of the center wall and used the bricks to build a facade across the false fronts to make it look like one building."

"I loved to go in that store when I was a kid. You remember it, don't you, Frannie?" Maybelle smiled at the older woman.

"Of course. It was a grand place, with the women's and girls' clothes on one side and the men's and boys' things on the other side."

"And they had one of those machines that x-rayed your feet," another lady said. "Remember how you'd try on shoes and stick your feet in that X-ray thing? Then you'd look through the viewer and wiggle your toes and see the bones move. It was supposed to help the clerk make sure the shoes fit."

"I reckon they could tell if they were too tight, but we could tell 'em that without all that scientific stuff. It was just a gimmick to get people to buy higher-priced shoes." Ed shook his head. "No tellin' how many of us wound up with damaged feet from the radiation. I only got to look at my feet a couple of times. Finally grew tall enough to look through the viewer and about a year later they were outlawed."

"I never did see mine. I was too little."

Maybelle sighed wistfully. "But Mama would lift me up so I could see my brother's."

Chance caught Emily's gaze, his eyes dancing. What was he up to? "Tell us more about the building, Chance." She smiled at those who had been reminiscing. "For those of us who don't have such fond memories of the store."

He stretched his legs out in front of him. "Each half has one large room that was the display floor and a smaller room at the back used for storage or office space. You could have the museum on one side of the building and the meeting room on the other. I think either of the back rooms would be large enough for a kitchen."

"What about the opening between the rooms? Could you close that off and put in a door or something?" Maybelle asked, her pen poised above her notepad.

"Yes. We could do a single or double door."

"It'll cost a bundle." Ed slanted him a calculating glance. "Unless you give us a real good price."

Chance shrugged lightly. "I'll do better than that. I'll lease it to you for a dollar a year, plus utilities."

Emily's jaw dropped. "What?"

"It's a great old building right downtown. I don't have much hope of selling it or leasing it. Even if I closed up the connecting wall, either side is too big for most businesses that might be interested in Callahan Crossing these days. I bought it and fixed it up for fun and because it was worth saving." He held her gaze. "Can't let the expert slip through our fingers while y'all waste time searching for another building. Might not be able to get her back again."

Emily glanced at his mother to see her reaction to his generous offer. Sue watched them with a speculative glint in her eye. When Chance winked at his mom, a slow smile spread across her face. He turned back to Emily.

"You'll have to check things out." Unexpected tenderness filled his eyes. "But I hope you'll find everything you want and need."

There was nothing unusual in his statement. Looking at the museum to see if it suited their needs was to be expected. But she had the distinct impression he was talking about more than the museum. Much more.

3

The next morning, Chance decided to eat breakfast at his parents' house instead of having a bowl of cereal or nuking a frozen sausage and egg biscuit in the microwave.

As his dad poured syrup on his French toast, he glanced across the table at Chance. "It's been a while since you dropped in this early. Good to have you here." A twinkle lit Dub's dark brown eyes. "I suspect Ramona's cookin' has something to do with it."

"Caught me." Chance nodded and grinned at the Callahans' housekeeper and cook. She and her husband, Ace, who was the gardener and handyman, had come to the ranch when Chance was two. "When I thought about it being Wednesday morning, I could just about taste French toast. Mine isn't nearly as good as Ramona's." Not to mention the crisp bacon fried just right.

"We're on the same wavelength." His brother, Will, two years his senior, had

41

already devoured half the food on his plate. "I could smell bacon cooking clear over at my place."

"You probably could." Ramona smiled fondly at both men from her spot a couple of seats over. Her husband, Ace, sat next to her. Their brown hair was liberally sprinkled with gray these days, but they worked as hard as they ever did. "Getting the smoke and grease out of here with the exhaust fan isn't just to keep from stinking up the house. It works magic to lure you boys over."

Chance tipped his head, looking at his brother. "It's a conspiracy."

"Yep. But I'm not complaining."

"Me either." Chance often ate with them in the evening, unless he was waylaid at a building site. When he worked at the ranch, eating dinner with them at noon was normal. He'd missed that lately. Not only the food — Ramona was a fabulous cook — but even more so, the time with his family.

His sister, Jenna, and her two-year-old son, Zach, used to eat almost every meal with their folks, even after they moved into the guesthouse a while back. But he knew he wouldn't see them much this week. On Saturday, Jenna had married Nate Langley, who worked on the ranch and had been

Chance's best friend since grade school. They hadn't gone on a honeymoon because they wanted to spend time as a family in their own home, just the three of them.

Jenna was also director of the local mission and was trying to get it set up again after it burned. For years it had served as the food bank, along with providing good used clothing and other items to folks in need around Callahan Crossing. Since the fire, their church was the food and clothing distribution center, but that couldn't last forever. They just didn't have the space for a long-term commitment.

He glanced at the clock on the wall: 6:15. For as long as he could remember, the Callahans sat down to breakfast at 6:00, except on Sundays, when they stretched it to 7:00.

"No Emily this morning?" Chance tried to sound casual as he cut through the stack of French toast with his fork.

His mother chuckled. "I think 6:00 is a little too early for her. She usually wanders out around 7:00. We don't mind. She is our guest, after all."

"Is she going to stay here the whole time?" *Please, Lord.*

"Yes. There aren't any available houses anywhere around to rent. And we enjoy having her here. Though she's offered to move

43

into the bunkhouse so she can work late and not disturb us."

Chance didn't like that idea. The building hadn't been used regularly in years.

"Is it in good enough condition for someone to live there?"

"I suppose." His mom took a bite of bacon, her expression thoughtful. "Ramona cleans it thoroughly every six months, so we only had to give it a little spit and polish before Ace set up some worktables for her. Everything works fine, including the appliances, though we'd expect Emily to eat with us. We turned on the icebox and the water heater. Some of the cleaners she's using are flammable, so we took out a couple of electric space heaters in case it gets chilly."

Chance was glad to hear that. If she was using anything flammable, it wasn't safe to even light the pilot lights on the gas heaters. The water heater was electric too.

"The mattresses on the cots are awfully old."

Will reached for the coffee carafe. "They were lumpy when we were kids and camped out in there."

"Well, I certainly wouldn't expect her to sleep on a cot." Sue frowned at her sons. "We'd move one of the guest beds out there."

44

"No." Chance's father shook his head. "I don't want her sleeping in the bunkhouse. It's a good place for her to clean things up, and even organize the pictures if she wants to. But sleeping in the same room with smoky things or where she's been using cleaners isn't a good idea."

"That's exactly what I told her when she suggested it." Sue beamed at her husband. "How come you're so smart?"

Dub raised one eyebrow, his eyes dancing mischievously. "So am I smart because you agree with me or because I figured that out all by myself?"

She shot him a saucy smile. "Both."

Chance glanced at Will and grinned. It was nice to know that couples could still tease and laugh with each other after thirty-four years of marriage. *That's what I want, Lord.*

"She's got a key, so she can come and go whenever she wants. It won't bother us a bit."

"Now that that's settled . . ." Chance's mom leaned toward him across the table, lowering her voice to slightly above a whisper. Her turquoise eyes were filled with curiosity. "So do I detect more than a passing interest in our pretty museum curator?"

He sensed Will stiffen slightly. *Uh-oh.* Was

45

his brother interested in her too? Of course, he was. Along with every single man in the county who'd laid eyes on her. He and Will had only competed for a female's attention once. They'd been in high school, and while they were trying to outdo each other to impress her, another guy slipped in and got the girl. Chance didn't plan to make that mistake again.

"Yes, ma'am, you do." Chance took a sip of coffee, setting the cup down carefully because suddenly his hand didn't feel quite steady. He glanced at his mother before focusing directly on Will. Might as well stake his claim then and there. "She's the one." His brother's dark brown eyes widened, and his mom gasped. Chance smiled wryly. "Though she doesn't know it yet."

Disappointment flickered across Will's face, but amusement quickly replaced it. "You goin' to just blurt it out to her? Or take things slow and easy?"

"No blurtin' unless I have to. But I can't go too slow, either. Not if she'll be heading back to San Ann-tone in two or three months." He turned to his mom. "I'm going to need your help."

"What do you want me to do?" She wiggled with excitement.

"Drag out this museum start-up thing.

46

Not enough so she gets frustrated and leaves, but enough to give me a little more time."

"I'll have to think about how to do that. Anything else?"

"Make her fall in love with me."

His mom got all misty-eyed. "Honey, that's between you and her. The good Lord sets the stage, but it's up to y'all to do your part so the play has a happy ending. I know one thing. Sparks flew between you two last night, and I'm not the only one who saw it."

Chance groaned softly. When he'd left — after two helpings of chocolate cake — most of the group had still been there. "Did anybody say anything?"

"Not to Emily. Not where she could hear them. But a few people commented to me about it, wondering if you two were an item."

Will slapped him on the back. "You might as well make your move pronto. Before noon, everybody in town will have you dating if not walkin' down the aisle."

"No time like the present. Or at least after she gets up." Chance had planned to try to spend some time with her today anyway. "I have a meeting at 10:00. Thought I might show her the building before that if it suits her schedule."

"I'm sure she'll want to see it. She's as excited about it as the rest of us." His mom leaned back and picked up her coffee cup. "I haven't been by there since you were putting in the new heating system."

"I didn't realize it had been that long. I basically have everything finished."

"When do you plan to show it to everybody else? I assume tagging along this morning is out of the question."

"Yes, ma'am, it is. But you set up a time when you can get everyone together who needs to okay it, and I'll meet you there."

"I'll arrange it."

Will scooted back his chair and stood. "Thank you for a great breakfast, Ramona."

"You're welcome. Come again, now that you know the way."

Will chuckled. "Yes, ma'am. Right at dinnertime." He lightly tapped Chance on the shoulder with his fist. "You gonna help me load hay on the truck while you're waiting on Emily?"

"And get all dirty? Nope. I'm going to sit right here, have another cup of coffee, and enjoy my mama's company." Chance picked up the coffee carafe, only to find it empty. "After I get a refill from the kitchen."

He and Will carried their dirty dishes into

the kitchen. Will rinsed his in the sink and put them in the dishwasher. Chance did the same. His brother paused at the back door, his hand on the doorknob. "How do you know she's the one?"

"I just do. When I saw her at the shelter the night of the fire, and she looked up at me, I felt like somebody hit me with a two-by-four. Those feelings have only grown stronger since then. I'm sorry if I'm stompin' on your toes." Chance couldn't resist teasing him a little. "But I did see her first."

"Yeah, I reckon you did. I knew you were interested, but I figured she'd be like all the others. Flash in the pan."

"Not this time," Chance said quietly. "Unless she's already got a boyfriend." He hadn't seriously considered that possibility. She wasn't wearing a ring and hadn't mentioned anyone in particular. "You've probably seen her more than I have since you're here every day at noon. Has she said anything about anybody else?"

"No. Come to think of it, I haven't heard her talk about much of anything personal. She's mentioned her grandmother a few times. Seems like she cares a lot for her. Mom asked about her family once at dinner. She said her father is a plastic surgeon in Dallas, and her mother runs a modeling agency. But that's it. I got the feeling they aren't particularly close. Hope it works out for you." Will turned the doorknob. "Don't rush in so fast that you live to regret it."

"I'm praying a lot. But I'm gettin' real tired of being alone."

"I hear you on that. Hey, maybe she has a sister." Will's expression was so honestly hopeful, Chance didn't even smile at the cliché.

"I'll ask. See you tonight."

Will nodded and walked out the door.

Chance poured a cup of coffee, pausing to contemplate another piece of the cake sitting on the counter. He decided after the syrup on the French toast, cake would be sugar overload. Ramona would probably stash a piece for him to enjoy later if he asked her.

The tap of boot heels on the wooden floor prompted him to turn around as his dad walked into the kitchen.

"Want some more belly wash?" Chance reached for the pot in the coffeemaker.

"No, thanks. Had my fill." His dad rinsed his dirty dishes and slipped them into the dishwasher too. He'd taught his sons early in life to help out in that way. Teaching his boys anything else about the kitchen had fallen to their mother or Ramona.

Chance ate at his own place fairly often because he didn't always get home in time to join them for supper. Sometimes he cooked, but more often he picked up something in town or heated up a frozen dinner. Will usually ate with his folks in the evening. Since Will and Dub managed the ranch together, they often discussed ranch business either during the meal or afterward.

"Are you and Nate about finished with the new fence at the Ross place?" Chance leaned against the counter, lifted the dark green mug, and gently blew on the coffee to cool it.

"Should be done by noon. Then we'll come get the horses and move his herd back. That ol' man was smart, cutting the fence and driving his cattle and horses down the highway away from the fire."

"I didn't think he could ride anymore since he had his hip replaced." The man they were talking about was eighty-nine.

"He hadn't ridden in about five years. But when a man's desperate, he gets creative. He used a stepstool to get on the horse. Had to find a big rock to get off."

Chance laughed, imagining the wiry old cowboy trying to find a rock big enough in their part of the country. "I'm still amazed the fire missed his house and barn."

"So is he. We figure the wind shifted at the last minute, but that big duck pond he put in at the spring helped too. It diverted the blaze somewhat." His dad relaxed against the cabinet to his left and studied him, his eyes narrowing slightly.

Chance resisted the urge to fidget. But it wasn't easy. When Dub Callahan had you in the crosshairs, it wasn't a comfortable position. "Somethin' on your mind, Dad?"

"You really serious about Emily?"

"Yes, sir."

"You don't know her very well."

Chance grinned. "You didn't know Mom well when you decided to marry her."

"True. Saw her at my cousin's wedding and knew right then and there that she was the woman I was going to marry."

"That's basically the way it's been with me."

"But I was heading off to war. That added more urgency to the situation."

"Have you had Emily investigated?" Chance didn't make a big deal out of it. About eight years earlier, a cousin had come for a visit and brought her new boyfriend. Their cousin adored him, and they'd all liked him. He'd been nice, friendly, and polite — until Dub caught him stealing

52

jewelry from the office safe. A safe with a combination lock and that was never left open. Turned out that by day, the boyfriend was a friendly auto mechanic and by night a thief. He had a rap sheet a mile long and had served time in prison both as a juvenile and an adult. Their cousin had been completely fooled, and so had they.

"Yeah, but don't tell your mother. She'd never let me hear the end of it. Don't mention it to Emily, either. I doubt she'd appreciate it. She's a sweet girl, a believer, and she's done so many good things for folks around here, I almost let it go. But I just couldn't."

"You've been taken in before. Obviously, since you gave her a key, we don't have to worry about anything."

"Never even had a parking ticket."

"How thorough is your PI?"

"Besides looking for a criminal record, he checked out her background a bit. Her father is a prominent plastic surgeon in Dallas. Caters to all the big money folks. He's Doyle Denny's son."

"The oil man?"

"One and the same. I think you met him a few years back when you went to that producers' meeting with me in Houston."

"Yes, sir, I did. He seemed like a good

man." Chance had met a lot of people on that trip, but Denny stood out, partly because he was six foot five. He was a geologist and a very successful wildcatter, drilling for oil, and finding it, in unexpected places around the world. Unlike some of the powerful and rich people at that meeting, Denny had been genuinely friendly and nice.

"He is. I haven't had many direct dealings with him, but when I did, he treated me fair and square. I've never heard anything bad about him. I never met Emily's father, though Doyle commented years ago that he'd spoiled him rotten and lived to regret it.

"Emily's mom is a former New York fashion model and runs her own very successful modeling agency in Big D. They're rich, high-society types. From what my man could learn, their net worth is somewhere around ten million."

Chance shrugged. The Callahan ranch alone was worth over five times that.

"Emily was valedictorian in high school. She had a 4.0 in college and earned a double master's in history and museum science from Texas Tech, which we already knew." His dad grinned and added, "But I don't hold that against her."

Chance smiled wryly. Dub was a big University of Texas supporter. "That's mighty good of you."

"Evidently getting a top job in her field is difficult due to a scarcity of positions. Her parents paid for her undergraduate degree, but Emily paid for her master's. Doyle set up a trust fund for her when she was born, likely a large one since she doesn't have much other income. The last couple of years, she worked part-time at a museum for a while and set up three other small town museums for a modest fee. She owns a nice three bedroom house in a good neighborhood in San Antonio."

"So you approve of her?"

"What I've seen I like." His father searched his face. "I just don't want you hurt. Her, either, for that matter."

"I suppose there's always that possibility. But it's a risk I have to take. Somebody told me a long time ago that fear of failure shouldn't keep me from going after what I wanted."

Smile lines appeared at the corners of his father's eyes. "Wise man."

"Yes, sir, you are."

His mom hustled into the kitchen carrying the rest of the dirty dishes. "Don't you have work to do, Dub Callahan?"

"I'll get there directly. I've been talkin' with my son." He slid his arms around his wife's waist and leaned down to rest his cheek against her hair. "Why are you in such a hurry to get rid of me this morning?"

Sue tipped her head, pressing lightly against his face. "Because Emily is stirring, and Ramona and I decided Chance should be the only one to talk to when she came in the kitchen."

"So Ramona and Ace have pulled a disappearing act." Dub released her and stepped back out of her way.

"That's right." Sue rinsed the dishes and put them in the dishwasher. "Ace headed for the barn, and Ramona is cleaning our bathroom." She shoved the door to the dishwasher closed. "I'm going to play on the internet. You can keep me company or take off."

His dad caught her hand as she started out of the kitchen and walked along with her. "You goin' to search for anything in particular on the internet?"

"News. Weather. See if I have any email. Maybe I'll find something fun to buy." She stopped and looked back at Chance. "There's some French toast in the oven for Emily."

"I'll tell her." He smiled at his mom.

"Thanks."

She grinned and slid her arm around his dad's waist. "Just tryin' to help."

4

A few minutes later, Chance heard the soft shuffle of slippers on the hardwood floor of the dining room. Shaking the drips of water off the frying pan he'd just washed and rinsed, he grabbed a dish towel with the other hand and turned toward the sound. When Emily walked into the kitchen, he froze, the dish towel splayed across the bottom of the pan.

She was wrapped in a heavy, rose pink terry bathrobe that almost hit the floor. Matching pink fuzzy slippers peeked beneath the hem of the robe with each step, as did blue flannel pajamas with tiny white flowers. Her hair was a little mussed, as if she'd attempted to smooth it down but hadn't tried real hard.

It was slightly below freezing outside but comfortably warm in the house. Yet, she was bundled up like they'd had a blizzard. Since it rarely got down to freezing in San Anto-

58

nio, it must've seemed like twenty below to her.

Her eyes widened when she saw him. She blinked, then focused sleepily on the coffeepot and put her feet in motion. "Coffee."

Chance hid a smile. Emily Rose was an absolutely adorable nonmorning person. Automatically drying the fry pan, he watched silently as she took a large mug from the cabinet and filled it with the hot brew. She added three teaspoons of sugar and stirred. He cringed. Opening the refrigerator, she removed a half gallon of milk and carefully added some to the coffee, turning it light mocha. She set the milk back in the fridge and picked up the cup, taking a tentative sip.

Turning to face him, she took another, larger sip. "You're here."

Chance chuckled and set the pan on the counter. "Yes, ma'am."

She stared at the pan for a few seconds. "You in trouble with your mom?" Another big sip of coffee. He could practically see the sleepy haze beginning to lift.

"No. Why?"

"Thought maybe she was making you do the dishes."

Chance laughed and tossed the dish towel on the counter. "My mama hasn't punished me in twenty years. Well, maybe fifteen. And doing the dishes wasn't on the list."

"What was?"

"Nothing related to chores. We did those anyway. No TV or video games for a week, maybe more depending on the offense. No going over to Nate's or having him over here. Or just plain being grounded when I got older."

"No basements," she muttered. "Lucky you."

A prickly sensation crawled along the base of his neck, and he slowly moved closer to her. "What about basements?"

"Nothing."

He stopped next to her and rested his arm against hers. "Come on, Em. Tell me what you meant."

"For minor offenses, I had to sit in the corner. But for big things, I was locked in a small storage room in the basement. Bugs. Spiders. No windows. Totally dark." He felt a shudder sweep through her.

He put his arm around her shoulders, holding her against his side. "You couldn't turn on a light?"

"It didn't have one. For a few minutes, I could see a sliver of light through the crack beneath the door. Then whoever hauled me down there would go upstairs and turn off

60

the light."

No wonder she didn't have much to do with her parents. If he ever met her father, he'd have a hard time not slugging him. "How long were you left there?"

She shrugged and took another drink of coffee. "I remember some of the TV shows that were on a couple of times, so I think fifteen to thirty minutes. Unless they forgot about me."

"Forgot . . ." He stepped around in front of her so he could see her face. How could anybody forget about a child? Or punish a kid like that? "How often did that happen?"

"Only once. I misbehaved when my parents were out, and my nanny threw me into the dungeon." She grimaced and stared at the mug. "I was there all night."

"Didn't you cry or scream for help?"

When she looked up, he caught a glimpse of fear in her eyes before she quickly masked it. "No. If I made too much noise, I'd have to stay there longer. Sometimes I laid down and tried to nap by pretending it was night-time. Except I had a night-light in my bedroom, so that didn't always work very well. Other times I told stories to an imaginary friend, mostly tales my grandmother had told me about little girls who were settlers back when Texas was a republic." A

61

smile eased the strain on her face. "I get my love of history from her. That night I talked until I fell asleep. My mother came and got me the next morning. I think she felt bad about it —"

"I hope so!"

"She fired the nanny, and they never put me in the basement again. I just had to stay in my room when I misbehaved."

"How old were you, that last time?"

"Six."

He wanted to hug her in the worst way, but she held that blasted mug in front of her like a shield. So he brushed a wisp of hair from her cheek, letting his fingers linger. She closed her eyes, seeming to take comfort in his touch.

"So it was the nanny who locked you in the basement. Did your parents know about it?"

She looked up at him again, sadness clouding her eyes. "It wasn't only the nanny. My dad started it. I don't think Mom knew about it until I was left there overnight. I still don't understand why he didn't see how traumatic his form of punishment was on me. Or how he kept the basement thing from my mother, though I honestly think he did. She was so busy with her agency, she didn't pay a lot of attention to things at home sometimes."

Now he knew he was going to punch the guy. Bust his nose. Then throw him in a small dark room for a few days. Forbid her to ever see him again. *Yeah, right. And she'd think I was a Neanderthal.*

"It didn't warp me too much." Her stomach rumbled, and she smiled. "See, I'm really pretty normal. Except I don't think I could handle small, dark spaces very well. I really haven't tested it, but other than that, I'm okay."

Chance couldn't help it. He leaned down and feathered a kiss on her forehead. "You're a whole lot better than okay." When he straightened, she stared up at him, wide-eyed. But he thought — hoped — he saw pleasure along with the surprise. "Ramona left you some French toast in the oven."

She blinked and turned toward the stove, her shoulder bumping into his chest in her haste to get away. "Good. I'm starving."

Chance mentally kicked himself for moving too fast.

"So what are you doing here this morning besides washing the dishes?"

"I thought you might like to take a look at the Morse Building. I have a meeting in town later, but I'm free before then."

Using a pot holder, she removed a plate

63

with two pieces of French toast and three pieces of bacon from the oven. "Great. I'm excited to see if it will work." She poured syrup on the French toast — skipping the butter, Chance noted — picked up her plate and mug, and headed for the dining room.

He tagged along, carrying his coffee. When he set the mug on the table and pulled out the chair for her, she looked up in surprise.

"Thank you." She sat down, and he scooted it forward slightly.

As he walked around to the other side of the table, she bowed her head, her lips moving in a silent blessing. He waited until *amen* to ease into his chair.

Spreading a napkin across her lap, she met his gaze. "Why are you so polite this morning?"

He grinned and slouched a little. "Am I impressing you?"

"Maybe."

He lifted his cup, looking at her over the rim. "I'm trying to."

"Why?" She nibbled on a bite of bacon, then broke eye contact and focused on cutting up her French toast.

"Because I want you to like me."

"I already do."

He set down the mug and leaned forward,

resting his forearms on the table. "Good. Emily, you're going to hear rumors about me."

"I already have. Several, in fact." She smiled and took a bite of French toast, her expression growing thoughtful as she chewed.

"Good things, I hope." He figured not everything was flattering. There were some folks in Callahan Crossing who resented the Callahans and their success. And a few people who just flat out didn't like him.

"Mostly." She paused and tipped her head slightly. "Everyone thinks highly of you, but I've been warned that you're a heart-breaker."

"Who told you that?" Even though he supposed it was true, he didn't like hearing it. Nor did he like people sticking their noses where they had no business.

"Several people. From what I hear, you date a woman once or twice, then they never hear from you again. But it's not too bad. Nobody has said anything about one-night stands."

"They'd better not — there haven't been any. I try to live my faith, Emily Rose. I mess up as much as anybody else, but not in that way."

She concentrated on her plate, swabbing a

piece of the egg-coated bread around and around in the syrup with her fork. A soft flush spread across her cheeks. "You've never been tempted?"

Chance wasn't sure where the conversation was headed, but he had a feeling it might not be good. "Sure, I have. But I've never dated anybody I cared enough about to let things get out of hand. I'm not saying it was easy, but God helped me.

"To be honest, being a Callahan helped too. We're minnows compared to a lot of ranchers and oilmen. But around here, we're the big fish in a small pond. Probably two-thirds of the women I've gone out with were a whole lot more impressed with my daddy's money than they were with me."

"I don't believe that." She glanced up and ate the soggy bite.

"Thanks, but it's true." Her sincere praise gave a boost to his ego, which according to most people didn't need increasing. "There's another side of being a Callahan too. I come from a line of honorable, Christian men, beginning with the one who came West in 1880 and founded this ranch. A Callahan's word is his bond. He treats people right and with respect. He honors his wife and the sanctity of marriage. It's a heritage and reputation I'm determined to live up to."

Emily leaned back in her chair and picked up her coffee cup. "So the people in your family have always been Christians?"

"Most of them. There were some folks several generations back who were pretty wild. One female cousin umpteen times removed ran off with an outlaw."

"You're kidding."

"Nope. The guy was killed in a shoot-out not long afterward, and she headed off to Chicago. According to family legend, she opened up a fancy saloon. But as far as I know, that was never confirmed."

"So you've always gone to church?"

"Starting two weeks after I was born. I can't even tell you when I accepted Jesus as my Savior. I've just always known it. What about your family? Did y'all go to church?"

"No. I went with Grandma Rose when I visited her, but my parents only go to church for weddings and funerals." She set the cup on the table and traced the grain of the wood with her fingertip. "I didn't become a Christian until my senior year in college, after I broke up with my boyfriend." When she met his gaze, he couldn't decipher the emotion in her eyes. "I haven't been as honorable as you, Chance."

Judging by her body language the last few

minutes, he'd thought that might be the case, but he still felt as if he'd been sucker punched. Obviously, he didn't hide his reaction very well because she winced.

"It's been different since Jesus found me." She shrugged one shoulder. "Maybe because I haven't really dated anyone for very long at a time, but I'd like to think I've changed."

He nodded and smiled, hoping it didn't look as forced as it felt. "The old man, or in your case, woman, is gone. Replaced by a new creature in Christ. He changes us all."

Now, if he would quit judging her and believe that. The conversation hadn't gone as he had planned, and his thoughts were bouncing around so fast he didn't know what to say.

"Do I have time to take a quick shower?" She pushed back her chair and stood, gathering up her dishes.

Chance looked at his watch. "Sure. My meeting isn't until 10:00. I'll go back over to the house and check my phone for messages." It was a lousy excuse, but he needed some time to clear his head, and that wouldn't happen if his mom noticed he was alone. "Give me a call when you're ready."

"Okay. I'll follow you in so I can go on to the old museum when we're done. I'll

68

hustle." She took care of her dirty dishes and headed down the long hallway to her room.

Chance carried the cup to the kitchen, absently slid it into the dishwasher, and grabbed his coat from the coatrack by the door, leaving quietly. He covered the distance to his place with quick strides, his breath puffing in little white clouds in the cold air. Though it would be in the sixties by afternoon, the clear night had brought a frosty morning.

He charged into his house, slamming the door behind him. All the houses in the family compound were far enough away from each other for that kind of noise not to disturb anybody. Shrugging out of the coat, he tossed it on a kitchen chair and stormed back to his office.

"This love at first sight stuff is a bunch of hooey." He'd taken everything he knew about her — all good — and decided she was perfect. But she wasn't. Nobody was. Not even him.

Pacing back and forth across his office, he raked his fingers through his hair. He was ready to explode. She'd slept with another man — maybe more than one. "And that's a big deal."

There, he'd admitted it. Out loud.

He dropped into his desk chair, leaned his head back against the cushion, and analyzed the situation. She was a Christian, so he'd assumed she'd grown up in a Christian home. He'd expected her to have always lived by scriptural standards and acceptable behavior. The kind of behavior *he* found acceptable.

A few years back, after his sister's marriage fell apart, he'd made a list of what he wanted in the woman he married. Strong, mature Christian held the top spot. In his mind, mature equaled long-standing.

He'd always believed that the woman he'd fall in love with would be as pure as newly fallen snow. That was number two on the list. Given the casual attitude of many people about sex, it had been a very high expectation.

Emily had been washed clean through Jesus. She was a new person, one whose sins were forgiven. In God's eyes, she was pure.

Was Chance Callahan so high and mighty that he couldn't forgive her, especially for something that she had done long before he met her? How could he expect her to live by Christian morals when she hadn't been a Christian?

But that wasn't the only problem, was it? It was something more elemental. More of

70

a man thing. And much more personal. He wouldn't be her one and only.

Chance leaned forward, propping his elbows on the desk, and rested his forehead against his loose fists. "Forgive me, Lord. I'm the one in the wrong here, not her. I'm disappointed, but that has as much to do with pride as anything. Help me let it go. She was honest with me, even after my grandiose speech about my piety. That says a lot about her character. My reaction doesn't say much for mine. Guide me, Lord. Help me make up for being a self-righteous jerk."

Feeling better because he'd gotten things out of his system, he called his finishing carpenter to make sure the helper had showed up that morning. They were about done with a house north of town that had been started the previous October. Then he answered the bricklayer's email, which had confirmed that the man could start on the decorative brickwork on the same house on Monday.

Gathering up a folder with some notes for his meeting, he wandered back to the kitchen and waited for Emily to call. He used the time to scribble off a grocery list and stared for a few minutes at his pathetically stocked pantry. There wasn't much use in filling it up for one person, especially when he ate a lot of his meals with the family or picked up something in town.

His cell phone rang, and he quickly unfastened the snap on the case attached to his belt. Caller ID told him it was Emily. *Make it good, Callahan.* "Hi, darlin'. Are you ready to go?"

"I am." She didn't sound offended or upset.

He breathed a little easier. "I'll be there directly."

Anticipation spiraled through him as he slipped on his coat, tucked the grocery list in the pocket, and picked up the folder.

His head was on straight. Now to get his plans back on track.

5

Emily looked up at the decorative tin ceiling fifteen feet above her head in the Morse Building. "Is it original?"

"Mostly. That was one reason I bought it. Back in the sixties, the previous owner put in a dropped ceiling with acoustical tiles. Wanted it to be more modern, I suppose. When I was looking at the building, I pushed one of the tiles up to see what was above it. I spotted that tin ceiling and got so excited I almost fell off the ladder.

"I had to replace some of the tiles because they'd been damaged when they put up the second ceiling. I found an outfit that makes reproduction ones in the same pattern."

"The new ones are made of tin, not aluminum?"

"Yes, though it took some searching. I was kind of amazed that I found exact replicas. So many of the ones used today aren't actually made of tin. I wish I hadn't been required to put in the sprinkler system. Those pipes detract from the ceiling. But it was necessary to bring it up to code."

Emily wandered over to the center red brick wall. Each of the outer walls was also made of the same red brick and, like this one, were a foot thick. All appeared to be in good condition. The fire hadn't reached this block, but the heavy smoke had blanketed the whole town for days. She was surprised the inside of the building wasn't coated with a layer of black soot. "The building must be well sealed. I don't see any smoke residue."

"Replacing the windows and door helped, along with caulking every nook and cranny. I had the thermostat set just high enough to keep things from freezing, so the heat pump hasn't been running much. I'd also changed the furnace filter about a week before the fire. It filters out just about everything and did a good job keeping the smoke out."

"We'll have to wash the outside of the building, but everybody in town is doing that. I'm sure I can recruit volunteers from the Historical Society to handle it. Did you have to repair any of the brickwork?"

"There were some places along the back wall that were missing big chunks of mortar. I studied up on it and used a lime-sand mortar."

"Good man." Emily shot him an approving smile, and he puffed up his chest and grinned back. Cement was a key ingredient in modern masonry mortar and was too hard to use with old bricks. It would cause them to deteriorate.

"I had to replace the floor, which is a shame. It was inch-thick, wide-plank pine. But a water pipe connecting the radiators sprung a leak a few years ago and flooded the place. It wasn't occupied, so no one noticed it until someone walking by spotted water seeping out the front door. By then, it had ruined almost the whole floor."

"This looks good, though. Is it old wood from another building?"

Chance shook his head. "It's new but finished to look old. I debated about using salvaged wood, but I couldn't find enough of anything I liked."

She noted the absence of radiators. There were vents in the floor, indicating forced air heat. "It's good you took out the radiators. That isn't the safest way of heating a museum."

He sauntered across the room to her side. "I didn't know it would be a museum when I took them out. Mainly I didn't want a repeat of the ruptured waterline. I thought it would make a good meeting hall, so I figured it would be nice if the middle was as warm as the sides."

"This building has a crawl space big enough to work in? Most don't."

"Even better. It has a basement. Along with running a general store in the other side, Mr. Morse was a whiskey distributor. He supplied saloons and fancy restaurants all across West Texas and the Panhandle.

"The basement made it fairly easy for me to run the ductwork for the central heating and cooling system. I installed a heat pump along with an auxiliary furnace for really cold winter days."

"Like this morning."

"This wasn't too bad. Only a little nippy. Really cold is when it drops down into the teens or lower."

Emily pretended to shiver. "This morning was cold enough, thank you."

"You're a wimp."

"No, I'm smart. I live where it's warm all year round. Mostly."

He chuckled and nudged back the brim of his blue cap with the local feed store logo on it. "It gets warm here too. Even hot."

"That makes it even more important to be able to keep a reasonably controlled temperature. The heat pump will help dehumidify the building too, and that's good."

"Don't want it smellin' all musty when folks come in."

"And we don't want things getting moldy."

Chance surprised her by grabbing her hand and drawing her closer to his side. Not that she minded. "So what do you think?" he asked. "Will it work?"

"Absolutely." She glanced up as a big smile lit his face. Walking toward the back of the building, she tugged him along with her. There were two doors, one single and one double. Opening the single one, she found a small bathroom. The new porcelain pedestal sink and Victorian high-tank toilet with a pull chain were a perfect style for the early days of the building. And a historical museum. "This is beautiful, Chance. You've done an amazing job with this whole thing."

"Thanks. I enjoyed almost every minute of it. Except for slicing my fingers a few times installing the ductwork."

"Ouch! That's not good."

"And there wasn't anybody here to kiss it and make it better." He pretended to pout.

"Poor baby." She inspected his big, strong hands. "All healed up anyway."

"Yeah, but it wouldn't have hurt nearly as much if a certain pretty lady had been around to offer sympathy."

She patted him on the back. "There, there, dear. Now, show me the storeroom. Does the other one have double doors too?"

"It does. They also have big metal roll-up doors at the loading docks in back. The building is set back far enough from the alley to facilitate truck deliveries. Or in the earliest days, wagon deliveries."

"Excellent. That will make it easier to bring in larger items."

"There are regular doors for each section too. And extra parking."

She smiled up at him. "This just keeps getting better and better."

"I'm not sure if the metal doors on the outside have been here all along, but it appears that Mr. Morse had the loading bays built into the building. The storerooms were a later addition, probably by Hampton's. I assume Mr. Hampton wanted double doors to make it easier to haul the clothing racks out onto the display floor." Chance opened the right side door. "Or it might have been because they couldn't get the shoe X-ray thing through a regular door." He flipped on the light and stepped aside so she could enter.

Standing in one corner of the storeroom was an old but beautifully maintained X-ray

Shoe Fitter. Emily gasped and ran across the room to inspect it. A light coating of dust covered it, but all the parts were there and in good condition. Scuff marks around the bottom and scratches from fingernails or jewelry on the top near the viewing ports told the tale of the hundreds, or perhaps thousands, who had used the machine over a decade or two.

"I don't know if it works or not," said Chance, clearly enjoying surprising her. "After I read some articles about it on the internet, I was too chicken to find out. Didn't want to risk burning my skin from the radiation. Since I'm full grown, I don't suppose it would stunt my bones like it could in kids, but who knows what else it might do."

"Exactly. Do you have the power cord?"

"I took it home. I didn't want to risk somebody finding it and firing the thing up."

"Good. That's where it should stay. Maybelle is going to be so excited when I tell her about it. Did you find anything else lying around?"

"Some wooden shelves in the basement." He pointed to the stairs in the corner that led down. "There was a box of decades-old newspapers in the other storeroom. I gave it to Mom. I don't know if she took it to the old museum or not."

"She did. It's one of the boxes we rescued." She walked out of the storeroom, standing outside the door as he turned off the light and joined her.

"Good. I hope they're useful."

"Definitely. It's always good to have newspapers available for research purposes, as well as displaying them occasionally."

He checked his watch and rested his hand at the small of her back, gently urging her toward the other room. "We'd better scope out the rest of it. I have to leave pretty soon."

The other side of the building was basically identical to the first, except it had no bathroom. That made the second back room slightly larger. She studied the big metal roll-up door. Like the rest of the building, there were no gaps around it for cold air to whistle in during the winter.

"Will this room be big enough to prepare for the tea parties?" Chance asked, checking to make sure the door was locked.

"They don't plan to do only tea parties." She looked sideways at him. "Men can have meetings here too."

"Don't need to." He rubbed the side of his nose with his fingertip. "We might have a confab at the gin, in the pasture, or in a field, or maybe park in the middle of the road to chat."

"And at the Boot Stop. I've seen a bunch of men there on several occasions."

"Most of the time those are just guys having a meal. Or maybe pie and coffee."

Resting her hands on her hips, she turned to face him. "You mean there are no men's groups in this town? No committees or organizations that get together?"

"Sure there are. But they all already have places to meet."

She tapped him lightly on the chest with her index finger. "You'll need to promote this meeting room to your buddies, Chance."

"Yes, ma'am. I don't know how much good it will do, but I'll try. Men get kinda set in their ways. And they aren't impressed by fancy sandwiches and salads."

"Do they always need food?"

"No." He grinned. "But it helps."

"I expect your mother and her friends will come up with something. We don't want to take business away from the Boot Stop or anyplace else, but there must be a need. Otherwise, the members of the Historical Society wouldn't have been so enthused about the idea."

She walked back into the main room. Chance closed the door to what would become their kitchen and leaned against the wall, watching her. They would have plenty of room for luncheons or meetings. She looked back at him. "Do you have the floor plans on your computer?"

"Yes. I can print off a copy tonight. Do you want a digital one too?"

"Both would be great. Once I have an idea of how many tables the society wants to put in here, I can start mapping things out with my CAD software."

Strolling over to the museum side, ideas for exhibits — if they found the right things — and where to put them filled her mind. Pausing, she studied the big picture windows at the front. While perfect for a store, they could be detrimental in a museum. "Did you replace these?"

"Yes. The old ones were single pane. Lousy on energy efficiency. The double pane ones will work a lot better."

"They'll also help keep out moisture, which is important. But sunlight deteriorates things." Though the building faced north, a beam of sunlight caught a small section of the window and came directly into the room. It probably wouldn't happen often, but over time it would damage whatever sat there. "We'll need to have the windows tinted to cut down on any potential

UV rays. There should also be blinds for better light control. There should be plenty of room in the society's budget for that."

"Fine with me. What about an office and a workroom?"

"We could put them along this wall. I don't think we necessarily have to have separate rooms for either one, but I'll leave the final decision up to the society."

"Do you have much to work with for the displays?"

"I have a list of things members intend to donate, so I can begin with that. They're starting to put out the word that we need more, so hopefully we'll get more contributions." She put her back to the windows and scanned the open space. "You're doing a wonderful thing, Chance. Being able to use this building will elevate the museum to another level. It's going to be good for the community."

"Heaven knows we need some good things to happen around here." He slid his arm around her waist in a light hug.

Which felt entirely too good.

"And I didn't want you to leave," he added quietly.

"I'll be leaving when it's finished in three or four months."

"That gives me time."

Turning her head, she looked up at him, her heart doing a little pitter-patter at his words and his intense expression. "For what?"

"To convince you to stay."

Two hours later, while she worked in the bunkhouse, cleaning items from the museum, Emily was still trying to wrap her head around Chance's words. What had he meant by them? He'd been awfully serious. But he hadn't elaborated, and she'd been too dumbfounded to push it.

Sure, she liked him. What woman who drew breath wouldn't? But he was a heart-breaker. Even his own sister said so, though Emily would never tell him that. She'd had her love rejected once and didn't intend to open herself up to that kind of pain again. They could be friends, maybe even date casually — if there was anything to do that classified as a date around here. But that's as far as it would go. As far as she'd allow it to go.

She had plans. A career she loved and wanted to take to the highest possible level. She was good at her job and had the recommendations to support her claim. All she needed was the opportunity to prove it in a position that could lead to advancement.

After a brief knock on the door, Chance's sister, Jenna, opened it, letting her two-and-a-half-year-old son, Zach, come inside ahead of her.

"Hi, Emily!" The cute little guy raced across the room to where she was working and stopped beside her chair. "What you doin'?"

Scooping him up in a hug, she received a quick one in return. "I'm still cleaning up things from the museum, trying to get the black smoke off them." He was a beautiful child with pale blond hair and deep blue eyes with gray starbursts radiating from the center.

Though he hadn't inherited Jenna's red hair and turquoise eyes, he favored her a great deal.

Like everyone else, Emily adored him.

He turned in her arms and studied the items on the worktable. "They in the fire," he said solemnly.

"Yes, they were, and they got all dirty. But some things have turned out okay."

He pointed to a pair of World War II binoculars. "What's that?"

"Those are binoculars. They make things that are far away seem bigger and closer. Let's go over to the window, and I'll show you." Setting him on the floor, she stood.

He walked beside her to one of the windows. She checked to see that the field glasses were still in focus from the day before, then folded them so the eyepieces were as close together as possible. Picking him up, she balanced him on one hip and held the glasses up to his eyes. "Look through here at your grandma's porch."

Zach looked through them and laughed.

"Move the binoculars around a little until you see the rocker."

As soon as she said it, she realized that was asking too much for such a little kid. Even though she held on, he moved them too much and too fast.

"No see it." He looked up at her with a frown. "You help."

"Okay. You look through, and I'll try to move them just a little bit." She glanced at Jenna, who was trying not to laugh. "This isn't easy."

Jenna grinned and settled in another chair. "Hey, you're trying. That's what counts."

Emily wasn't so sure of that. Zach was getting frustrated. "Can you still see the porch?"

"Yeah." Though she held the binoculars, his little hands curled around them. "Grandma!"

Jenna laughed, and Emily joined her.

"That's right. Grandma is on the porch. Does she look close?"

"Uh-huh." He started wiggling. "My go see Grandma."

Emily set him on the floor and glanced out the window again. "I think she's coming over here."

Jenna stood and walked over to help Zach open the door. "Have you talked to her since you went to see Chance's building?"

"Yes. I told her that it should work great. How did you know I went to see it?" Emily followed them out the door, deciding to leave it open for a few minutes and air out the bunkhouse.

"Mom called." She paused, making sure that Zach was running straight to his grandmother. "She's more excited about you and Chance going to look at it together than she is about the building."

"Is your mother a matchmaker?"

"Not usually. At least not too much." Jenna turned to Emily. "But I'm sure she sees what I do."

"Oh?" Emily tried to be nonchalant. "What?"

"That he's crazy about you." Jenna watched her mom and Zach for a minute. They'd stopped to observe something in the grass. "He's never been this way with anybody else, Emily. He lights up whenever you're around. I think you like him too."

"Yes, I do. But I'm not looking for a serious relationship. My course is laid out."

"Sometimes the course we set for ourselves isn't what God has in mind. Look at Nate and me. Don't be so set on what you think is right that you miss what God has for you."

"I'll keep that in mind. Did you find a building for the Mission?"

"I did. It's on Second and Alder. It's a thousand square feet bigger than the old one and brick. Lots of parking. And it's still in an area that will give folks a bit of privacy. Some people would rather not have others know they're coming to the food bank."

"I can understand that. Did you buy it?"

"No, the owner wants to lease it. His rent is fair, and he has no objections to the changes I want to make. I've ordered a big refrigerated display case and a freezer case. So we'll have plenty of room to keep the dairy products and frozen meats. They'll be delivered next week, along with the shelving units and worktables. We should have things set up and everything moved from the church in a couple of weeks. I'll call the district food bank this afternoon and get back on their distribution list."

"Do you need me to come help at the church this afternoon?"

"I think we have enough people lined up," Jenna said. "Pastor called a little while ago and said some folks from a church in Mississippi rolled in about 10:00 with a rental truck full of canned goods and clothing."

"Mississippi?"

"They said they'd been helped after hurricanes, and they wanted to help somebody else. Money is still coming in every day to the Fire Victims Fund at the bank. It's amazing."

"There are a lot of good people in the world. We sometimes forget that when there are so many bad things on the news." Even Emily's parents had sent a thousand dollars to the fund, which she appreciated. Her father and mother had some faults, but they did help many worthy causes.

Emily hadn't told them, or anybody, that she had contributed five thousand dollars to the fund. And why not? She could afford it, and she had already developed a close connection to the people of Callahan Crossing. But she was glad she had already given her donation before her mother mentioned theirs. Otherwise, she would have questioned herself. Had she given that amount because it was what the Lord led her to give? Or was she trying to outdo her parents?

She had a strange relationship with them. Always trying to make them proud of her but rarely succeeding. At the same time, she seemed to look for ways to prove to herself that she was as good or better than they were.

A psychiatrist would probably have a field day analyzing her.

6

That evening, Chance sat across the dining room table from his mother, sister, and Emily. The three women were huddled together looking over the museum plans he'd drawn up. He stifled a yawn and glanced at his watch. Only 8:00, but he was ready to crash.

He'd had a long, busy day. The meeting that morning had been fruitful, gaining him a new client. The Parson family had lost their home and almost everything else in the fire, but they had good insurance and would be able to start on a new house in a few weeks. They'd studied the sample building plans he had available and had taken several variations home to study. He encouraged them to make any changes they wanted, and he'd do his best to accomplish them if they were structurally feasible and fell within their budget.

After a quick burger at the Sonic, he'd spent the afternoon working on the cleanup, not stopping until dark. He missed dinner with the family and picked up some fried chicken, potato salad, and half of a small watermelon at the grocery deli. Such was the life of a bachelor. After dinner and a quick shower, he'd printed out a copy of the museum floor plans and sent a digital version to Emily via email.

Now, here he was, half-listening to the conversation as they discussed how to set things up. He was more interested in watching the light shimmer in Emily's golden hair. She had abandoned her usual workday ponytail, letting it hang loosely around her shoulders. His fingers itched to touch it, to see if the gentle curls were as soft as they looked.

Did she know how pretty she was? Her eyes were the color of the bluebonnets that filled the pastures in the spring. The soft blush on her cheeks reminded him of the flush of a newly ripening peach. He was no dummy. He knew some of that sparkling color had been brushed on. But he had seen her without makeup that morning. The added blusher only lightly enhanced her natural coloring.

Her face was nicely shaped, and her nose was perfect. Maybe too perfect. If it was her dad's handiwork, he was very good. But he would be, nipping and tucking the Dallas elite.

Chance decided it didn't matter if her nose had been sculpted a bit. It suited her. His gaze moved down to her mouth. Nice. Kissable. Smiling. He looked up, relieved to see she hadn't caught him studying her.

A childish giggle drew his attention to the living room, where his brother-in-law, Nate, was giving Zach a horsey ride on his back. Crawling around on the floor, Nate glanced up at him and grinned. Chance had never seen a man as content with a ready-made family as his friend.

Chance was happy for them and for little Zach who finally had a daddy who loved him. Nate was already talking about adopting Zach if they could get past all the legalities. Chance prayed they could.

"I think that will work just fine."

His mom's words penetrated his thoughts and he looked back at her. "No changes?"

Jenna laughed and glanced at Emily. "See, I told you he wasn't paying any attention to us."

"More fun to watch your son." Chance grinned at his sister and leaned forward, trying to decipher some notes and lines Emily had made on the drawing. He thought he caught the gist of what they wanted, even though he was looking at it upside down. "What did I miss?"

"We'll need to add cabinets and counter space in the kitchen along with the refrigerator and an industrial dishwasher. Possibly a warming oven would work too." Emily turned the sheet around so he could see her scribbles and the lines she had sketched in. "There is room for a long, narrow island in the middle. We're debating about using stainless steel worktables with a shelf on the bottom or having a cabinet with a couple of shelves to give more storage space."

He studied the drawing for a minute. "You'll have a safety issue with open cabinet doors, especially if someone has a cabinet or drawer open along the wall too. Nobody would be able to get through. I don't know if they make stainless steel worktables with two shelves, but you could have an island cabinet built with two shelves and no doors. And don't forget the basement. There's plenty of room for storage down there." As Emily's eyes widened, he paused. "Or not. It isn't heated, and it wouldn't be handy for everyday use. But the society might be able to use it for something."

Turning the sheet back around, Emily tapped her lip with the edge of her index finger, totally distracting him. Dragging his gaze away from her mouth, he looked up and met his sister's twinkling eyes. He frowned, warning her not to say anything. She grinned and nodded minutely.

"You can order the cabinets?" asked Emily.

"Cabinets, sink, appliances. I'll get all of it for you wholesale. I might finagle some kind of discount if you go with the worktables, but you might do better shopping around for those and the other tables and chairs."

Emily looked at Sue. "Let me play with this on the computer and see how many tables we can fit in the meeting area."

"I'll get the Historical Society together later in the week and organize some committees after folks have toured the building," said Sue. "I'm sure they'll be thrilled with it. Except for using your software to draw out the ideas, you shouldn't have to deal with the meeting room and kitchen. We'll handle that. You need to concentrate on the museum itself."

"Works for me."

His mom relaxed against the back of the chair. "You two make a good team."

Her comment was a little blatant, but he agreed. "That we do." He winked at Emily. Leaning forward to stack up the papers, she rolled her eyes, and he almost laughed out loud. His mom had turned away, watching Zach run around the living room, so she missed Emily's reaction. It was probably a good thing.

Chance pushed his chair away from the table. "I'm going to mosey on home. Hey, Zach, I'm leaving. Can I have a hug?"

His nephew walked around the end of the couch and into the dining room, his pace half the speed it had been earlier. It was a sure sign the little guy was running out of steam. When Chance picked him up, Zach wrapped his arms around his neck in a sweet hug, then laid his head on Chance's shoulder.

"You tired, buddy?"

"Uh-huh."

"Maybe it's time for you to go home and go night-night."

Zach raised his head and leaned back a little to look him in the eye. "You go night-night too?"

"Pretty soon. I have a few things to do first."

"You go night-night in your bed. I go night-night in my big boy bed."

"That's right. Those are some long sentences." He really was missing too much time with his family. Hugging the little boy again, he looked over his head at Jenna.

96

"When did he start putting so many words together?"

"Just the last couple of days. And you'll note that he said *I,* instead of using *my* for everything. He doesn't always do it, but he's learning."

"That he is."

Zach pushed on his chest. "I go see Papa."

"Okay. Good night."

" 'Night." When Chance set him on the floor, he walked over to his grandpa. "Night-night, Papa."

As Dub picked him up and hugged him, Nate stood. "Looks like we're headin' out. You ready, honey?"

Jenna gave her mom a quick hug, then stood. "I'll get Zach's coat while he tells everybody bye."

She came around the table and gave Chance a hug too. "Spend a little more time around here, bro. We miss you."

"I miss y'all too. Things will get back to normal when I finish my part of the cleanup."

"Then you'll be running every which way building houses."

"I'll be running more crews than ever, that's for sure. But I have good folks lined up, so I should be able to get home in time for supper more often."

Jenna wiggled her finger, motioning for him to bend closer. When he leaned down, she whispered, "You can't court your lady if you aren't around."

"I know. Believe me, I intend to correct that situation as soon as possible. Starting Sunday afternoon if the weather co-operates." He straightened, and Jenna stepped back.

"Good. Time's a-wastin'."

"Don't I know it."

Emily stacked up the drawings and notes they'd made. "I need to go out to the bunkhouse for a little while and check on some things I was cleaning this morning."

"Mind if I go with you?" Chance walked around the end of the dining table. "I haven't seen any of the things you salvaged."

"Don't mind a bit. Let me put this in my room and grab my coat."

Sue rose too. "I'd better go get some sugar before our baby boy heads for home."

"I'll wait here and catch him again as he goes by." Even if Chance saw that kid two or three times a day, he finagled a hug at every opportunity. Holding that little guy and sharing the special love between them was a precious thing. He praised God that Jenna and Zach had been blessed with a loving family. How hard it must be for single parents who didn't have that kind of family support to nurture and care for a child alone.

By the time Emily returned, he had been the beneficiary of another big hug around the neck. Zach held out his arms to Emily when she stepped up beside them. When she took the little boy and held him close, Chance's throat tightened.

Zach straightened, resting his arm on Emily's shoulder. "You show Uncle Chance the bin . . . bin . . ."

"Binoculars?"

"Yeah. Binoculars."

"He can look at them, but it won't do him any good to look through them tonight."

"Why?"

"Because it's dark. You can't see much through them without light. He needs to use them in the daylight."

"Oh." Zach swiveled around in her arms to look at Chance. "You use the bin . . . binoculars in daylight."

"All right. I'll do that. Sleep good, buddy."

"Okay." Zach turned to Nate, who stood patiently waiting beside them. "I go night-night now, Daddy."

At the word *Daddy,* Nate's smile practically lit up the room. He reached for Zach and set him on the chair seat. "Okay, but let

Mom put on your coat."

As Jenna stuffed the wiggling child into his coat, Chance caught Nate's eye. "Careful, you're gonna bust your buttons."

"Good thing all my shirts come with snaps." Nate glanced at his family. "Or Jenna would be sewing buttons on every day."

Chance looked back at his parents and brother. "Good night, y'all."

"Good night." Though his parents didn't speak in unison, it was close.

Chuckling at Will's lazy wave, Chance followed the others into the kitchen and grabbed his coat. He, too, was blessed by having a loving family. They agreed on most things, but if they couldn't come to a resolution on something, they chose to amicably disagree.

Outside, Jenna and her family headed across the yard and followed the dirt road to their house. Chance and Emily took a different path, winding around a couple of winter-sad flower beds and along the side of the vegetable garden dotted with bare stalks of something or other until they reached another road.

The bunkhouse had been built far enough away from the main house to ensure privacy for the rancher as well as the occasionally rough-and-tumble cowboys. The ranch house had been moved a few times over the years, but Emily was working in the original bunkhouse.

The light from Emily's flashlight led the way. Chance had a smaller one in his coat pocket. On a full moon night, he wouldn't have used one. But a quarter moon didn't illuminate the landscape enough to avoid the ruts or occasional rock.

"Have you had any time for a tour of the ranch?"

"I haven't seen it all, but Will drove me around a couple of days ago."

Chance grimaced in the darkness. Definitely a good thing he'd declared his intentions, to his family at least. "Where did you go?"

"To Red Ridge and a couple of other pastures. I don't remember their names. We stopped at an old house, but there wasn't much to see. It's about to fall down."

"That would be Uncle Jack's place. He and our great-great-grandfather Aidan established the ranch, but they didn't get along too well. They built their houses so they couldn't see each other. Jack was flamboyant and a big spender. Aidan could make a nickel go so far the buffalo got sore feet."

Emily laughed. "I hadn't heard that one. I've studied his photographs in your father's office. You look a lot like him. Though not as stern."

"My grandpa agreed with you. He said I had Grandpa Aidan's eyes. He always made a big deal out of it because nobody else along the way has had green eyes."

"Tell me more about Aidan and his brother."

"They were both hard workers and smart businessmen, but Aidan was constantly harping on Jack about spending too much. They came out here in 1880, near the beginning of the cattle boom. It was open range then, but they bought some land, mainly to make sure they had a secure water supply. One section has a creek running through it. They named it Jack's Creek, and the name stuck. The other section has Aidan's Spring."

"Where Nate and Jenna got married."

"That's right. They camped at the spring the first year or so and took care of the cattle. They built a one-room shack at their campsite and went through two winters living there. By then they'd made some good money, so they decided they should each have a house. Living at the spring provided water, but it was more secluded than either

102

of them wanted. So Jack built his place, and Aidan built a two-room dogtrot up here."

"The old house on the other side of the barn."

"Yes. At first he hauled water from the spring. Later he put in the windmill. He and his wife, Clara, lived there until their second child was born. By that time, he and Jack had made a fortune, but Jack was tired of Texas. He wanted to live the good life, be a rich cattle baron without the cattle. So Aidan bought him out.

"Jack went to England and found an aristocratic wife. Bought her, basically. Her father needed money, and Jack was happy to provide it in exchange for a lady wife."

"Did he stay in England?"

"No, they moved back to the States and settled in Boston. Some of their great-grandkids came out to visit when we were in high school. They were my dad's age and nice enough, but a little snooty. Jack might have been flamboyant, but he was shrewd. He invested wisely, and so have his off-spring. They're probably worth about the same as we are, but I think they considered us hicks."

"Have you ever visited them in Boston?"

"Nope. And I don't plan to. Me and cities don't get along. Too much traffic and too many people."

"I love being in the city. Going to the museums, concerts, theaters, restaurants, and even the occasional sporting event. Don't you find cities exciting?"

"Oh, sure. Dodging idiot drivers going eighty on the freeway in heavy traffic gives me more excitement than I see in a year around here." In a normal year anyway. The range fire that hit town held enough excitement and fear for a whole lifetime.

She laughed. "Don't tell me you're scared of a little traffic."

"I'd rather ride a bull than spend ten minutes on the expressway in Dallas. I was there on business last year and had to go through the High Five. I thought sure somebody was going to bump me, and I'd go flying off into space."

"Why, Chance Callahan, I didn't think you were afraid of anything."

"Anybody in their right mind should be scared of a freeway interchange with five levels."

Right now what made his stomach burn was the thought that her love for the city might be a tall horse to saddle.

7

When they reached the bunkhouse, Emily unlocked the door and flipped on the light. "Where did Aidan and Clara live after the dogtrot?"

"He built her a house in town. She and the kids lived there most of the time. He stayed at the ranch during the week and went to town on the weekend. Several ranchers had homes in town so the wives could be around other women, and the children could go to school."

"Does your family still own the house in town?"

"No. My grandfather sold it after his parents died. He and Grandma preferred living out here." Chance followed her inside and closed the door. "Of course, they also had a Model T Ford and used it to go to town and back. He improved the road they'd used for years with the wagons."

"Which benefited the neighbors too." Emily took off her coat and draped it over a chair back.

It was warm in the room, so he slipped off his coat too, and laid it over another chair. He scanned the items spread out on three six-foot-long tables and shook his head. There were some dishes, vases, knickknacks, and various metal items, all cleaned. "I'm sorry we ruined so many things with the water, but it couldn't be helped."

"I know. The water didn't do as much damage as the smoke. Many of the textiles are too old for the type of cleaning necessary. This is about a third of what I think I can restore. We also have the pictures and records you and I saved. We need to get some good donations. I want to make a ranching display. Your dad said I could have his great-grandfather's saddle and tack, along with some old tools."

"Make sure he gives you a branding iron."

"I will. I'd like to collect branding irons from all the ranches around here and hang them on the wall of the exhibit."

"Good idea. I can't wait to see it."

"Ed's great-grandfather was a lawyer. He has several things, including furniture and law books, that were in his office. Another member of the Historical Society has a collection of drugstore items that belonged to an uncle in the 1920s. Those are typical displays, but I'm hoping we can find something unique to the area."

"I see you were able to clean up the mastodon bones. Aren't those unusual?"

"Yes. There aren't too many museums around here that have any prehistoric items. But I'm worried. Don't tell anybody else, especially not your mom, but I'm still concerned about having enough donations to make it a viable museum. I had my doubts, even before the fire. Now . . ." She drew a deep breath and released it slowly.

"That doesn't sound like the Emily Rose I know. The one whose faith never wavers."

"You don't know me as well as you think you do, Chance. I do trust in the Lord. But my faith in people isn't nearly as strong."

Chance brushed a wisp of hair off her cheek, letting his fingertips linger for a few seconds. She looked up at him with a wary expression. "You've been hurt. By your nanny. Your parents. Probably that boyfriend you mentioned. Others?"

She turned her head but didn't move away. "More than I can count. This morning you said many of the women you dated had been more interested in your family's money than they were in you. I understand that completely, only perhaps in a slightly different way.

"My folks have a lot of money. I was expected to move within a certain circle of friends, date a specific group of boys. If I befriended anyone outside the clique, both my new friend and I paid for it.

"There were only a few people in the group who were nice and who I still count as friends today. The rest of them were about as nice as scorpions."

"Ouch. But you still hung out with them?"

"Until I went off to college. I didn't like them, but I didn't want other people to get hurt because of me. So I hovered on the fringes as much as I could and spent most of my time studying. Things were better in college. My parents didn't have much control there. I was very careful not to tell anyone who my parents were."

"What, no Ferrari?" he teased.

She met his gaze, her expression somber. "I left it at home."

Chance studied her face. "Are you serious?"

"Completely. My mom drives it when she's in the mood."

"Hmm, and I thought my pickup was hot stuff." He grinned at her, wanting her to feel at ease.

"Well, it is. For something you haul hay

and lumber and who knows what else in." A tiny twinkle lit her eyes, and he felt a small victory. "I could still beat you in a race, though."

"That's a no-brainer," he said with a laugh, making her smile.

She pulled out a chair and sat down, her smile fading. Chance grabbed another chair and moved it over so he could face her, resting one arm on the table.

"My not-wealthy strategy backfired when my folks unexpectedly decided to drop in to see me in the spring of my senior year at Tech. They were in Lubbock for a medical association meeting and decided to check up on me. It was the first time they'd come to see me at school since I was a freshman.

"They drove up in Dad's Porsche, and Mom was wearing her typical designer clothes. I doubt the outfit and shoes cost less than five grand. I have no idea how much her jewelry cost. My boyfriend was so shocked, I thought he might faint. Then my mom commented that surely with the money from my trust fund I could afford a much nicer place. To say they weren't impressed with my modest one bedroom apartment is an understatement."

"You hadn't told your boyfriend about the trust fund?"

"No. I told him I had a monthly allowance to live on." She grimaced and toyed with a silver matchbox on the table. "In a sense that was true, but it was a self-imposed limit. I've had full access to the money since I turned twenty-one."

"So he was ticked because you hadn't been honest with him. I can understand that."

"So could I. I knew I'd have to tell him the truth eventually, but I liked my normal, everyday life. I'd caught myself in a trap and couldn't figure out how to explain it. I expected him to be mad, and he was. Thankfully, he waited until after my parents left to blow his top. I was ashamed about lying to him. But that turned out to be the last thing that bothered him."

Chance figured he knew what angered the bum the most, but he let her keep talking. He had a feeling that she hadn't shared this with very many people.

"He was angry because I hadn't lavished money on him. Because I was a cheapskate. He thought I should have given him all the electronic toys and gadgets he wanted. Eaten at nicer restaurants. Gone out partying or to sports events. Gone to the Bahamas on Christmas break. Or traveled around Europe."

"Didn't want much, did he." Chance shook his head.

Emily sighed and laughed a small laugh. "Not much. We couldn't resolve things. We'd been together six months, and the breakup hurt. At least he moved in with some buddies and didn't find a new girl-friend for a while. So, yes, he hurt me. But I hurt him too. I regret that."

She lifted one shoulder in a light shrug. "Now, I don't pretend to be something I'm not. I don't make a big deal out of having money, but I don't keep it a secret either. My trust fund came from my grandfather, and he is very generous."

"So you really don't have to work." Which meant she might not be too anxious to race back to San Antonio if he gave her a good reason to stay in little ol' Callahan Cross-ing. Not that they had the kind of entertain-ment she was used to, but surely there were some community activities she'd find enjoy-able.

"Technically, no. But it doesn't hurt to earn more money. And I love what I do. I have my five-year plan all laid out." She wrinkled her nose. "Though it's looking longer now. My ultimate goal is to become the head curator at a top-notch museum. But I have to land a job as an assistant curator first and work my way up."

It didn't matter whether it was five years or twenty, Chance didn't like her plan. "Helping small museums like ours is a good thing. Couldn't you keep doing that?"

"I could. I probably will until I'm hired in a full-time position. But this is the bottom rung of the ladder."

"And you want to go all the way to the top."

"Exactly. I intend to be a success. I need to be."

"Why?"

She frowned and met his gaze. "It's part of who I am. I've always wanted to be the best at whatever I attempted. And, well, it's expected."

"By your parents?"

"Yes. By everyone in my family except Grandma Rose."

"Your mom or dad's mother?"

"Mom's. That side of the family is nice — normal. Grandma Rose lives in Eden. I get my love of history from her. She tells me I don't have to be the best. If I do my best and wind up second fiddle, that's okay."

"Sounds like good advice to me. I think I'll like your grandma Rose." And maybe her other grandfather who provided for her. He was going to have a problem with her parents. That probably didn't bode well.

Smiling, she tipped her head slightly. "I think she'd like you too. I'm going to go see her on Sunday. Why don't you come with me?"

"I'd love to go with you." He could always take her for a drive around the ranch another day. "What time do you want to leave?"

"At 8:30. I want to get there in time to go to church with her."

"I'd like that. Do you want me to drive?"

"Only if you're too macho to ride shotgun."

Chance narrowed his eyes. He had the feeling she was testing him, maybe to see if he would try to squash her independence. "I don't mind being the passenger."

"No backseat driving."

"No, ma'am." He might not be above a little front-seat driving if necessary, but he didn't think he should mention it right then. Glancing at his watch, he decided he'd better get home. "I need to call it a night. Have an early getup in the morning."

Emily stood and he followed. "Are you hitting the bulldozer at the crack of dawn?"

"Not quite. Dalton wants me to stop by before I head out. He wants to talk about building his house. Then I'll hop on my trusty dozer. I can't help much longer. I need to concentrate on building projects."

They moved to the door, and Emily looked down at the floor. "Thanks for coming out here with me. Sorry I talked so much."

"I'm not. I want to learn all about you, Emily."

She met his gaze, a hint of sorrow in her eyes. "I think you just did, including the sordid details."

"Nothing sordid about it." He lightly tapped the end of her nose with his fingertip. "And there's a whole lot left to discover."

A tiny smile lifted her lips. "It's my turn to learn about you."

"Not much to tell. You have the advantage of seeing me with the family. That basically sums up who I am."

"I doubt that. We'll see on Sunday." She wiggled her eyebrows as he opened the door.

"It's liable to be a boring conversation, but I'm game." Since he'd met her, he'd already learned things about himself he hadn't known. Who knew what else lurked in the shadows?

Deputy Sheriff Dalton Renfro had been staying at the Callahan Ranch since his house burned. He'd bunked at Will's place for a few days, then moved into the camp house Nate vacated when he and Jenna got married. Nate left the furniture, stereo, and television. Considering Dalton had lost everything except his horses, which his father had rescued, the clothes on his back, and his patrol car, he was thankful for all of it.

He'd gotten up extra early to tend to his horses because Chance was coming by to talk building plans. His home had been only two years old, and he'd done much of the work on it himself. He didn't have the heart to put all that time and effort into a new one.

The horses were fed, and he'd finished mucking out the stalls when he spotted Chance's headlights coming down the dirt road. Putting away the pitchfork, he walked back to the house, reaching the porch about the time Chance pulled up. He waited outside until Chance joined him on the porch.

"Mornin'." Chance grinned as they shook hands. "Hope I'm not too early."

"Nope. All the critters are fed and watered, including me." Dalton stepped back, opening the door wide. "Want some up-and-at-'em juice?"

"Sure. I could use another cup." Chance

followed him into the kitchen. "How are you doing?"

Dalton glanced at him, then took another mug from the cabinet. "You want the truth, or what I tell everybody else? What everybody tells everybody else."

"The truth." Chance pulled out a chair and sat down.

Dalton felt his gaze as he poured them both some coffee. "If I was any lower, you could use me for a throw rug." He joined his friend at the table. "Pastor Brad says it's usual for depression to show up a while after something like the fire. At first people are busy surviving — finding a place to stay, dealing with the insurance, FEMA, the bank, or whoever so they can try to put their lives back together. They don't have that much time to grieve for what they've lost. But I thought I was handling it okay."

"You've been so busy working and helping other folks, you probably haven't had the time or energy to think about things too much. When did it hit you?"

"Yesterday afternoon. I drove out to my place to see it after they finished the cleanup. There's nothing left of the house and barn except a little bit of ash and one brick. One brick from the whole house. The big mesquite tree in the backyard is gone.

That ol' tree shaded the whole house in the late afternoon. Now there's just a burned stump sitting there to remind me of it. The pastures are black. Every bit of the fencing is gone. It's worse than when I bought it. At least then there were grass and fences."

"As soon as we get some rain, the grass will grow back. And we'll help you put up new fencing."

"I appreciate that, but y'all have done too much already."

"Dalton, you're a friend and a brother in Jesus. It's our privilege to help you. You know you can stay here as long as you want. It's beneficial to have someone living here."

"What if you hire another hand?"

"I don't see that happening anytime soon. Buster and Ollie will probably be here until they retire, and that's years away. Nate is part of the family now, but he still works as much as he did before he and Jenna got married."

Nate divided his time between cowboyin' and helping his father run their cotton farm. Dub and Will managed the ranch, and Jenna did the bookkeeping, among other things. Chance helped out during roundup and when he wasn't busy with construction.

Though Dalton knew he wasn't imposing on the Callahans, he still felt like a freeloader. But he wasn't all fired up to start building his house, either.

Chance took a drink and relaxed against the back of the chair, mug in hand. "What else is going on?"

"I can't dredge up any enthusiasm to rebuild. I want to make a few changes from what I had, but I can't seem to concentrate on the plans long enough to figure out what they are. I tried studying those alternate plans you gave me, but after five minutes, they all start looking alike."

Chance laughed, almost spewing his coffee all over the table. He swallowed and hopped up for a paper towel to wipe a dribble off his chin. "There are only two of them that are similar. There are eight totally different options."

"So you said when you gave them to me." Dalton slumped in the chair, more tired than he wanted to admit, even to himself. "I reckon I just don't want to think about it now."

"Then don't."

"But I promised you the job."

"I've got plenty of work. If you aren't in a hurry, I'll just shift someone else up in the schedule."

"You sure it's okay to stay here a while?"

"Until you're ready to move, whether it's

ALLEN PARK PUBLIC LIBRARY

five months from now or a year or two."

"I want to pay rent. Otherwise, I'll go camp out in the pasture and you can give this house to a family who needs it."

"Do you know of any family who doesn't have a place to stay?"

"Haven't heard of any. Folks are either getting a FEMA trailer so they can stay on their property, finding a place to rent, or staying with family or friends."

"Like you are with us. You'll have to take up the rent discussion with Dad. But you might as well save your breath. He'll tell you to use your money to buy another pickup. Didn't you have that Ford about six years?"

"Five. But it was a year old when I bought it. Lucky for me, some guy couldn't make the payments and had to give it back. The insurance won't pay for a new one, that's for certain. But I have some money stashed away. Thankfully, the bank didn't go up in smoke."

"Even if it had, your stash would be covered." Chance drained his mug and set it back on the table.

Relieved that he could put off the house decisions for a while, Dalton relaxed. That had been weighing on him. "I was in town yesterday and saw you and Emily at that

ALLEN PARK PUBLIC LIBRARY

building you're redoing. Y'all were lookin' mighty cozy."

"How cozy?"

"You had your arm around her."

"You could see that from the street?" Chance frowned thoughtfully.

"I was walking by on the sidewalk. I noticed movement inside and stopped to see who was there. Don't worry, there wasn't anybody else around right then. Nobody to crank up the gossip mill."

"It's already chugged to life. Mom tells me there were sparks flying between me and Emily at the Historical Society meeting the other night. Several people made comments to her about it."

"Are you going to ask her out?" Dalton liked Emily. If he'd been in a better frame of mind and better situated, he might have asked her out himself.

Chance met his gaze directly. There was an intensity in his eyes that put Dalton on alert, and he sat up a little straighter. "I'm going to marry her."

"You're kidding." Dalton studied his friend's face. "No, you aren't. Didn't y'all just meet the day of the fire?"

"Yep."

"Have you proposed?"

"Nope. But I will when the time is right."

Grinning, Dalton shook his head. "Mighty sure of yourself, aren't you?"

"No, but I'm sure of the Lord. I think he's picked her for me. At least I hope he did because I'm crazy in love with her."

"I'll buy crazy." Dalton laughed and took a sip of coffee. "I envy you. Not that I want to date Emily, but that you've found someone you like so much. I hope it works out for you."

"Thanks. What about you? Are you interested in anybody?"

"Don't have anything to offer a woman right now."

"Nothing tangible at the moment, but the potential is there. Maybe that's why you can't get excited about the house. You need a wife's input."

"Where am I supposed to find a wife? You already got dibs on the only new woman to come to town in a coon's age."

Chance stood and carried his mug over to the sink, rinsing it out. Dalton watched in amusement as he opened the dishwasher and stuck the cup in the top rack.

Walking back to the table, Chance rested his hands on the back of a chair. "Maybe you need to take another look at the ladies who've always been here."

"Like who?"

"Lindsey."

Dalton stared at him, even as a picture of the cute blonde flashed through his mind. "Lindsey?"

"If you think on it long enough, it'll dawn on you." Without another word, Chance sauntered out the front door.

8

On Sunday morning, Emily made one last survey in the mirror. Hair combed. Lipstick not smeared. Earrings and necklace matched her sweater — no mean feat since she'd changed her mind three times about what to wear. She wanted to look nice for her grandmother.

"Okay," she muttered. "Admit it. Grandma would be happy as long as I wore something that matched, was clean and in good condition. I dressed up for Chance."

Closing her eyes, she groaned softly. "What am I doing? Why am I trying to impress him?" She couldn't remember the last time she'd been so stressed over choosing an outfit. It also wasn't the first time he'd seen her in something other than jeans and a comfy top. She'd dressed nice the previous Sunday too. And she hadn't even worried about it.

That was before they'd had a little time to

themselves. Before he put his arm around her and said he wanted to convince her to stay. Before something shifted in their relationship.

Turning sideways, she checked to make sure that her coral pink cotton sweater and gray light wool slacks weren't too tight. Would he think she was trying to show off her figure? Did he even think she had a figure worth showing off? Turning farther, she looked over her shoulder, trying to see how she looked from the back. Was her mother right? Was she getting saddlebags? Did she need liposuction?

"Emily Rose Denny, stop it!" She spun around, facing the mirror, and glared at herself. "Quit right now. You look fine. Relax and enjoy the day. The man has seen you at your worst, and he still keeps hanging around."

Technically, she was the one hanging around the Callahans. But Chance didn't have to go with her today. He could have easily come up with a dozen excuses not to. "Calm down and get out of here so you aren't late."

She put on a short, soft white wool jacket, grabbed her purse, and walked briskly down the hallway.

As she entered the living room, Dub came

out of his office across from her. "Headin' out?"

"Yes, sir."

"There's a cold front moving in this evening, and the roads might turn icy. Try to get in before dark."

"All right. Thanks."

Dub nodded and smiled. "Drive safe."

"Always. This time especially. I don't want Chance deciding he has to take over."

"I doubt he'll give you too much hassle. Will might be a different story, but Chance is pretty laid back about most things. Have a good time."

"We will."

Emily went out the back door and across the driveway to where her van was parked. As she pulled around in back of Chance's house, he came out the door, pausing to pull it closed behind him. Her heart skidded to a halt for a mini-second. *Whoa . . .*

He usually wore well-used jeans, a western shirt, cowboy boots or heavy work boots, and sometimes a cap. Nothing fancy, just normal, everyday clothes. She'd seen him dressed up the previous Sunday — good black jeans, a soft white western shirt, and highly polished black cowboy boots. He'd been handsome enough to make all the women in church take notice.

Today, he'd kept the black jeans and boots but added a green western shirt and a black western-style wool sport coat. Topping it all was a black western hat. Funny, she'd expected a white hat — didn't the good guys always wear a white hat? But the man looked amazing in black.

When he reached the van, he took off his hat and got in, leaning between the bucket seats to lay it upside down on the backseat. He straightened and met her gaze. "Mornin'."

Emily croaked a reply and stared as he fastened his seat belt. The combination of black coat, green shirt, dark brown hair, and those green eyes would befuddle any woman's brain. Reaching for her water bottle in the holder in the console, she took a long swig and amended her earlier assessment. The man didn't merely look amazing; he was knee-weakening gorgeous.

"Grandma's going to love you." She set the bottle back in the holder and shifted into drive, forcing her mind to focus on the task at hand.

"Oh yeah? I scrub up good, huh?" His eyes danced merrily.

"And you know it. You're going to give her and her cronies something to talk about for at least a week."

126

He frowned. "Is that all?"

"I said at least." She shot him a smile as they drove past the ranch house and down the dirt road. Noting the speculative gleam in his eyes, she looked a little closer. "What are you scheming?"

He casually scratched the back of his neck, his expression changing to pure innocence. "Maybe I should really give them something to talk about. Like kiss you when I know your grandma is watching. Maybe even in front of her friends."

"Don't even think about it." *Don't you, either, Emily Rose.*

"But I like to think about kissing you." The twinkle was back in his eyes.

Her mouth went dry. She wasn't about to admit that her imagination had gone there a few times too. "Well, don't."

He watched her for a minute, nodded once, and rested the back of his head against the seat. "You're right. The first time I kiss you shouldn't be in front of an audience. It should just be you, me, and the moonlight."

For a second, she halfway considered booting him out of the van. She needed to end this before it got started. *Too late.* Besides, when had she become such a chicken? Before she could come up with something to change the subject, he did.

"You look nice this morning."

Nice? That's all she got for her trouble? "Thank you."

"You're always pretty, even when you're grubby."

She sneaked a peek in his direction. He watched the road as they approached the ranch entrance, then slid his gaze toward her, his expression tender. "But today you're beautiful."

"Thank you." Much better. "I always try to look nice for Grandma." Well, she did. She just didn't usually try quite so hard. Now if Gram didn't say anything about it, she'd be all right. She doubted she'd be so lucky.

"Did you go to the museum with Mom and the rest of the gang yesterday?" As she turned onto the highway, he pulled down the visor above the windshield.

"Yes. They love it. They're so excited about it and grateful. I didn't mention the treasure hiding in the storeroom. You should have heard Maybelle's scream when she spotted the X-ray Shoe Fitter. Half of them wanted to plug it in and check their feet. I was glad the electrical cord wasn't there."

"She'll probably ask me for it the next time she sees me. I'll refuse and tease her a little. She'll give up after a few tries."

"Good. Now, tell me your life story, Callahan."

Chance laughed and shifted slightly. "In twenty-five words or less?"

"Nope. We have a couple of hours, so go for it."

"Not that much to tell. I've lived on the ranch all my life. Even when I was a kid I liked to play with trucks and bulldozers. I've always been interested in building things. I started working for a local contractor the summer before my junior year in high school."

"Did you work on the ranch too?"

"Sure. Learned to ride a horse when I was four and started helping with the roundup when I was eight. We've always had plenty of things to do here, both fun and work. A lot of the time, it's a combination of the two. Pitchin' in around the ranch was a part of growing up. We figured every kid did it."

"Unlike this little rich girl who never even washed her own clothes until she went off to college."

"I never did my own laundry until I moved out." He smiled, his expression nostalgic. "I started to toss everything into the washer at once, then decided I'd better ask Mom how to do it. The first thing she told me was to put my new red shirt in with a couple of old ones and not anything else. But I accidently got a white sock mixed in."

"Did it come out pink?"

"Yes, ma'am. I sure was glad that was the only thing that was ruined. It would have been embarrassing to wear a pink T-shirt to the construction site the next day."

"I would have made a similar mistake, except with a purple shirt, if I hadn't called Grandma Rose before I did my first load. I waited until my roommate left for class so she wouldn't overhear how inept I was."

"And ask questions."

"Exactly. So your dad didn't object to you working somewhere else?"

"No. He and Mom have been great at letting us choose our own interests. Dad made it clear, though, that he preferred I live out here instead of moving off somewhere else. I wouldn't have it any other way. I love living at the ranch. My house is the first one I ever built."

"No way. That can't be your first one."

"Guess I should rephrase that. I'd worked in construction for about eight years, learning the various trades. It's the first one I did as a general contractor. Did most of the work myself, unless the task took more than two hands or one back. I didn't do the plumbing, either. Hate to mess with plumbing. But almost everything else is my handi-work."

"It's beautiful."

"Thanks. I'm proud of it, even if I made a few mistakes along the way. There are things I'd do differently now, but nothing big enough to want to build another house."

"Did you design it too?"

"I started with a basic design that I bought, then changed it to suit me. After I finished mine, I built Will's. I tried to make them complement the ranch house, but not have anything so similar that it looked like a suburban development."

"Jenna and Nate's house would have really stuck out then."

"That was another reason not to make them cookie-cutter. It was our grandparents' house. Mom used it as a guesthouse for a while, then Jenna and Zach moved in last fall. Jen's always loved it, and she was ready to be on her own. Her divorce was hard on her. It took a while for her to make peace with the whole thing."

"She's told me a little bit about it. How does someone get over that kind of hurt?"

"The only way is with the Lord's help. We did what we could, but it took the Lord and the love of a good man to completely set her free from the past. Nate has loved her forever, so she has no worries about him taking off for greener pastures. They're both content with all creation."

Emily slowed down as they approached a pickup driving slowly along the wide bar ditch between the highway and a barbed wire fence. A cow trotted along in front of the truck.

"Looks like Milt's got a hole in the fence." Emily slowed down even more, keeping her eye on the cow. She'd been in West Texas long enough to know that the animal might take a notion to cut across the road in front of her without any warning.

Chance lowered the window as they crept alongside the truck. "Need any help?"

The middle-aged, skinny cowboy gave him a big grin. "Naw, even if it would be fun to see you chase that cantankerous critter and get your fancy coat all dusty." He glanced back at the cow, then leaned down a little to peer at Emily. "Mornin', Miss Emily."

"Good morning, Milt," Emily called, smiling at him. She'd met him the night of the fire when he came into the shelter for a short rest from fighting the blaze.

"Where y'all headed?"

"We're going to Eden," said Chance. "To visit Emily's grandmother."

Milt grinned again. "Watch out, son. Being introduced to the grandma ranks right up there with meetin' the parents."

"I'm hoping so." Chance winked at Emily and waved at Milt as they eased past the pickup and the cow. Rolling up the window, he chuckled. "Milt ought to know. He's married to wife number three."

"Think this one will stick?"

"Maybe. They've been married about five years, I think. He was pretty wild in his younger days, but he's settled down a lot. Probably because the current missus isn't somebody he met at a honky-tonk."

Reaching the speed limit, Emily flipped on the cruise control and rested both feet on the floorboard. "What do you like to do besides build things and play cowboy?"

He lifted one eyebrow. "I don't play cowboy. I is one."

She laughed and turned the heater down a notch. "I know. I didn't mean anything derogatory. I know you work hard at both jobs. But what makes you tick?"

"My heart?" He placed one hand on his chest and tipped his head as if he were listening. "Still going strong. Tick, tick, tick."

"Isn't thump, thump, thump more like it?"

"Don't be such a stickler for semantics." He surprised her by reaching out and trailing his finger along her cheek. "Now, it's thumping."

So was hers. Since her face turned pink, the dratted man undoubtedly knew it too. "Okay, how do you spend your time besides working and flirting?"

He grinned. "I play the guitar."

"Are you any good?"

"Good enough to play with the worship team at church. I alternate months with a couple of other guys. We only have one piano player but have a surplus of people on the guitar."

"You have some good vocalists on the team too. I've enjoyed the music."

"Maybe you should join them."

"Not a good idea. I'm not a bad singer, but I'm not good enough to be in front of a microphone. Stick me in the middle of the congregation where I can blend in with everybody else, and I do fine. How about you? Do you like to sing?"

"Like it, but I'm not very good. I'll stay with you in the middle of the congregation. The cows don't seem to mind my melodies, though."

"The cows?"

"Sometimes I'll sing to them if we're holding them in a trap and waiting on another bunch to be brought in."

Emily envisioned the wire mesh cage a neighbor had used to trap a stray cat. He had put a bowl of food inside, and when the cat went in to eat, it tripped a wire and the door slammed shut. The poor cat was terrified. "How do you trap cows?"

"By putting them in a fenced pasture. Generally, the pastures on our ranch are big —"

Emily nodded. "Will said each one might be five to ten thousand acres."

"That's right. In this country, the grass can be sparse, so it takes more land than in a lot of places to support a cow. The traps are only a half section to a section." When he saw her puzzled expression, a tiny smile lifted one corner of his lips. "A section is 640 acres."

"That still seems big to me. Don't you have to round them up again?"

"Sometimes. Usually, a couple of riders will hold them fairly close together while we're waiting on the rest of the cattle. When the other cowboys bring them in, we herd the whole bunch to wherever they're supposed to go. Depending on the time of the year, we might simply be moving them to fresh pasture. Most of the time we're either rounding them up to brand and vaccinate the new calves in the spring roundup or separating the calves from their mamas in the fall roundup. You'll see the whole process in late April or early May when we have our roundup."

"That will be interesting. I've seen roundups in the movies and on TV but never in person."

"Some shows are more accurate than others, but I'm sure you have the gist of it."

Over the next hour and a half, Emily learned that Chance had taken some business and accounting classes at the nearby community college, but he'd never had any desire to get a degree or go off to a university like his siblings. He'd spent most of his work time learning various aspects of the building trade from the man whose company he eventually purchased.

These days, he focused more on supervising and running the business than swinging a hammer. Emily had the impression that he missed the more physical part of the job.

When they pulled up in front of her grandmother's farmhouse, a slender woman stepped out onto the front porch. Her beloved Rose wasn't quite five foot eight like she used to be, but she had maintained her height better than some older women Emily knew. Rose waited as they got out of the van and stretched out the kinks. "Good morning, Mr. Callahan."

"Mornin', ma'am." Chance sent her one of his "make 'em swoon" smiles. "Please call me Chance. Mr. Callahan is my daddy."

Her grandmother laughed and nodded. "Welcome, Chance."

Emily shut her door and walked around the front of the vehicle to where he waited politely. They strolled up to the porch, and Emily gave her grandmother a hug.

Gram stepped back and gave them both the once-over. "You look lovely today, my dear. Dressed up a bit more than you usually do for your ol' grandma." She winked at Chance. "Reckon it has somethin' to do with this handsome man. Doesn't she look pretty this morning, Chance?"

Emily's face grew hot.

"Yes, ma'am, she does. But she always looks pretty, no matter what she's wearing."

"I do like your young man." Gram caught Emily's elbow and ushered her toward the house as Chance scurried to open the screen door for them.

"He's not my young man," Emily muttered as they stepped into the living room. "He's just a friend."

Grandma Rose patted her arm and leaned close to her ear. "And I'm the queen of England."

9

"Emily girl, you get prettier every time I see you." A tall, stout woman who appeared to be about the same age as Grandma Rose wrapped her pudgy arms around Emily and squeezed. The hug only lasted a couple of seconds before the sweet-faced lady zeroed in on Chance. She took a small step closer, crunching the gravel in the church parking lot beneath her sturdy black shoes. "And who is this fine-looking young man?"

"This is my friend, Chance Callahan. Chance, this is Bertie Sparks, Grandma's BFF."

Bertie was clearly taken aback. "Say what?"

Emily grinned and slid her arm around the woman's waist. "Her best friend forever."

Bertie huffed out a breath. "Whew. I thought you were calling me her big fat friend. Which I am, but I'd be put out if you said so."

"Oh! I'm sorry. I didn't mean anything like that at all." Her expression mortified, Emily shot Chance a little "help me out here" glance.

"Pleased to meet you, ma'am. So you've known Miss Rose a long time?" Chance shifted slightly closer, drawing the woman's gaze with his body as well as his voice.

"My goodness, yes." Bertie turned her full attention toward him, Emily's gaffe hopefully forgotten. "We've been friends since first grade. The things I could tell you about her." She smiled and tipped her head coyly, slipping her hand around his arm, urging him to start slowly walking toward the church building. "Could tell you some things about Emily too, but I won't. I want to hear about you. Are you Dub Callahan's boy?"

"Yes, ma'am. Do you know my father?"

"No, but I knew your grandfather." A wistful smile flitted across her face. She glanced at the church and grimaced slightly. "Since I'm goin' to church, I reckon I'd better be more truthful. I only met William once, but that was enough to set my girlish heart to dreaming. He was a very handsome man."

Chance chuckled, thinking that his grandfather had definitely made a lasting impression on the lady. "Yes, ma'am, he was. He was also a good man. I miss him."

She nodded, then waved at someone across the parking lot. Chance looked over at Emily and her grandmother, who were walking alongside them. Rose shook her head, her expression filled with fond amusement as she watched Bertie and him.

"You going to take over the ranch someday?" When a middle-aged woman approached, Bertie shook her head and made a shooing motion with her hand. The woman scowled and spun on her toes, stomping off toward the building.

"No, ma'am. My brother, Will, is the man for that job. I just help out when they need me."

She glanced at Emily, then looked up at him in consternation. "Then you won't inherit all that money?"

"Bertie!" Emily and Rose spoke at the same time, glaring at her.

"Well, somebody should ask before things get serious between these two! And I know neither of you will." She glared back.

"I don't run the ranch, but I'm a partner in all the family enterprises."

"Them oil wells too?"

"Yes. And I have my own business." He

leaned back slightly so he could smile at Emily and let her know he wasn't offended by the woman's nosy questions. He wasn't telling her anything that wasn't public knowledge anyway, at least in Callahan country. He'd also noticed that Rose was listening to every word.

"Doing what?"

If they slowed down any more, they wouldn't make it inside before the service started. "I have a construction company, build mostly houses but occasionally do some commercial work."

"So you can provide well for a wife and family?"

Emily groaned softly.

"Yes, ma'am." Chance met Emily's gaze and silently mouthed "very well." The love of his life frowned, but her grandmother grinned.

They were barely seated before the worship leader told everyone to open their songbooks, so Emily and Chance only spoke to a few people. After the service, Rose's cronies seemed to dart toward them from every nook and cranny of the church, cornering them before they left the sanctuary. He didn't know elderly ladies, some with canes and one with a walker, could move that fast.

They fussed over them for a good fifteen minutes until Rose finally declared that it was time to go home and have dinner before the roast burned. His stomach was grateful for the announcement, but no more so than his head. He had a soft spot for little old ladies, but this bunch tested his ability to keep up with the conversation. They talked all over each other, and his mind was spinning trying to keep up.

Mixed in with the exclamations about how lovely Emily was, how handsome he was, and how great they looked together was sincere concern about the folks in Callahan Crossing. According to his dad, the Fire Victims Fund had received several monetary donations from Eden, good-sized ones from churches and other organizations and several from individuals. The town was only about twice as big as Callahan Crossing, but they were generous and caring. As had been people from all over the country.

When they returned to Rose's farmhouse, Chance took off his coat and rolled up his shirtsleeves. "What can I do to help?"

Rose tied her apron behind her back, narrowing her gaze. "You know how to cook?"

"A little. I'm good at taking directions."

"Oh, I like that in a man." Rose laughed

and pointed to the second drawer at the end of the cabinets. "My Joe wasn't much for following orders, mine or anybody else's. But I loved him anyway. Grab a couple of aprons out of that drawer and give one to Emily. Can't have y'all ruinin' your Sunday clothes. There's a blue and yellow one that should fit you better than the others."

Chance dug through the drawer, finding a pretty pink ruffled apron for Emily. The only blue one had bright yellow sunflowers but at least no ruffles. He figured he could use it without too much embarrassment. When he held it up, he suspected it was one of Bertie's. Emily's slender grandmother could wrap it around herself a couple of times.

He tossed the frilly pink thing to Emily and slipped the blue bib over his head. Tying the apron strings around his waist at the back, he looked up and caught Emily and her grandmother exchange a smile. If wearing a silly apron was all it took to please these two important ladies, he wouldn't complain a bit. "What do you want me to do?"

"Take the roast and potatoes out of the oven. Then you can mash the potatoes while I make the gravy."

Chance picked up two pot holders sitting

beside the stove and opened the oven door. When he saw the size of the roast, enough to feed at least six, he smiled to himself. Rose was typical of most farm women; she knew hardworking men liked to eat. He set the roasting pan on top of the stove and retrieved a covered casserole filled with peeled potato chunks and water. Interesting. He'd never thought about cooking the potatoes that way in the oven with the roast. His mom and Ramona always cooked them on top of the stove when they were making mashed potatoes.

He set the casserole on the stove and turned to Rose. "I'm good at the mashing part, but I've never paid any attention to how much butter and milk Mom puts in."

She handed him the potato masher. "Emily can help with that part. She's a good cook."

"Oh yeah?" He looked at Emily across the room as she turned from the open refrigerator with a half gallon of milk. "I'll have to invite you over so you can cook me dinner."

Emily set the milk on the counter next to an orange butter dish, which held a fresh stick of butter. She sashayed over to his side, carrying a large glass measuring cup. "I might take you up on that. Do you like sushi?"

"I've never tried it. And I don't intend to. Raw fish — yuck."

"I thought you were tough." She smiled up at him, her eyes alight with a teasing glint.

"I am. But I like my meat cooked."

"You just want to see me slaving over a hot stove."

"Not necessarily. You could use the grill." He lightly nudged her arm with his elbow and motioned toward the cup. "Do you want me to pour the potato water in that?"

"Yes." She moved over a few steps, setting the cup in the sink.

Chance laid the potato masher on the counter and followed her, carrying the pan of potatoes. He drained the water into the wide-mouth cup and set the pan on a pot holder she'd quickly slid over to him. As he started mashing the potatoes, she plopped a big spoonful of butter into them, then poured in some milk. "Mom's right," he said. "We make a good team."

"This isn't exactly rocket science, Callahan."

"No, but we aren't sloppin' milk all over the counter, either."

Out of the corner of his eye, he noted Rose taking an orange and white platter from the cabinet. When she lifted the roast from the pan and set it on the platter, he asked, "Do you want me to slice that when we're done here?"

"Let it sit while I make the gravy. Then you can slice away." She covered the nicely browned rump roast with a sheet of aluminum foil.

"Yes, ma'am." Chance mashed the last lumps out of the potatoes. "Do they need more milk?"

"Just a tad." Emily added a little bit, and he swished it around with the masher. "Perfect. Now set the pan back on the stove so they'll stay warm."

He would have done that anyway, but he didn't mind that itty-bitty order from his woman, especially when she lightly laid her hand on his back as she set the lid on the pan. No, sir, he didn't mind it at all.

Setting the pan on the back burner, he turned it on warm and stepped out of Rose's way as she browned the flour in the roasting pan. "Now what?"

"You can help Emily set out the salads and get our drinks. I have iced tea, soda, or milk. And water, of course." Rose stirred the flour-drippings mixture and slowly poured in the potato water.

Chance wondered when she'd picked up the cup from the sink. He'd been so focused on the potatoes — and Emily — that he hadn't even noticed.

"Iced tea sounds good to me." He tagged after Emily, holding out his hands when she opened the fridge.

Her eyes twinkled again when she handed him a big clear glass bowl of orange Jell-O salad. "Grandma likes orange," she whispered.

"I noticed," he whispered back. "This looks good," he added in a louder voice. And it did. Mandarin oranges, pineapple, coconut, and nuts mixed in with Jell-O and either whipped cream or sour cream was bound to be tasty.

Emily carried a bowl of broccoli salad, which also looked good. When his stomach rumbled, she giggled.

We're going to have so much fun cooking together when we get married. He barely kept the words from tumbling out.

She paused, holding the broccoli bowl a few inches above the table. "What are you thinking, Callahan? You look happy as a cat in a creamery."

Chance laughed and Rose chuckled. "Do you use my sayings all the time, girl? Or do they just come out when you're here?" her grandma said.

"They show up now and then. Much to

my parents' dismay."

Rose snorted and gave the gravy a stir for emphasis. "They're too uppity for such things. It would do your mama a world of good to remember her roots."

Emily slid her arm around Rose's waist and laid her head on her grandmother's shoulder. "And to remember you. Have you heard from her since that call on Christmas?"

"Nope. If I'm lucky, I'll hear from her on Mother's Day. The token acknowledgment as usual." Rose cleared her throat but kept stirring the gravy with dogged determination. "Don't know where I went wrong with that girl."

"It's nothing you did or didn't do, Grandma. Fame and fortune is what changed her. And my father."

Even with what Chance knew about the man, he was surprised at the bitterness — that seemed to almost border on hatred — in Emily's voice.

"I don't understand that, either." Rose turned off the burner and nodded to Chance. "There's a good knife in that drawer and a cutting board in that skinny cabinet down there. You can start slicing now."

"Yes, ma'am."

"Clark's parents are good folks, even with all their money. But that daddy of yours . . ."

Emily stepped away and removed a couple of bowls from the cabinet, setting them near the stove. She glanced at Chance, as if apologizing for the discussion.

He tried to silently tell her not to worry. Her grandmother needed to vent, and he had the feeling that Rose didn't voice her opinions on these things very often. Except maybe to Bertie. He figured Rose's BFF knew all her joys and heartaches.

"Grandpa blames himself. He says he spoiled Dad rotten from day one." She looked at Chance again. "My father is an only child, and was born when my grand-parents were in their midthirties. They were so thrilled to finally have a baby, Grandpa said they went overboard indulging him."

"And lived to regret it." Rose poured the gravy in a bowl, and Emily scraped the last of it out of the pan with a rubber scraper. "I reckon they see your parents more than I do." She caught Chance's eye. "They're in Dallas too."

He focused on cutting up the meat, but there was no way he could shut out the conversation. Evidently, Rose wanted him to hear what was being said. He wasn't so sure Emily agreed with her.

"They don't see them much more. Mainly at charity events or things like that. Now that Grandpa Doyle and Grandma Iris have started going to church and are involved there, they really don't have much at all in common with Mom and Dad."

"Your mother knows better. She was raised in the church." Rose sighed heavily. "Not that it made any difference. Miranda was too beautiful for her own good." She picked up the bowl of gravy and carried it to the table as Emily dumped the potatoes in the bigger bowl. "Ran off to New York the day after she graduated from high school."

Chance set the platter of roast on the table and quickly pulled out Rose's chair, helping her scoot it in after she sat down.

"Why, thank you, Chance. I don't remember the last time a man helped me with my chair." She tipped her head slightly, reminding him of Emily, and smiled. "Not that I need the help, mind you."

"No, ma'am, I'm sure you don't." He would have assisted Emily too, but she'd already set the potatoes on the table and slid into her place. "But my mama taught my brother and me to be gentlemen." He took his seat and sent her a smile. "If we didn't learn it from her, Daddy made certain we got it."

"Well, they did a good job. Would you like to ask the blessing?"

"I'd be happy to." Chance closed his eyes and bowed his head. "Heavenly Father, thank you for this food and for Miss Rose's work in preparing it. Thank you for a good drive down and the great church service this morning. Please bless our time together and this food to our nourishment. In Jesus's name, amen."

Emily and her grandmother joined in with a soft "amen."

As they passed the food around and filled their plates, Chance scanned the antiques-filled room. "Are all these family heirlooms?"

"Many of them are. Though I've been known to stop at a flea market or antiques store now and then."

Emily laughed, wagging a finger at Rose. "Along with estate and garage sales. Don't let her kid you, Chance. She and Bertie own Days of Old Antiques and Collectibles on the town square. They have all sorts of goodies in there."

"I'll have to let Mom know. She likes to shop for antiques. We have a lot of old family things in the ranch house. Furniture, pictures, old ranch record books." He noticed Emily's eyes light up. "Mom hasn't told you about them?"

"No. She's probably afraid I'll abscond with them. Which I might." She cut a bite of roast. "How far back do they go?"

"The first one is a little notebook of expenses for 1880. My great-great-grandfather didn't own any land then, was running the herd on free grass." Chance scooped up some potatoes and gravy. "I'm not sure you'll convince Dad to part with them. They cover the whole history of the ranch."

"I can't wait to look at them. I'll be thrilled if he will loan even one of them to the museum."

"Maybe between us we can get him to agree to a loan. Once you have everything set up and he sees how great it is, he might be more willing. He wasn't impressed with the old one. He didn't think they'd be safe."

"I agree. A book like that should be kept in a locked glass case where people can see a sampling of the entries but can't handle it. If someone wanted to use it for research, they'd have to do it under supervision. Though even that might be prohibited, depending on the condition of the pages. The ideal is to transcribe them, so people have access to the copy."

Rose spread some butter on a roll. "Emily tells me you're donating a building to use for the museum."

"Actually, I'm leasing it to them."

Emily added some salt to her potatoes. "For a dollar a year."

"Plus utilities."

"That's very generous of you, Chance." Grandma Rose studied him with keen, thoughtful eyes. "You must be very interested in Callahan Crossing's history."

"I am. And the museum is one of my mother's pet projects."

"You like to make your mother happy?"

"Whenever I can. This time it was easy. I didn't have anyone interested in the building and didn't expect to. So I figured I could earn a bunch of brownie points with Mom." He grinned at Emily. "Maybe some with the museum lady too."

"A few." Emily gave him a mischievous smile.

Chance noted Rose's lifted eyebrow as she watched the exchange and caught a hint of a smile before she took a drink of iced tea. He was pretty sure he'd earned a few brownie points with Emily's grandma too. But he didn't think it had much to do with donating the building.

10

Early the following Wednesday afternoon, Sue burst into the bunkhouse where Emily was cataloging items. "Grab your coat and come with me. I just got a call about a potential large donation. But we have to hurry or Alicia Simpson might send something good to the dump."

"I'll be right there." Emily saved her work on the computer, stuffed a spiral notebook into her large leather bag, and slipped on her coat. Racing out the door, she hopped into Sue's SUV and dropped the bag onto the floorboard. Sue took off before she had her seat belt on. "Who's Alicia Simpson?"

"Sally Tucker's granddaughter. Sally died last month at 102 years old. Mrs. Simpson is in town to clear out the house. She saw the ad we put in today's paper about needing items for the museum. Sally's father, Doc Bradley, came to Callahan Crossing in 1892 and was a prominent physician for forty years. He also owned some ranch land west of here in the Permian Basin oil patch."

"Like yours?"

"Ours is west of here too, in a different part of the basin, but just as rich in oil." Sue smiled and shook her head. "Of course, Aidan and Doc Bradley didn't know anything about the oil when they bought the land. They wanted it for grazing. Doc and his wife built a beautiful Victorian home on Third Street in 1904."

"Is it the Queen Anne on the corner? Sage green with sienna trim and roof?"

"That's the one. It's listed on the National Registry of Historical Places as the Bradley-Tucker House. Sally was meticulous in maintaining it. After her folks passed on, she and her husband moved into it. He died years ago, but she stayed here, even after her daughter married and moved to Houston. She lived by herself until she was eighty-five, then hired a live-in housekeeper. Bless her heart, she managed to stay in her home until about six months ago.

"Mrs. Simpson gave me the impression that she wasn't interested in keeping many of her grandmother's things other than her jewelry. She inherited her mother's portion of the estate some time back, but I suppose she'll get the rest of it now. Not that she deserves it." Sue frowned. "Sorry, that wasn't nice. But neither she nor her mother made much effort to keep in contact with Sally. Sally's daughter came to see her once a year on her birthday, but rarely any other time. Neither of them called more than two or three times a year. They were both too busy to bother with her."

Emily felt a twinge of guilt. She often went three or four months without contacting her parents. Of course, it wouldn't kill them to call her. When she had finally been able to get in touch with them a few days after the fire, her mother had been genuinely relieved that she was all right. Miranda had also been concerned about those who had lost so much, but minutes later, she'd gone right back to denigrating Emily's job.

Just like you denigrate hers.

Emily drew a quick breath. Where had that thought come from? She sighed softly. There was no need to question it. She'd felt the Holy Spirit's prodding before, not on this issue but on others. She had never considered how judgmental and critical she'd become of her mother's career.

During her childhood, she thought her mother was a beautiful princess living a glamorous fairy-tale life. As she grew older and participated in some fashion shows, she learned it was far from a fairy tale. Modeling could be grueling, with long hours and photographers, runway managers, or egotistical clothing designers making ridiculous demands of the models.

What bothered Emily now about her mother's business was the very thing she'd thought so wonderful when she was a little girl. The glamour, the emphasis on beauty, feeding the fashion obsession of women and girls, and the useless materialism of the whole thing.

"Uh-oh, I think I lost you somewhere about a mile back."

Emily turned toward Sue. "I'm sorry. What did I miss?"

"Nothing important. I was just wondering how much of Miss Sally's things we'll actually wind up with. She had some wonderful antique furniture that belonged to her parents and an amazing silver set they had received when they were married in 1900."

"We could set up a parlor scene or a dining room scene. Or both. We have the room now. I'm hoping she kept some of her father's early medical records or equipment. That would make a terrific addition."

"I wouldn't be surprised. Sally had a great respect for her father and her family's history. She was also something of a pack rat."

Excitement danced across Sue's face. "There's no tellin' what we'll find." She glanced at Emily with a smile. "So how was your visit with your grandmother?"

"Good. It always is. Grandma Rose is as steady as they come. She was quite taken with Chance. Of course, he was Mr. Charisma."

Sue chuckled. "That boy can charm the gold out of your fillings when he wants to. I'm sure he wanted to make a good impression on your grandmother."

"Oh, he did. And on her friend Bertie too. Bertie said she had a crush on Dub's father years ago. She only met him once, but she still had a dreamy expression when she talked about him."

"William Callahan was a man who turned women's heads. For that matter, so are Dub and the boys. But there was something special about William. When he talked to someone, he had a way of making them feel like the most important person in the room. Is Bertie married?"

"She's a widow, like Grandma. But she was happily married for over forty years. So she didn't pine away for William."

"That's a relief." Sue slowed as the speed limit dropped outside of town. "Chance really liked your grandmother too. He told me about her antiques store. I'll have to make a trip to Eden one day soon and have a look."

"She'd enjoy that. Though if you want to meet her, you'd better call and see when she'll be there. They have a couple of people who work in the shop part of the time while she and Bertie look for other merchandise. It's really more a hobby than anything, but they have good things."

They pulled up in front of the lovely old house. There were several old homes in Callahan Crossing, but this was the grandest that Emily had seen.

As they got out of the SUV, a tall, slim woman with expertly highlighted soft brown hair stepped out onto the porch. She looked around fifty, but she'd had a few facelifts. Emily could spot such things in thirty seconds, as easily as she noted the designer clothes likely purchased at Neiman Marcus in Houston or perhaps Bergdorf Goodman on a trip to New York. Michael Kors ivory trousers with a brown and black geometric tunic, easily a two thousand dollar outfit. No wonder Mrs. Simpson didn't want to be bothered with cleaning out the house. She'd likely never touched a dust cloth. Had she even cared enough to bring someone to help?

As Emily neared the steps, she assessed the other woman's shoes. Prada half boots, around five hundred dollars. Who was she trying to impress? The electrician working near the top of the power pole down the street? Or the folks at the Boot Stop if she lowered herself to eat there?

Emily was quite content in her faded jeans and blue cotton sweater purchased at JCPenney, but if her mother had witnessed the scene, she would have died of mortification because Emily's clothes weren't high priced. It wouldn't matter whether or not she knew the woman on the porch — Alicia Simpson was rich. And she had expensive taste in clothes, which was her mother's primary criteria for judging anyone.

Given that Emily could spend two thousand on a pants outfit if she wanted to, she was rather proud she hadn't done so in years.

Sue was dressed in her usual Wranglers and western boots, though she'd taken a few minutes to change into a lovely yellow cashmere sweater. Emily was certain she had not found it at Penney's.

She felt another twinge of guilt. Why did it matter what they were wearing? She was critical of her mother for judging people by how they looked and what they wore, yet she was doing the same thing. *Lord, forgive me. Please help me to quit thinking this way.*

"Good morning, Mrs. Simpson. I'm Sue Callahan, head of our Historical Society. This is Emily Denny, a curator from San Antonio, who is setting up the museum for us."

"Good morning." Mrs. Simpson smiled graciously and held out her hand to Sue as they walked up the porch steps. "Thank you for coming out so quickly. I hope there's enough here that you can use to make the trip worthwhile. I'm afraid I have no interest in old things, so I don't have any idea if it will suit your purposes. I don't know values of the furniture, but I expect most of it is high quality. There are a few pieces that probably should be tossed, but I'll leave that decision up to you. I've set aside some family photos that the housekeeper will ship to me. And as I mentioned on the phone, I've also taken Grandmother's jewelry. Gaudy old pieces, but the gems will be lovely in different settings."

She opened the door and stepped back, motioning for them to go ahead of her. When Emily walked into the entryway and glanced into the living room, she barely stifled a gasp. Everything in the room dated from the 1890s to the early 1900s.

161

"Told you," Sue said with a wide grin.

"Grandmother left some things to her housekeeper, Linda, but she's already taken those except for the television. She's going to pick it up the next time her son comes to visit." Mrs. Simpson led them into a smaller sitting room down the hall. Here, the twenty-first century reigned. Two pretty blue recliners faced a large screen LCD television. A long sofa table sat against the wall, holding a combination stereo-radio and a stack of music CDs. A cordless phone rested in the charger on the small round table between the chairs, and a tattered Bible lay beside it.

"You're welcome to anything you think would benefit the museum. Linda will handle the distribution or disposal of whatever is left. She's already taken the newer linens and useable household items to the church donation center. She was careful to leave anything that you might want." Sally's granddaughter smiled and traced one finger over a crocheted doily. "I'm glad she has a sense for that kind of thing. My interests have always been in modern art and decor, so I would have been lost without her."

"This will be a wonderful boon to the museum," said Sue. "Much of what we had in the old one was lost in the fire."

"Excellent. I know Grandmother would be pleased to see her family legacy remembered." Mrs. Simpson glanced at her watch. "I have to leave in a few minutes, so let me give you a key to the house. There's one in the kitchen."

Sue and Emily followed her into the large kitchen, which held an old round oak table and four chairs. Though in reasonably good condition for its age, the nicks and worn finish told its history. "This has been around a long time," Sue commented.

Mrs. Simpson's lips twisted in a mild reflection of distaste. "I have no idea why Grandmother kept that ugly thing. It seems so out of place with the other furniture. Perhaps Linda can explain it. She's on her way over." She took a key from a hook above the kitchen counter and handed it to Sue. "Feel free to come and go as you please. Just make certain the house is locked when you leave. The neighbors keep an eye on the place. Linda will let them know that you'll be here and will possibly be moving some things out."

"We'll be moving a lot of things out," Emily murmured as she inspected an icebox sitting in one corner of the kitchen. "I suspect the table and chairs, along with this icebox, were purchased by your great-grandparents when they were newlyweds. The time period is right."

"Well, that might explain it. Grandmother was rather sentimental. Linda probably knows." She moved to the kitchen counter and wrote a note on a tablet, signing it with a flourish. "This gives you authority to start going through things and take what you need. I'll have my attorney draw up a legal document and send it to you. Here is his business card." She handed the card to Sue. "I'll let them know that you'll be calling to give them your mailing address and if there is anything specific you need included in the permission."

Sue tucked the card in the pocket of her jeans. "We'll keep an itemized list of what we use and have everything appraised. Do you want me to send the list to your attorney or to you?"

"Send it to my attorney. He'll pass it on to whichever accountant handles such things." Mrs. Simpson smiled at Emily. "It was nice meeting both of you. I apologize for racing off this way. We have some friends who arrived in town unexpectedly, so I must get back to Houston. I don't want to miss my plane. If you have any questions or run into problems, consult with Linda."

"Are you going to sell the house?" Sue

casually walked with her back down the hall. Emily tagged along behind them, curious to hear the answer. If the Historical Society could get this beautiful treasure, it would draw more visitors to Callahan Crossing.

"Yes, though I don't suppose we'll get much for it. Things are so cheap out here, and it's so old. It probably should be torn down."

Emily bit back a cry of dismay. Tearing it down would be a disaster.

"Would you consider donating it to the Historical Society?" Sue held her hand behind her, fingers crossed.

Emily figured that was more a signal to say a quick prayer than a wish for good luck. *Please, Lord. Help us save this beautiful jewel.*

"What would you use it for?"

"As part of the museum. I'm hoping to set it up as it would have been when it was first built. Or at least early in its history. Displays in the museum are nice — and we'll be thankful for each one — but a home gives visitors better insight into how people actually lived. It puts their lives into better perspective."

Mrs. Simpson shrugged lightly. "I suppose it would make a good field trip for school-children."

"Yes, it would. It would certainly make that section of history more interesting."

Their benefactor's expression grew thoughtful. "Would you take it as is? I don't want to be bothered with having things repaired."

"I think we could, though we'll have to have it inspected first. I'd be in a pickle if I agreed, and we discovered it was about to fall down or something. It's not a decision I can make on my own anyway. The Historical Society will have to vote on it."

"That's my only condition. I'll be delighted if you'll take it off my hands. Let my attorney know whether or not you want it."

"I'll give him a call as soon as we make a decision. It may take a few weeks to have the inspection done and get everyone together to vote on it."

"Not a problem." Alicia Simpson hurried out the door, tossing them a graceful wave. "Ciao."

Sue looked at Emily as the woman drove off. "Did she really say chow?" Her eyes twinkled, revealing that she knew Mrs. Simpson was saying good-bye. "If I'd known she was hungry, I would have brought her a hamburger from the Sonic."

Emily laughed and closed the door. "*Adios* seems more appropriate out here." Considering Mrs. Simpson's social set, her laughter faded. "But I doubt that is in her vocabulary. It certainly doesn't seem to be in my mother's."

"Perhaps we should invite your parents out for a visit and loosen them up."

Emily shook her head. "Please don't. Everyone would be miserable within an hour."

"Are they really that bad?"

"I'm afraid so."

Sue murmured something that sounded like, "That could be a problem."

Emily wasn't sure she understood correctly. "I'm sorry. I didn't catch what you said."

"It's nothing. Just thinking out loud." Sue slid her arm around Emily's waist and grinned. "What are we doing standing here? Let's explore."

11

"It's incredible, one of the best Queen Anne's I've ever seen." Emily spread pictures of Sally Tucker's house across the big brown ottoman coffee table in front of Chance. The whole family had settled in the ranch house living room after dinner so Sue and Emily could tell them more about it. With a little silent cooperation from his kin, Chance nabbed the spot on the couch next to Emily.

He picked up a photo of the house from the front. It was a grand structure. He had admired it for years and had visited Miss Sally several times. He liked the old lady. She appreciated his interest in her home and gave him permission to wander through it to study the architecture.

Now he was jealous of the old Victorian. That was pretty bad. Maybe he had a right to be a little out of sorts. He didn't even know if they still wanted his building. Emily had been so excited about it the week before, but neither she nor his mom had mentioned it once this evening. And her eyes hadn't sparkled quite this much when she'd talked about his building.

Of course, it was empty. The Bradley-Tucker House was filled with wonderful stuff. Even Emily had used the word *stuff* when she'd run out of breath trying to describe it.

"But we have to have it inspected." His mother looked at him, narrowing her eyes.

Here it comes. I've been demoted from answer-to-our-prayers-wonderful-building-giver to lowly building inspector.

"And we need it done right away." His mother smiled gently, using an expression she knew he never could ignore. "We don't want to agree to taking it if it's going to fall down."

"You also don't want to give Mrs. Simpson time to change her mind." Chance sighed softly, mentally running over his full schedule for the next day. He was done with the debris cleanup, but he had appointments with clients and potential clients all day. Glancing at Emily's hopeful expression, he knew he'd rearrange everything if necessary to make her happy. "I could do it early in the morning." He held her gaze.

"But it will have to be at first light." She winced and he almost laughed. Instead he reached over and patted her hand. "Sorry, that's the best I can do. My schedule is tight. But you don't have to be there. I just need a key."

"No, I'll go, but I may not be too alert."

"I'll bring a thermos of coffee."

"With lots of sugar."

He'd rather sweeten her up with hugs and kisses, but that might not do much for her coffee. "Two thermoses, then. One black and one syrup."

"With a little milk."

"Maybe I should just pick up a mocha latte and have them add a Sonic Boom espresso shot?"

"Perfect."

"Boom," cried Zach, throwing his hands up in the air.

As Chance joined in the laughter, he caught his grinning mother lightly nudge his dad with her elbow. Was she thinking about her cute grandson or was she expressing her excitement about him and Emily? Better assume the latter and head her off before she made a comment. "Do y'all still want my building?"

His mom opened her mouth to speak, but Emily beat her to it. "Oh, my goodness, yes.

Miss Sally has a century of things stored in her home and the two double garages out back. Far more than we could ever display in the house. It may take us a month to go through it all."

Chance relaxed against the back of the red leather couch and silently thanked the Lord for answering his prayer to keep Emily there longer. "I've always loved that old house. Thought a lot of Miss Sally too. I used to visit her on occasion."

"You did?" His mom's eyebrows rose. "I didn't know that."

"Started when I was in high school. She let me study the architecture anytime I wanted. I'd spend time with her too. She was a neat lady, interested in what was going on at school and in what I wanted to do when I grew up." A bit of wistful sadness touched his heart. "She encouraged me to follow my dream and was proud when I opened my company.

"I don't think I'll find any major issues. I inspected the house for her every year and occasionally fixed some things. She had the exterminator come out regularly, so termites didn't dare set up residence. At the first sign of a problem, she'd call whoever she needed. If it was a squeaky board, she called me."

"I can't wait to see the inside," Jenna said,

pausing to give Zach a hug as he drove one of his little cars along the coffee table past her. "It sounds beautiful."

"It is. The woodwork was done by a true artist. I hope we can find the architect's drawings and notes along with who the builder was." Emily propped her feet up on the ottoman. "Unfortunately, the craftsmen weren't always recorded."

"I've seen the drawings, though I don't know where she kept them. She still had them two years ago. There was a list of materials too, and a few bills from the suppliers. I don't recall seeing anything about the people who did the actual work." Chance watched Zach wander across the room to the corner where his folks kept the little guy's toy box.

"Did she have anything from her father's medical practice?" Nate asked, also keeping a relaxed eye on his son. "It would be cool if you found some old medical equipment."

His mom curled her legs up on the couch. "Linda thinks there are some things stored somewhere, but she didn't know if they were in the attic or one of the garages. She's never come across it, although Miss Sally told her years ago that she had kept everything except the exam tables from her father's office. His big mahogany desk is in the study downstairs."

Zach came back, carrying a drawing tablet. He smiled at Chance and wove his way past all the adults' legs until he reached him. "You draw a picture for me?"

Chance noted surprise flash across Emily's face. "Sure, buddy." Scooting toward Emily until their shoulders and hips touched, he made room for Zach on the couch. He picked up the little boy and settled him on the other side of him. "What do you want me to draw?"

Zach grinned impishly, his eyes shifting to Will. "Uncle Will all muddy."

"Ah, you're thinking about when he fell in the mud at the stock tank last week."

"Uh-huh." Zach nodded and grinned at Will before he leaned forward and said to Emily, "Him was all dirty."

Chance turned the pad sideways, pulled a pen from his shirt pocket, and started drawing.

"I'll have you know I didn't fall in the mud. That ornery bull pulled me down." When his dad laughed, Will frowned at him. "You could've helped."

"I told you that bull would come out of the tank when he was ready. He wasn't nearly as bogged down as you thought he was."

"He might have been more cooperative if you'd roped him too."

"Couldn't. I was laughin' too hard when he started pullin' you into the tank."

Chance sketched quickly, starting with the ground, sloping it gradually downward, making a flat bottom, then sloping it up on the other side so he could add water. In some places, it was called a pond. In West Texas, it was a tank. One he had built with his bulldozer. "I don't have room to show the whole tank, just part of it. Okay?"

"Okay." Zach watched him intently.

Chance sensed that Emily did too. He drew a longhorn bull, cartoon style, standing in water up to its knobby knees. When he added a clump of mistletoe hanging from the bull's exaggerated long horns, Zach giggled. "That's why Uncle Will thought he couldn't get out. That ol' bull had been standing there so long he was raisin' mistletoe."

Even Will chuckled.

He drew Will sprawled on his backside on the bank, digging in his heels and clinging to a rope that he'd thrown over the bull's head. "He had to make a great big loop to go over those horns, didn't he?"

"Uh-huh." Zach spread his arms as wide as he could. "This big."

"At least," Will murmured dryly.

Chance glanced up at his older brother and grinned.

Will tried hard not to smile, but he wasn't successful. "Be kind, bro. Be kind."

"Oh, I am." Chance chuckled as he covered the cartoon Will in mud. A big glop of it was about to slide off his cap, which had been knocked sideways.

Zach shifted around until he was sitting on his knees so he could see better. He giggled and pointed at the mud on Will's head. "It gonna hit his nose."

"It might slide down and hit his ear."

"No, his nose." Zach leaned against his arm, making it a little harder to draw. Chance didn't say anything. Moments like this with his nephew were too precious to worry about something so trifling.

"Yep, I think you're right. First his nose and then probably his mouth. Then he'll spit and sputter."

"He did some of that, all right." Dub sent his oldest son a teasing smile. "And said a couple of words that made my ears burn."

"They weren't that bad." Will squirmed a bit and glanced at his mother — and at Emily.

Chance raised an eyebrow. Will looked at him and shrugged slightly. He supposed he

175

couldn't blame his brother for not wanting Emily to think badly of him.

"Should I add Papa watching the whole fiasco?"

A tiny frown creased Zach's forehead. "What's that?"

"Fiasco?"

Zach nodded.

"Mess. As in Uncle Will messed up."

"Yeah. Draw Papa."

"I bet he was laughing. What do you think?"

"Uh-huh."

Chance drew his dad standing over to one side, laughing broadly and slapping his knee with his cap. Just for fun, he added a big mesquite tree and a wide-eyed, open-beaked mockingbird perched on a branch, watching them.

Zach giggled again. "The bird's laughing."

"Yes, he is. What about the bull?"

Zach shrugged and held out his hands in front of him in a classic I-don't-know gesture. He looked so sweet that Chance gave him a one-armed hug.

"The bull is bored." Emily pressed against him as she leaned closer to look at the drawing.

Chance relished the moment, promising

himself there would be a million more like this.

"Or maybe he's thinking about pulling Will into the water. What do you think, Zach?"

The little boy studied the picture for a few seconds. "Yep."

Chance laughed and moved his arm from around the boy so he could carefully tear the drawing from the sketch pad. "I reckon that ol' bull wants to give him a bath."

"Give Uncle Chance and Emily a hug." Jenna smiled adoringly at her son. Chance didn't think any mother anywhere loved her child more. "Then show everybody else the picture and give them good-night hugs too."

"Okay." Zach put his arms around Chance's neck and squeezed him tight. "Thank you for the picture."

Chance's eyebrows went up. The kid had been saying thank you for things for a while. But he didn't think he'd ever heard him use it in a sentence unless prompted by someone. "You're welcome, buddy. Tell your mom to hang it up in your room."

He picked Zach up and handed him to Emily, noting that the hug he gave her was a little longer than what he'd received. Smart kid.

After she set Zach on the floor and he

went over to show Will and his grandparents the drawing, Emily slipped her hand beneath Chance's forearm, curling her fingers around it. "On Sunday, you didn't mention that you were an artist," she said quietly.

"It wouldn't be any fun if you learned everything all at once. I have to spread it out so you'll stay curious."

"So that's your strategy."

"Yes, ma'am." He slid his hand up to capture hers. "Think it will work?"

She laughed softly and tickled his palm with her thumbnail. "For a while. What happens when you run out of surprises?"

"It won't matter then."

"Why not?"

"Because we'll be old and gray and so used to having each other around that we wouldn't know what to do with ourselves if we were apart."

12

Emily sipped her supercharged mocha and stared at the hole in the foundation where Chance had disappeared into the crawl space of the Bradley-Tucker House. The awful thought of sliding the cover back in place and leaving him there for a few minutes to contemplate his transgressions crossed her mind. But she couldn't do it, not with spiders and bugs and walls that grew closer by the second. She shivered, set the cup down on a wrought iron bench, and buttoned up her thick wool sweater. No matter how angry she was, she would never shut him or anyone up in such a confining space even with a flashlight.

Besides, angry was a slight exaggeration. Irritation fit her feelings more accurately. How dare he stir her up last night with that talk of becoming old and gray together? She had worried and fretted almost all night, only to wind up with dark circles beneath her eyes and a strong urge to conk him in the head and knock some sense into him.

Didn't he understand that she had a career waiting to happen? That getting to know each other didn't mean happily ever after? It meant becoming friends, enjoying each other's company — in a platonic way — and maybe seeing each other two or three times a year after she moved back to the city. Which city remained to be seen since it depended on where she went to work. She was not supposed to spend her life in Callahan Crossing, where a hot date was going to the Boot Stop for dinner and dancing the night away at the honky-tonk north of town.

Nothing serious could develop between them, even if a tiny part of her heart longed for love and a too-handsome-for-her-own-good cowboy/builder. Shaking her head, she smiled at herself. That's how she thought of him. Cowboy-slash-builder. Equal parts of the whole. She'd yet to see him on a horse, but she had no doubt that he would be comfortable in the saddle and as proficient at herding cows as he was with a bulldozer or hammering a nail.

Ah-choo! Or crawling around in the dirt beneath houses.

She leaned over so her voice would carry

180

better into the shallow cavern. "Are you all right?"

"What?" His reply was faint and muffled.

"Are you all right?" She called louder but didn't move an inch closer to that awful hole.

"Yeah."

She heard some sliding noises.

"Yuck!"

"What's wrong?" Shading her eyes with her hand, she tried to peer farther into the darkness.

"Cobwebs." He sounded closer now, accompanied by scraping noises and a glimmer of light. The wobbling light grew brighter, and a hand holding the flashlight came into view. A few seconds later his head and shoulders appeared in the entrance as he pulled himself out of the crawl space. A few more wiggles and scoots and he was kneeling in the cement-framed hollow beside the house.

"Eww! There's a spider on your cap." Emily grabbed the stocking cap off his head and threw it on the ground, stomping on it. The spider fled in terror, but she stepped on the cap one more time for good measure.

"I think he escaped." Humor tinted Chance's voice as he climbed up to ground level and stood.

181

"He might have had a partner in crime."

"From his perspective I'm the one who committed the crime."

"What?" She frowned and shook her head in confusion.

"Home invasion. His home." He smiled. "Beneath the house."

"I get it." Annoyed at his smug expression, she glared at him. "Don't exterminators zap spiders too?"

"They do. But it appears they haven't been here in a month or two. You'll need to check with them and restart the service if it's been discontinued."

"Okay." When he shoved the wooden cover back over the entrance, she took a good look at him. He was coated in dirt, cobwebs, and a half dozen dead bugs the spiders had in their pantry. "You're filthy."

He pulled off his leather gloves and tossed them on the bench. Glancing down, he inspected his dark brown coveralls. "That's why I wear these over my clothes." He pointed to a yellow-handled narrow broom lying on the dried-up grass. "And bring something to brush off with. Would you do the honors, Miss Emily?"

"I'd be delighted to, Mr. Callahan." She noted his wary expression as she picked up the broom. Perhaps she'd sounded a little too enthusiastic. "Do you want me to start with your head or your shoulders?"

"Just shoulders and back," he said quickly. "I'll wipe off my head and face in a minute. I have a whisk broom in the truck that I can use for the rest of it."

She began to brush with vigor, stirring up a dust cloud and making him cough.

"Whoa!" He turned and grabbed the broom handle, halting her in midswipe. "I appreciate the effort, but we're going to choke to death."

"I'm fine."

"Well, I'm not." He tugged on the broom, but she held fast. She'd been rather enjoying herself.

He frowned and tugged again. "Am I on your nasty list?"

"Whatever makes you think that?" She strove for an innocent expression.

"You're applying that broom like a rug beater and I'm the rug."

"Oh." She released the offending object and backed up a step, aware that she didn't appear the least bit contrite. "Sorry."

"No, I don't think you are." He brushed at a large dirty spot on his lower pant leg. "You've been about half aggravated all morning."

"I have not."

He raised an eyebrow and kept brushing.

"I've been wholly aggravated."

"Why?"

Emily stared at him. He honestly didn't have a clue. "Remember last night? You talking about us growing old together?"

"Oh, that." His smile was so sweet she wanted to throw something.

"Yes, that. Hello? Remember my career? I don't want to get involved."

He paused, resting the broom bristles on the ground. "Don't you?" he said softly.

"No."

"Then why did you take me to meet your grandmother?"

She'd been asking herself the same question. "I thought she'd like you."

"Did she?"

"Yes. But just because we went to see her —"

"And spent the day together."

"Doesn't mean I intend to get serious."

"Sometimes what we intend and what happens are completely different things."

"I want us to be friends, to enjoy each other's company while I'm here."

"And when you go back to the city, you'll just forget about me?" A glint of anger flashed through his eyes.

"No," she said honestly. "I could never

184

forget you."

He leaned the broom against the back of the wrought iron bench and stepped closer. "There's something special between us, Emily Rose. You know it."

Yes, she did, but she wasn't going to admit it.

He smoothed a loose strand of hair back over her ear. "All I'm asking is to see if God has something in mind for us beyond friendship."

"I have everything all planned out, Chance."

"What about God's plans? Don't you think he might have something even better for you?"

"The Bible says he gives us the desires of our hearts. Running a big museum is what I want more than anything." Wasn't it? Seeing the intense emotion in his eyes, she wasn't quite so sure.

"There's another way of considering the same verse — that he puts the desires in our hearts and fulfills them. Did the goal of working in a big museum come from him, Emily? Or did you sort through your interests and decide it was what you wanted to do? Were you willing to let him lead you?"

"I didn't know God when I started college and chose a major."

"What about after you were saved? Did you ask God if you were doing the right thing?"

She lifted her chin a notch, meeting his direct gaze head-on. "Yes, I did. I asked him to block my way into the master's program for museum science if he didn't want me pursuing this. But he opened every single door. I know I'm in the right career." *So there.* A childish thought, but it was the way she felt at the moment. She was proud of herself for not saying it out loud and looked away so she wouldn't be tempted to do it anyway.

What had happened to her cool reserve, the sophistication she'd achieved under her mother's careful tutelage to survive in their world? Where the slip of the tongue or an unguarded expression might lose a valuable client, destroy a potential business deal, or offend a large benefactor to a favorite charity.

Why did he turn her upside down and inside out? It wasn't only Chance, she realized. It was his family, the whole town. Most of the people in Callahan Crossing weren't afraid of showing their emotions, good or bad. They were steadfast in their beliefs, honest in their feelings. They were real. Like Grandma Rose. And they were

186

changing her.

Or was God using them to change her? To mold her into more of the person he wanted her to be. Not the little kid who felt like sticking out her tongue at Chance and saying "Neener, neener, neener." But the woman who had discovered a depth of compassion she hadn't known she possessed until the fire. The woman whose hard heart was being softened because she was in the midst of a family who loved each other deeply despite their occasional disagreements.

Chance ran his fingers through his hair and sighed, drawing her attention back to him. "I know you're in the right career, Emily. Your love of what you do is obvious in the way your face lights up when you talk about the museum or this old house. Your belief in the value of history can't be denied, especially after you saved those documents and pictures from the fire."

He inched closer, curving his right hand around her waist. "But why does becoming the head curator of a big city museum have to be the ultimate prize? Is it the only thing that will make you happy?"

"I want to be a success." The drive that had brought her this far lent an edge of stubbornness to her voice. Or was it the desperate need to show her parents that they were wrong? To prove to them that she was important but on her own terms. That what she had chosen to do was important.

"Is that the only measure of success?" He eased his left hand around the other side of her waist.

"The only one that matters." If he was trying to distract her, he was pulling it off.

"Liar," he said softly.

"What?" She stared up at him.

"If that were true, you wouldn't care how good a job you do setting up the museum."

"Of course, I would." When had she rested her hands against his chest?

"Because if you didn't do it well, it would be a black mark on your resume."

"Yes. But that's not the only reason." She frowned up at him, wishing he'd stop lightly rubbing his thumb against her side. No, she didn't. She just wished it wasn't scrambling her brain. "I take pride in my work. I want it to benefit others, to teach them about the diverse history of this wonderful state."

"So every small museum has value."

"If it's done right."

"And there's a need for you to help people make their museums the best they can be. Which in turn makes you successful."

"Rungs on the ladder." Was he bending

down? Her gaze settled on his lips. They were slowly moving closer.

"Leading to the top."

"Right." She swallowed hard and tried to calm her racing heart.

"There's more to life than being at the top, darlin'," he whispered. "A whole lot more."

Hang her goals. She wanted to kiss him in the worst way. A little breeze ruffled his hair. A small gray clump floated down on a cobweb, dangling in front of his ear and swinging in her direction since he was leaning toward her.

Catching her breath, Emily pulled back.

"Don't chicken out on me, sweetheart."

She cleared her throat. "There's a cocoon-wrapped bug caught in your sideburn."

Chance smiled ruefully as he dropped his hands, straightened, and stepped back. "Reckon that kind of ruins the moment." He flicked his fingers across the side of his face, knocking the spider's boxed lunch to the ground. "I'm too dirty to be holdin' you anyway. Sorry."

She didn't know how to reply, so she grabbed her latte and took a long sip. He gathered up his gloves and the broom and walked over to his truck. She picked up the poor stocking cap that she'd ground in the dirt and followed, not wanting him to think she was mad. Surely, he realized she'd been a willing participant to their almost-kiss.

He wiped his head and face with a towel as she walked up and draped the cap over the side of the truck bed. "Did I get it all?"

His hair looked adorably rumpled. "I think so." She stretched around to see better. "Wait, there's a little bit of cobweb on the side of your neck." She reached over and plucked it off, trailing her fingers lightly over his skin. His gaze met hers, and her mouth went dry.

"Thanks." His voice sounded a little husky.

At least he could speak. She nodded and stepped out of his way.

He untied his tennis shoes and slipped them off, standing on the cement driveway in a pair of white socks that looked brand-new. Had he worn a new pair to impress her? She wouldn't put it past him. In a way, it was sweet.

He tossed his shoes into a heavy duty plastic storage box on the backseat. Shrugging out of his coveralls, he rolled them up — dirt, bugs, and all — and put them on top of the shoes. The whisk broom remained tucked away somewhere. He added his stocking cap to the container before removing a pair of cowboy boots from the floor between the seats. Leaning against the truck, he pulled them on.

Emily chugged some more of the latte, which had cooled down enough to drink quickly. "Did you find any problems?"

"There are a couple of sections of drain pipe that need to be replaced. No holes or anything, but there is some corrosion where they connect. I'll call a plumber to take care of it. But the structure looks good. No sign of termites or dry rot." He looked up at the roof. "She had a new thirty-year roof put on fifteen years ago, but I see a couple of shingles missing. I'll have my roofer fix it and make sure there's no damage underneath. We can check for leaks when we look at the attic. Did you go up there yesterday?"

"No. We didn't get around to it. Linda said she hadn't been up there in about five years, not since her knee got bad."

"All those stairs were hard for her. They lived on the first floor these last several years since it has two bedrooms and a bathroom. Linda's daughter came over every few months and cleaned the second floor rooms for her. Linda has needed a knee replacement for a while, but she refused to get it while Miss Sally was alive. She didn't want to leave her with anyone else."

"She's still putting it off." Emily set her empty cup in the back of the truck and moved to the edge of the driveway to pull a few weeds. "Now, she wants to wait until everything with the house is taken care of. She doesn't want to be out of commission if we need her, which I think we will. She knows a lot of the family's history, things Miss Sally told her over the years."

"Miss Sally was a good storyteller. I told her several times that she should write a book. She'd just laugh and wave her hand and say all those journals and account books would have to suffice."

Emily straightened and tossed a scraggly clump of grass onto the mini-weed pile. "She has journals?"

"I don't know how many or where they are. I'm not even sure who wrote them." Chance pulled a short comb from his back pocket and leaned down in front of the outside mirror, combing his hair. When he was finished, he tucked the comb back in his pocket and noticed she was watching him. "Do I look presentable?"

"Yes. Though I kinda liked the rumpled look."

"Oh yeah? I'll let you mess it up again." He glanced at his watch and sighed. "But not now. I need to sprint through the rest of the inspection if I'm going to make my first appointment." He caught her hand and tugged her toward the house. "Come on, darlin'. You can search for family skeletons while I look for cracks and mildew."

"You lead such a glamorous life."

"Not usually." He opened the back door and followed her inside. "But I've worn a tux on occasion. I can hold my own with the rich and powerful."

"I'm sure you can." And it would be something to see.

13

On Saturday evening, the guys got together at Will's to watch pro basketball. Since the girls were celebrating their friend Lindsey's birthday, Nate brought Zach along. The little guy took turns pushing the bulldozer around on the hardwood floor and driving off with an imaginary load of dirt in the dump truck. Sometimes he stopped the dozer and used the toy crane to pick up blocks and put them in the truck to haul away.

Chance had given him the construction set, so he was pleased that it was one of his favorite toys. He was also tickled because it annoyed his brother, who was convinced he was trying to turn Zach into a builder instead of a cowboy before he reached age three.

He looked around the room at his friends and silently thanked the Lord for life being good. There hadn't been any problems with the Bradley-Tucker House, so the Historical Society had approved the donation at a hastily convened meeting on Thursday night. His mother got the ball rolling with a call to Mrs. Simpson's attorney first thing Friday morning. His mom and Emily were chockful of glee.

"Pizza's ready," called Will, setting two pans on the wide counter that separated the kitchen from the rest of the great room.

"About time." Chance hopped up from the sofa and headed for the refrigerator. "Nate, you want root beer?"

"Water's good for me."

"I want root beer," Zach said.

"No, buddy. You need to stick with water too. That's what I'm having."

"Okay. You fix me pizza?"

"Sure will."

Dalton rested his hand on Nate's shoulder as they walked toward the kitchen. "You're good at this daddy stuff."

"He makes it easy. Not perfect, but he's really a good kid."

"Married life agrees with you."

"There's nothin' better." Nate washed his hands and dried them on a paper towel. Taking a glass from the cabinet, he filled it with water from the cold water dispenser on the front of the refrigerator. "Chance thinks he's next to get hitched."

"That's what he says, but I don't see him taking Emily out on any dates." Will set a stack of paper plates and napkins on the counter beside some regular forks. If a fork was needed, plastic didn't cut it.

"Haven't had the opportunity. But she took me to Eden to meet her grandmother." Chance handed Dalton a Dr Pepper and opened one for himself. "That's a biggie in my book."

"Mine too." Dalton washed his hands at the kitchen sink, opened the soda, and took a drink. Setting it on the counter, he looked over the pizza. "How'd you and Grandma get along?"

"Good. Charmed the socks off her and her best friend."

"What about her parents? When are you goin' to meet them?" Nate asked as he cut a slice of Canadian bacon and pineapple pizza into child-sized bites.

"I don't know. She doesn't seem to like her parents much. To be honest, from some of the things she's said, I don't think I will either."

"How come?"

"They're rich."

Dalton chuckled and put a couple of slices of Miller's Grocery Everything-On-It pizza

196

on his plate. "So are you."

"Yeah, but they act like it. Flaunt their wealth, rub elbows with the rich and famous."

"Which y'all have done on occasion." Nate motioned for Zach to come to him. "Come wash your hands."

Just for fun, Chance held out his hands and inspected them. "But they're clean. I washed them this morning."

"Don't go puttin' ideas into my son's head." Nate motioned toward the sink. "Be a good example to your nephew."

"Yes, sir." Laughing, Chance dutifully washed his hands. They probably needed it anyway. Drying them on a paper towel, he held them up to show Zach. "Squeaky clean."

His nephew grinned as Nate lifted him up to the sink and scrubbed his hands with some soap. "Kid, you sure got grubby from playing with imaginary dirt."

"Will probably needs to mop the floor."

"What's a mop?" Will helped himself to the food.

"That thing our cleaning lady uses when she shovels out your house and mine." Chance wadded up a napkin and tossed it at his brother. Will batted it back. They'd hired a high school neighbor to clean their places every couple of weeks. She did a good job, and it made their lives easier.

Chance tucked a napkin and fork into his shirt pocket before sliding a slice of each kind of pizza onto his plate. He moseyed back into the living room area, watching Nate settle Zach in his little chair at the coffee table. The chair had been Will's when he was that age. Chance had an identical one from his childhood at his house. It came in handy when his sister and family were over or on those rare times when he babysat.

Will and Dalton took their seats on the couch and tucked into the food. Nate glanced at Chance as he started toward the kitchen.

"I'll keep an eye on him." Chance winked at Zach. He didn't think Nate had any worries about the boy abandoning his food. Zach loved pizza.

The Dallas Mavericks made a score, and Zach threw his hands up in the air. "Touchdown!"

"That's a basket, buddy. Touchdown is football." Will smiled at his nephew as the San Antonio Spurs raced down the court. "Now, the Spurs made a basket, a three-pointer."

"Three-pointer." Zach nodded and stuffed

another bite of pizza in his mouth.

"So when are you going to take Emily out?" Will asked. "If you don't make a move soon, I'm going to."

Since his brother had a mischievous twinkle in his eye, Chance thought he was kidding. On the other hand, Will had admitted that he was attracted to her. "You do, and I'll take you down and sit on you."

"Oh yeah? You and who else?"

"Now, boys," Dalton drawled. "Behave yourselves, or I'll pin my deputy badge on and arrest you for disturbing my peace."

Grinning, Will waved his hands in the air. "Oh, I'm so scared. You scared, Chance?"

"Naw. We can still whup him."

Dalton grinned lazily. "So when are you going to ask her out?"

"Already did. Since the weather's supposed to be good, I invited her on a picnic tomorrow." He looked pointedly at the deputy. "It's Valentine's Day."

"Noticed that on the calendar." Dalton picked up a half slice of pizza from his plate and took a bite.

"So?" Chance asked.

"What?" Dalton frowned and wiped a string of cheese off his chin.

"Remember what I told you the other day? Didn't you take that under advisement?"

"I've been thinking about it."

"What'd you tell him?" Will reached for his soda.

"That he should ask Lindsey out."

"Good idea." Will glanced at Nate. "Didn't Jenna say we should come over at halftime for some cake?"

"Yep. Perfect opportunity to speak to the lady."

Groaning, Dalton leaned his head on the back of the couch. "I've been set up."

"Past time for you to act." Chance grinned at his old friend.

"Come on, guys. I'll get around to it when I'm ready."

"Time's a-wastin'," Nate said, wiping pizza sauce off Zach's face with his napkin. "Besides, the lady likes you."

"She does?" Dalton sat up straighter. "How do you know?"

"I don't think you were supposed to tell him that," Will said.

"Just slipped out. My bad." Nate's smile wasn't in the least repentant.

Chance laughed and shook his head. "You've been hanging around with my sister too much."

"Yeah, and lovin' every minute of it."

"Nate, how do you know she likes me?" Dalton set his plate on the coffee table, one piece of pizza untouched, a frown drawing his eyebrows almost together.

"Jenna told me. Women talk about that kind of stuff."

"I suppose they do." Dalton picked up his plate, then set it down again. "This isn't the kind of thing to spring on a man when he's stuffin' his face with pepperoni and Italian sausage." He dug a roll of antacids out of his front pocket and popped two into his mouth.

"Are you all right?" Chance watched him closely. His friend had been under a lot of stress since the fire. He didn't want them to add to it. But Lindsey would be good for him.

"I'm okay. After a burrito for lunch, I should have stuck with the Canadian bacon and pineapple."

"Go make a trade. We don't care. It's not like you've eaten half of that piece already."

"Wouldn't care if he had," said Will. "I can always cut off that part."

Dalton walked into the kitchen and switched slices. "I don't think Lindsey is all that interested in me." He sat down, looking at Nate. "She's friendly in a polite sort of way. But she doesn't flirt or anything."

"She's a little shy sometimes. She's a good

woman," said Nate. "And a good friend to Jenna."

"She helped Jenna a lot after she first moved home, pulled her out of her shell when we couldn't." Will stood and headed toward the kitchen for a refill. "But I think she gets a little tongue-tied around a certain deputy."

"So how come y'all know all of this, and I never noticed?" Dalton rearranged the pineapple on the pizza, spreading it out.

"We have keen powers of observation?" Chance grinned when Nate and Will laughed.

Dalton frowned in consternation. "I thought I did too."

"Well, you know what they say . . ."

"What?"

"Love is blind."

"I'm not in love." Dalton's frown had darkened to a scowl.

"Not yet," Nate said quietly.

Though her insides were quaking, Lindsey Moore smiled and blew out the candles on her cake. When Dalton Renfro had walked through the door wearing a deer-in-the-headlights look, she'd wished she were home polishing her toenails. Or riding the exercise bike she never got on, though she really needed to. Even weeding her mother's rosebushes in the dark would be better than this humiliation.

Someone had told him.

Maybe not that she'd loved him since they were in high school but that she was interested in him now. He'd barely noticed her back then, and it hadn't changed much. He'd greet her at church or around town with a friendly smile. But he'd never been interested enough to do more than comment on the weather or something equally mundane.

The Callahans and Nate had obviously decided Dalton needed a little — no, make that a *big* — push in her direction. Bless their hearts, they meant well, but for the most part, the poor man looked as uncomfortable as she felt.

Still, he joined in singing "Happy Birthday" with enthusiasm. She hadn't known he had such a beautiful bass voice. The smile he gave her when she successfully blew out all twenty-eight candles was sincere. Lindsey relaxed a little bit.

That only lasted until she'd distributed the slices of chocolate birthday cake with strawberry filling. Somehow everyone else had wandered off to the living room, leaving her and Dalton alone in the kitchen.

Lord, please don't let me say or do something stupid.

He motioned toward the cake's icing decoration of an artist's palette and a paintbrush. "What do you paint?"

"Murals. So far most have been in kids' bedrooms, but Maisie hired me to draw one on the front of her antiques store."

"That's great." He paused, frowning mildly as he cut a bite of cake with his fork. "The only place you can put a mural on her building is on the false front."

"That's right. It will cover the whole wall of the fake second floor. I start on it Monday." In spite of her nervousness, excitement bubbled up. She cut herself a small piece of cake and put it on the crystal dessert plate. "I'm hoping other store owners will be so impressed that they'll hire me to do more on their buildings."

"How are you going to work up there?"

"I'll use one of my dad's scaffolds. We've already gotten approval from the city council, the constable, and the fire department to use it. I've worked on a scaffold when I helped my dad paint houses — the regular kind of painting — so it won't be hard."

"What kind of mural are you going to do?" He took a bite of cake and actually seemed interested in what she had to say.

Amazing.

"An 1880s wash day. The wife scrubbing some pants on a rubboard, a black cast-iron kettle over the wood fire, a couple of rinse pots, sheets on the clothesline, a kid and a dog running around. That kind of thing. Maisie has given her approval to the sketch I drew out."

He smiled and leaned his hip against the kitchen counter. "That sounds perfect for Maisie's place. I hope you get to do more of them. They would make downtown a lot more interesting. Are you still working at the bank?"

"Yes. Have to keep my real job. But I'm taking a couple of weeks vacation to work on the mural. If I'm not finished with it when it's time to go back to work, my boss said I could go to part-time and only work a couple of days a week until it's done. He wants to train someone to fill in during vacations this summer, so she could work on my days off."

Dalton nodded. "And he wouldn't be out any more money. I bet he loves the idea."

"Maybe a little too much." Lindsey picked up her plate and fork. "Sounds like the game has started. Shall we join the others?"

"In a minute." He set his dessert on the counter and straightened, stepping closer.

Lindsey thought surely he could see how hard her heart was pounding. Weren't law officers trained to notice such things? She couldn't say a word. Just looked up at him, probably like a grown woman with a school-girl crush. But she couldn't help it. The feelings she had for this good, noble man came from the depths of her heart.

"I think our friends are trying to set us up."

A hot flush filled her cheeks, and she lowered her gaze to somewhere around the first button on his western shirt. *Don't cry. Not now.* "I didn't know they had this planned. No one told me you were going to be at Will's." Somehow she managed to look up at him. "I'm so sorry."

"Don't be. And don't be embarrassed." His expression softened, and an intriguing light warmed his eyes. "Maybe they've done us a favor. Would you go to dinner with me tomorrow after church?"

"Yes, I'd like that."

"Maybe drive over to Sweetwater?"

"Sweetwater's good. I haven't been over there to eat in a while."

"It will keep the gossips from burning up the phone lines and email for an hour or two." He grinned and turned to pick up his cake again. "I think they must have spies scattered all over three counties. Sometimes they know which bad guy I'm chasing before I do."

Lindsey laughed and started toward the living room. When she felt his hand rest on the small of her back, gently guiding her to take one of the two open places on the couch instead of the empty chair, she was afraid she really might cry.

This time with happiness.

ALLEN PARK PUBLIC LIBRARY

14

On Sunday afternoon, Emily sat in the rocker on the Callahans' back porch, waiting for Chance to pick her up for their picnic. It was a gorgeous sunny day, around sixty-five with a light breeze. Wintertime in Texas was unpredictable. The high might be thirty-five one day and sixty or seventy the next. It tended to sometimes get colder at night in West Texas than in San Antonio or even Dallas, but days like this made up for having to bundle up.

Dub had taken Sue out to dinner to celebrate Valentine's Day. Ditto Nate and Jenna with Zach, and even Dalton and Lindsey. They'd all gone to various restaurants in Sweetwater or Abilene and weren't back yet. Will was the only one left alone.

She felt bad about that, but if it bothered him, he hid it well. He'd planned to pick up a bucket of fried chicken in town, relax in his recliner, and watch a suspense thriller he'd rented. When she'd quietly voiced her concern after church, he said Valentine's Day was for sweethearts and that they needed him tagging along like a duck needed an umbrella.

She'd wanted to point out that she and Chance weren't sweethearts; this was their first real date. Being on Valentine's Day made it seem more important than it was. Even to her. Dinner out in a restaurant would have been nice. Just the two of them going on a picnic was special.

When she saw his pickup pull away from his house, she walked out to the road and playfully stuck out her thumb as if hitching a ride.

He stopped in front of her and lowered the passenger side window. His smile held a hint of flirtation. "Need a lift, purty lady?"

"Depends. Where ya goin', cowboy?" She rested one hand on her hip and pretended to chew gum.

Grinning, he motioned toward the southeast. "Thought I'd wander up into the hills for a spell. Thar's some mighty fine scenery up thataway. Brung along dinner. I'll share with ya."

She made a big show of deeply sniffing the unmistakable aroma of fried chicken. "Do I smell chicken?"

"You do. Slaved for the past hour fryin' it up."

Emily opened the truck door and climbed in. "Right. Are you sure you didn't have Will pick some up for you when he stopped at the grocery store?"

"Caught me. I did bake the cake, though."

"Really?" She leaned forward to see his face better as he put the truck in gear and drove around the house. He appeared sincere.

"Yes, ma'am. Banana nut cake and from scratch too. It's a family favorite. Mama got the recipe from Grandma so no tellin' how long it's been around. It's easy to make."

"Jenna says you're a good cook."

"Huh. I figured I did okay. At least she didn't get sick after eating at my place. But I didn't make anything fancy. Remind me to thank her."

"Simple things are as good as gourmet, especially when prepared with love. She said she hung out at your place a lot after she first moved home."

"She did. Sometimes I could get her to eat some steak or something else from the grill, but more often we had a box of macaroni and cheese, pinto beans, and corn bread, or scrambled egg sandwiches. Jen needed comfort food then. When she ate, which wasn't nearly often enough. She was in rough shape when she moved back home."

"She's happy now."

"That she is. Did you notice Dalton and Lindsey sat together in church this morning?" He wiggled his eyebrows.

She nodded. "Yep. I heard her tell Jenna that he's taking her out to dinner in Sweetwater."

"Hot dog! Our little matchmakin' scheme worked."

"At least they're taking a step in the right direction." She watched the scenery for a minute. When she glanced at him, she found him studying her. "What?"

"Two things. Did I just hear you say *yep?*"

"You did. I've been hanging out with the Callahans too long."

"Is that bad?"

"No." If her parents heard her talk that way, they'd be appalled and say she sounded like a hick. "It's good. What's the second thing?"

"Are we taking a step in the right direction?"

"I don't know." Looking out the window, she considered the question before turning back to him. "I like you a lot, Chance. But I have goals and dreams."

"Ever dream of me?" One side of his mouth lifted in an endearing, lopsided smile.

"Yes." The word spilled out before she had time to come up with a better answer. Though anything else would be lying. "I dreamed about you the other night, after you inspected Miss Sally's house."

"Was it good?"

"Depends on how you feel about being attacked by a giant cockroach."

He made a face and shook his head. "Definitely not good. Did I win?"

"Don't know. I woke up right after you jumped out of the crawl space and that six-foot bug stuck his head out from under the house."

"You really do have a problem with dark, closed spaces, don't you?"

"Yes. Not fond of spiders and bugs, either."

"I noticed. Not even dead ones."

"Not if they're about to hit me in the face."

"I'll keep that in mind. Have you dreamed of me any other time?" The man was entirely too persistent.

"I think about you occasionally."

"Daydream?" His expression practically brimmed with hope.

212

"Not exactly. Okay, sometimes. Look, let's don't go there. I don't have to tell you all my secrets any more than you've told me all of yours."

"Good point." He turned left, crossing a cattle guard and going down another dirt road. The hills and a long flat-topped mesa were directly in front of them, about a mile away. "The land is pretty dreary now, but it will be filled with wildflowers in the spring if we get good rains. If the rains are sparse, the flowers will be too. Unless there's a drought, we'll have plenty of flowers to brighten it up."

As they neared the first of the hills, the reddish-brown dirt and sun-dried golden grass of the flat land gave way to a mix of brown and white earth. Small scruffy green cedar trees, leafless gray-brown mesquite trees, and green prickly pear cactus somewhat dulled by the winter's chill were scattered across the swells and dips of the landscape. The shadowed gray of the mesa made an artistic backdrop for the subtle swaths of gold, gray, and green.

"It's pretty this way too, though it's more subtle, almost like a sepia photograph. Springtime must be spectacular. Even without the wildflowers, the bright green of the mesquites and the yellow and orange blossoms on the prickly pear will bring it to life."

He smiled and sighed quietly. "There isn't an inch of ground on this ranch that I don't love. In good times or lean, this is still the best place on earth." Steering with one hand, he reached for the water bottle in the console. He pulled open the pop-up top with his teeth and took a drink. "I suppose you think the city is better." Pushing the top closed with his thumb, he set the bottle back in the console. He'd thoughtfully provided one for her too.

"Better in some ways. I love the historic section of San Antonio, the restaurants and shops. My neighborhood is quiet, if you don't mind kids playing in the street or the teenager down the block with his loud muffler. Home is a nice place to retreat from some of the hustle and bustle. But it's not like here. I wonder what Aidan's wife, Clara, thought of the silence. Did she find it comforting or did it cloak her in loneliness?"

"I expect loneliness, particularly when Aidan was out working the herd or gone on business. We're a ways from town, so it wasn't easy for her to go visiting or attend the weekly meetings of the Ladies Aid Society. After the kids started to school, she only lived out here between terms. A lot of ranching families split their time between homes in town and homes on the ranch."

He slowed the pickup and shifted into four-wheel drive, bouncing along a narrow, winding road that led up and through the hills. The road turned at the base of the mesa, going up the side of it in a long sloping climb. At the top, he stopped so she could look back at the way they'd come.

In the distance, the trees of the Callahan compound appeared like a small oasis in the desert. Farther away, the ranch camp house where Dalton lived was a tiny white blur. Chance drove a bit farther and stopped again. "Those two little dots in the distance are Buster's and Ollie's houses."

Turning, he guided the pickup toward the other side of the mesa. The land was relatively flat, but shallow ravines cut through their path now and then, making for a rough ride.

"Sorry about bouncing you around like you're on a buckin' bronc. I wouldn't put it past Will not to try to watch us with his telescope."

"He wouldn't do that, would he?" Smiling, she shook her head. The brothers teased each other a lot, but she didn't think either of them would infringe on the other's privacy.

"Probably not, but I want to show you the view from the other side. Jack's Creek is down in the valley. Down there at night, you can't see a single light except for the stars and moon."

"So it's the way it was when Aidan and Jack first moved here."

"Exactly. If we wait until after dark to go back to the house, you'll have a feeling for what it was like. Or we can come back again if you have things you need to do."

"I don't have anything that can't wait until tomorrow, but I didn't bring a coat. When the temperature drops, it will be cold unless we sit in the pickup and run the engine. And that burns gas."

He chuckled and drove around a big rock. "For a rich lady, you sure are frugal. At least with other people's money. I tossed a couple of quilts in the back. We can wrap up in them if we get cold and still look at the stars. If you don't want to stay, just say the word when you're ready to leave."

She moved around, leaning against the door, facing him. "Do you always plan ahead for all contingencies?"

Slowing down for another bump, his gaze briefly shifted toward her. "I plan as best I can, taking the options into consideration, but you can never prepare for everything. Life is like herding cattle. You may think you have them under control, but it only takes a few seconds for something to go wrong. One spooked critter causes the whole herd to stampede."

"You've actually been in a stampede?" She glanced out the windshield when he stopped the truck but quickly returned her attention to him.

"Several. The first one was when I was fifteen. We have big pastures, but if you don't get the cattle under control quick enough, they'll try to run right through the fence. They might even tear it down, but they'll get cut up bad in the process."

"Do you stop them like in the movies? Race ahead and try to turn the lead cattle?"

"Exactly. If you turn the leader, the rest will follow." He shifted into park and turned off the ignition. "You get them going in a tight circle, back into the herd, and they'll all slow down. Sometimes it takes a while to stop them from milling around, but they're moving slow enough by then that they won't get hurt."

"Is it as dangerous as it appears in the movies?"

"People can get hurt. There's always the

risk of a horse stepping in a hole and you both going down. Or getting thrown for some other reason. The fall might break a bone, which can be bad if it's your back or neck. Usually, it's just an arm or leg."

"That's bad enough."

"True, but that can happen tripping over an uneven sidewalk. The worst danger is being trampled by the cattle."

"So you actually could get killed." She supposed she should have known that, but she'd thought it was some movie trick to make it look more perilous. A chill crept down her spine.

"Plenty of jobs are dangerous. You were in danger when you were cleaning out the old museum. It could have collapsed on you."

"I didn't know it. Well, not until you pointed it out to me."

"You still went back in there to finish up."

"Only once. There's a difference between doing something I needed to despite my fear and trembling and being an adrenaline junkie."

Frowning, he took off his cap, tracing the tractor logo with his index finger. "An adrenaline junkie is a race car driver, a bull rider, or a skydiver. I don't chase stampeding cows because I want a rush. I do it because they'll get hurt or killed if I don't."

"What about working on the front lines when y'all were fighting the wildfire? If the wind had suddenly switched, you and your bulldozer would have been toast."

He put the cap back on and reached for the door handle. "It was something I had to do despite my fear and trembling. Enough shoptalk for now. I'm ready to eat."

Emily thought she might have made him mad, though she couldn't tell. Did he ever get really mad? Foot-stomping, shouting angry? No, guys didn't stomp their feet. But they shouted a lot. At least her dad did. He was an expert at flying off the handle and letting everyone in the house know about it. She'd often wondered if he exploded at work too, or if he saved it all up and let loose at home.

The only time she'd seen a hint of anger in Chance was at Miss Sally's when he talked about her going back to the city and forgetting about him. There had definitely been a glint of anger in his eyes at that moment, though he had tamped it quickly.

Emily climbed out of the truck and walked around the back to the driver's side. Chance stood outside the back door and leaned inside. She stopped a few feet away where she had a view of his scowling face. He was taking too long to get whatever he was after

219

and muttering under his breath. When he drew back out of the pickup and straightened with a patchwork quilt, he was still frowning.

"Can I help?" She took a tiny step closer.

"Can you handle this?" At least he didn't snap at her.

"Sure."

He thrust it into her open arms and ducked back inside the truck, pulling out a wicker picnic basket.

Emily didn't want to ruin their afternoon together. "Chance, I'm sorry. I didn't mean to offend you." His frown darkened again. "It scares me when I think about you doing something dangerous and possibly getting hurt. I spoke before I thought."

His frown faded, and some of the tension in his stance eased. "That must mean you care about me."

"Of course, I do, you big lug. You're my friend."

One dark eyebrow arched. "Still just a friend, huh?"

"That's right. A good friend." Who could become much more if she'd let him. And that would cause all sorts of problems.

"Spread the quilt out over there. I'll bring the food. We'll see if the way to my woman's heart is through her stomach."

Emily laughed, knowing he'd accepted her apology. She really should point out that she wasn't his woman. But a quiet little voice — which sounded surprisingly like Grandma Rose — told her to shush and enjoy the afternoon.

How many opportunities would she have to go on a picnic on the top of a mesa with a real, live, very handsome cowboy-slash-builder?

15

Half an hour later, they were both stuffed with fried chicken, potato salad, and banana nut cake. As Chance had hoped, she was impressed with his simple dessert.

"I'd like the recipe." She added her paper plate and napkin into the plastic bag he held out for her. They'd already put the food away in the cooler with plenty left over if they wanted a snack later. "It's not some old family secret that's passed down from generation to generation with everyone sworn to secrecy, is it?"

"Nope. Even if it was, I'd share it with you." He stuffed the garbage in a compartment in the toolbox in the back of the truck.

"That's sweet."

Which was what he'd hoped she'd say instead of getting on him about breaking secrets.

Emily had spread the quilt where they had a good view. She drew up her knees and wrapped her arms around them, staring off across the ranch. "It's so peaceful here."

"It's like this most places on the ranch away from the houses. Except in the fall when we separate the calves from their mamas. Several hundred cows and calves all bawling at once makes a ruckus that can be heard for miles. The old-timers say that's what makes them hard of hearing, and I halfway believe it."

"Only halfway?"

"Enough to wear earplugs when working around the pens. Do you want to stretch your legs?"

"Sure. Though I'm not walking down off this mountain."

Chance stood and offered her his hand, pulling her up beside him. "I'm not sure it technically qualifies as a mountain."

"Well, it's high enough to be a mountain in my mind, especially if I'm walking. And high enough to make me dizzy if I get too close to the edge."

He'd hadn't thought about that. "I didn't know heights bothered you."

"They don't unless I'm staring at the bottom of a thousand-foot cliff."

He chuckled and took her hand as they walked along. "It's more like two hundred feet, if that. Do you ski?"

She glanced up at him. "No. Why?"

"So you haven't been to the top of any real mountains."

"That's not what you asked me. I've been to Aspen, but I don't ski. Neither does my mom. We spent our time in the spa and the shops."

"Ah, so you like to be pampered."

"I indulge occasionally."

"Nothin' wrong with that. Or with having some girl time with your mom."

She drew to a halt and was quiet for a few minutes, looking at the scenery. Chance hoped she was around in the spring to see it. He loved the place, but he was honest enough to accept that it wasn't at its best in the wintertime. Or the heat of summer. Or even fall, for that matter. But springtime was beautiful.

"Maybe that's what I need to do," she said softly.

"What's that?" He stepped behind her, sliding his arms around her waist, gently drawing her back against him. When she leaned her head against his shoulder and rested her hands on his, he briefly closed his eyes, savoring the moment.

"Have some girl time with my mom. It will be a while before we could get together. She's trotting the globe for the next month, hitting all the shows for Fashion Week."

"If it's a week, how come she'll be gone for a month?"

"It's a week in each place. New York, London, Milan, Paris."

"Maybe you should go to Milan or Paris and surprise her." Not that he wanted her out of his sight for more than a day, but it sounded as if she was missing her mom. That was odd, given the way she got along with her parents, but a lot of people in Callahan Crossing seemed to be reevaluating their priorities and relationships since the fire.

She laughed and shook her head. "You make me sound like a jet-setter."

"You aren't?" he teased.

"Not like my folks. I've traveled quite a bit, but I'm not one to impulsively fly off to Paris for a few days. She'd be too busy to spend any time with me anyway. It's a business trip, and practically every minute is filled. I might call her though. I've been thinking about her a lot this week and about my not-so-Christian attitude toward my parents."

"What brought this on?" He rested the side of his face against her hair, letting the subtle floral scent of her shampoo surround him. He could stay right there for an hour or two.

"It's kind of convoluted."

"I've got all afternoon."

"When Sue and I were on our way to the Bradley-Tucker House the first time, she mentioned that Miss Sally's daughter and granddaughter rarely came to visit her and only called her two or three times a year. That made me feel a little guilty because I often go three or four months without calling my parents."

"Do they call you?"

"Rarely. If they do, it's usually to see if I've gotten a job or to give me a bad time because I don't have anything good or permanent. Or simply to complain about my chosen career."

"Under those circumstances, I wouldn't want to talk to them, either." What a difference between his parents and hers. His folks hadn't always liked every crazy idea he'd had as a kid, and his dad had been hard to live with sometimes. But they'd always supported his decision to be a builder, even when things were slow.

"During that same conversation with Sue, it hit me that I've given my mother a bad time about her career for years. Maybe if I hadn't been so snotty about something she

226

loves doing, she might not have been so negative about my career."

"Sounds like the Lord's trying to teach you something."

She shrugged, and Chance felt the movement against his chest, momentarily distracting him. *Stay focused on the conversation, Callahan.*

"Yes, I think he is. And there's more. When I met Miss Sally's granddaughter, I instantly noted that she'd had some facelifts."

"Bad ones? Was she kinda bug-eyed or the skin pulled so tight it looked like it was about to snap like a rubber band?"

She laughed softly and tipped her head to look up at him. "Nothing like that. She looked good, but I've been around my father long enough to recognize when work has been done. He wanted me to join him in the practice, remember? So he started teaching me about plastic surgery when I was in junior high."

"How? Did he work on you?" Chance winced the second he blurted out the question. It had hovered in the back of his mind for days, but that wasn't the way to ask it.

She pulled forward, and he released her, holding his breath. When she turned around to face him and smiled, his breath came out in a whoosh. "Sorry, darlin'. That was a stupid question."

"But an understandable one." She grabbed his hand and tugged as she turned back toward the pickup.

He'd blown it. Now, she wanted to leave. "It's none of my business one way or the other."

"Isn't it? You're dying of curiosity to know what improvements I've had made."

Oh, man! She might be smiling, but she was ticked. It was obvious by how tightly she was holding his hand. "If your dad did anything, he's excellent. You're about as close to perfection as any woman I've ever seen."

Emily jerked her hand free and stepped in front of him, her eyes flashing as hot color spread across her cheeks. "What a crock! I never thought you'd lie to me, Chance Callahan."

Frowning, he absently scratched the back of his head where his cap was pulling the hair. "I'm not lying, sweetheart. I mean it. Sometimes when I look at you, you take my breath away because you're so beautiful."

"I am not beautiful!" She spun around and jammed her fists against her hips. After a couple of deep breaths, she turned back to face him, crossing her arms. "My eyes are too close together, and my lips aren't full enough. I do have nice cheekbones, but my face is too round. I should have liposuction on my hips and thighs and will need a tummy tuck in a few years. Sooner if I keep eating Ramona's cooking. The only perfect thing about me is my nose."

"Which is the one thing your father worked on," Chance said quietly.

"Yes."

Tears glistened in her eyes, but he figured she'd rather hang glide off the mesa than give in to them. Or have him mention it. He took a step closer and carefully settled his hands at her waist. She honestly didn't know how lovely she was.

"Is that your father's assessment or your mother's?"

"Dad's, but Mom generally agrees with him. She suggested collagen for my lips." Emily twisted those oh-so-kissable lips in disgust and stared at his chest instead of looking him in the eye. "And the liposuction. Of course, Dad thought I should include a few more areas for lipo. He also thinks he should reshape my jawline and my chin."

"Emily, for such intelligent people, your parents are nuts." That brought her gaze up to his. "It's true that your nose is nice. Your

229

daddy did a good job on it, though I suspect he had something pretty good to work with."

She shook her head. "No, I agreed with him on the nose. I inherited my grandpa's, and it was way too big with a funny knot on the end. Dad fixed it the summer before I started high school, and I was very grateful. I'd been self-conscious of my old one."

"Well, they're wrong about everything else."

She started to protest, but he laid his finger lightly across her lips and shook his head.

"When I look at your eyes, I don't measure how far apart they are. I see a field of bluebonnets in the spring, and it lifts my heart. I notice the way they light up when you're watching Zach or talking about history. I'm reminded of your compassion as you helped folks out after the fire, and the sweet, gentle welcome you gave me that first night when I walked into the shelter.

"As for your face being too round or your chin needing work — hogwash." He lightly traced his fingertips along her cheek and jaw. She uncrossed her arms, letting them fall to her sides. He leaned back and slowly ran his gaze over her. "The only reason you'd need lipo would be to become one of those skinny models who are just skin and bones. Most men, me included, like a woman with a few curves. And sweetheart, you have the right curves in the right places."

That earned him a roll of those beautiful eyes, but she didn't appear nearly as upset as she had a few minutes earlier.

He moved closer, tightening his hands minutely at her waist. "As for your lips . . ." He focused on them, and his heart rate kicked up a few notches. "Puffy ones are highly overrated. Yours are perfect to look at." He glanced up to make sure she wasn't about to hit him or something and discovered that her eyes had gone all soft and expectant. *Oh yeah.* "And perfect to kiss."

Lowering his head slowly, he gently touched his lips to hers — and felt his world shift on its axis. She flattened her hands against his chest, then slid them up around his neck. Deepening the kiss, he drew her even closer, rejoicing in her touch, her eager response.

After several wonderful moments, he finally straightened. Her head might be determined to have a big city career, but her heart was saying that life with him in Callahan Crossing would bring her happiness. His challenge was to help her heart to overrule her head.

He kept his arms around her, sighing contentedly when she rested the side of her face against his chest. Remembering his promise on the way to her grandmother's, he said, "Sorry I didn't deliver on the moonlight."

"It's out there somewhere." She sighed too, and snuggled a little closer. "Nothin' wrong with a kiss like that any time of the day."

"Happy Valentine's Day."

"Happy Valentine's Day to you too. This has been nice."

He dropped a kiss on her forehead and eased away from her. "The day's not over. This date has just begun, darlin'." He caught her hand and gently urged her back toward their picnic spot. "I don't know about you, but I'm ready for some of your chocolates."

"I didn't bring any chocolates."

"No, but I did." He grinned, happy with life. "Heart-shaped box and everything."

She tapped him on the arm. "You aren't supposed to tell me about it, silly. You're supposed to surprise me when you give them to me."

"That's the way it works? I've never given a girl anything on Valentine's Day, except for the little cards everybody in the class exchanged in grade school. Wait, I take that back. I gave Sue Ellen Nixon a special card in the seventh grade, one with hearts and stuff on it."

"Was she impressed?"

"For about five minutes. Then Jim Pratt gave her an even bigger one — and a little box of chocolates. That sealed the deal as far as she was concerned. She never looked at another guy after that, and they got married right out of high school. He went to work for the oil company and they moved away, but when I saw them last fall at homecoming, they were still together."

"Wow, all that from a box of candy."

"And it was only a little four-piece sampler."

When she looked up at him, her eyes twinkled merrily. "How big is mine?"

"Thirty pieces."

She stopped and stared up at him. "Thirty?"

"I'm making a point."

"I see." She started walking again.

"I was also hoping you'd share."

"I think I can spare a few pieces."

"Thanks. Before we got sidetracked, you were talking about your mom and Mrs. Simpson, and maybe something else the Lord is teaching you?"

She nodded but didn't look up. They were walking through a rough stretch of ground. "As soon as I saw Mrs. Simpson, I immediately knew who designed her outfit, that she had on Prada half boots, and how much everything cost. I was critical, wondering who she was trying to impress, and instantly disliked her. I was proud of myself for not spending that kind of money on clothes, though I can. But she's a nice woman, despite not giving her grandmother the attention she should have. I've concluded that I'm a reverse snob. I'm as judgmental about rich people as my mom is about the middle class on down. And I shouldn't do that."

"I know some rich people who are mighty annoying and think they have rights other people don't." They were back on smooth ground for a short stretch, so he could watch her more than where his feet were going.

"My dad is one of them. But I also know some Joe Sixpacks who have the same attitude."

"So do I. What are you going to do?" Chance stepped down into a ravine and turned to lift her off the steep embankment. He didn't release her the instant her feet touched the ground. She kept her hands on his shoulders a little longer than necessary, so he didn't think she minded. Taking her hand, he helped her up the other side.

"First off, I'm going to stop being critical of her career and the way she is. She's worked hard for what she has achieved. Sure, a lot of the money now is my father's, but she'd made her way before she met him. Plus, she's put up with a lot of garbage from him. At least I'll try to be more understanding. It's not a switch I can turn off and on, but with God's help, I can do it."

"Atta girl." He'd try to do the same, especially since he hadn't met her mother.

"I'm also going to take an interest in some of her charitable projects. She used to ask me to come to her parties or dinners, but I turned her down so much she finally quit inviting me. So I may invite myself to a charity auction and gala she's heading up in April." She looked up at him and hooked her arm around his. "Maybe I'll take a handsome friend."

"No fancy party for me if I'm just a friend. You have to promote me to beau."

"All right. But it's nothing serious."

"I can live with that for now."

They had reached the truck. She plopped down on the quilt, grabbed her water bottle, and took a long drink. Setting it beside her,

235

she looked up at him with a smile. "I'm ready for chocolate now."

"Yes, ma'am." He pulled the large box with a gold ribbon out from underneath the second quilt on the backseat. Handing it to her, he grinned. "Sweets for the sweet."

She checked the little yellow rose-shaped sticker before untying the ribbon. "Yellow Rose Chocolates. I've heard of them, but I didn't think they were around here."

"They're in Austin. Jenna discovered them when she was at the University of Texas. She sent a box home for Christmas one year, and we've been customers ever since."

Emily opened the box and grinned. "Truffles. Yum."

He figured she'd say more than yum when she took a bite. She offered him one, but he shook his head. "You go first."

She picked out a dark chocolate one and handed the box to him. Biting into it, her eyes widened for a second, then drifted closed. She chewed, swallowed, and looked at him. "This is incredible. I've never had anything like it."

"Told you they were good. What kind is it?" Some were solid, some had fillings or nuts. There was quite a variety in the box.

"Dark chocolate with raspberry filling. Real raspberries." She ate the other half and licked her fingers. "What did you get?"

"Haven't tried one yet." He was having too much fun watching her. Finally picking one, he took a bite. "Milk chocolate with orange. One of my favorites."

"I think they're all going to be my favorite." She took another one and *mmm-ed* softly as she ate it. "I'll have to send some of these to Grandma Rose for her birthday." Her face lit up. "I'll order some for Mom's birthday too. Chocolate is her one indulgence."

"That's a good way to let her know you care."

"Yes, it is." She smiled happily, shoving her hair out of her eyes. The wind had picked up, lowering the temperature.

"We'd better pack up and get off of here before the wind gets any higher, or our stuff will be littering the pasture below."

Emily scrambled to her feet and carried the candy box to the pickup. "Can't lose these."

Laughing, Chance waited for her to gather up the water bottles before shaking the twigs and dried grass off the quilt and folding it up. He laid it on the backseat. After she climbed into the truck, he shut her door and jogged around to the driver's side.

"Where to now?" Emily rubbed her hands

together after he got in the pickup.

"Are you cold?"

"A little bit. The wind is nippy."

"I'll crank up the heater in a few minutes. We'd only get cold air now. Do you want a quilt?"

"No, I'll be all right."

He started the truck and turned around, bouncing across the mesa to the road. "It will likely be warmer when we get down to the pasture. There's more wind up here."

"Are we going where you can't see any lights at night?"

"If that's okay with you. We can head back to the ranch house if you'd rather."

"I'm in no rush."

"Good. I'll throw in a minitour of this part of the ranch." He concentrated on the road as he drove down from the tall, flat-topped hill. "In other words, we might as well check on the cattle while we're over here."

Emily laughed and stretched out her legs. "A rancher's work is never done, right?"

"Right. We'll find a pretty spot to park, and I'll serenade you with my guitar. Instrumental only, unless you want to sing along. Later, we can climb in the back of the truck, bundle up in the quilts, and watch the stars come out."

"So is this a typical date out here in the sticks?"

Chance shrugged. He hadn't brought all that many girls, or women as he got older, out here on the ranch. "I've taken a few girls driving around but no picnics on the ranch. I've escorted a few ladies to the church picnic on occasion. Next time we go riding around, I'll bring a pistol, and we can practice shooting it."

He'd never done that with a woman other than his sister, who'd learned to fire a pistol along with the rest of them. He would enjoy teaching Emily. It would give him another opportunity to put his arms around her while he showed her how to do it. If she was going to become his wife and live on the ranch — and he was determined she was — she'd need to know how to protect herself.

"What do you shoot at?"

"We have a target set up on the side of a cliff. That way, if we miss, it just goes into the dirt. Will, Nate, and I put up the first one when we were in junior high, but it's been replaced many times since then."

"You started hunting when you were in junior high?" Her frown didn't bode well.

"None of us hunt. Dad was never into it, so Will and I never gave it more than a passing interest. We were always busy with school activities or working with the horses and cattle. But you need to know how to shoot accurately out here, in case you come across a rattlesnake or a rabid animal.

"We haven't had much of a problem with rabies in this area for several years, but it's always good to be prepared. It only takes one sick animal to attack you, and that could ruin your whole day."

"And a lot of days afterward." Emily shivered and turned on the heater. "That's scary."

"It was bad for a while, but on a scale of one to ten, the concern now is a one. Rattlers are a different story."

"I know to watch for them from visiting Grandma Rose."

"Usually I take my dates to the city for dinner and a movie so we don't have to worry about snakes. Or maybe go bowling. Do you bowl?"

"I've never tried it."

"Woman, you've been deprived. I'll have to take you sometime."

"Okay, but for now, snuggling in the quilts and watching the stars sounds nice."

Chance winked at her as he drove along the dirt road bordering the pasture. "It sure does."

16

On Monday, Emily, Sue, and half a dozen others started going through the Bradley-Tucker House. They meticulously recorded everything. Later, a smaller committee, along with Emily, would divide the items into three categories — keep, think about, and let Linda handle it. Emily would determine what would be used in the museum to start with and what would stay with the house.

She was impressed with their organization. Sue divided them up, two people to a room, and by midafternoon on Friday, they had completely inventoried the downstairs. Sue, Frannie, Maybelle, and Ed were antiques experts. Where some of the others stated things like "pretty blue bowl," they would usually show the maker, pattern, and general time period.

They agreed to wait until Monday to start on the second floor. Emily figured that would go fairly quickly too. The garages would take longer since there were hundreds of boxes, many not labeled. They would save the attic for last. Emily, Sue, Ed, and Jim were the only ones who could go up and down the steep stairs above the second floor, and Jim could only help occasionally. Emily hoped to start setting up some exhibits in a few weeks while the others finished the sorting.

After everyone left, she worked at the kitchen table for a while, entering the lists in the computer and making notes. When her cell phone dinged, she picked it up, noting she had a text message from Chance. Smiling, she read his note.

"Still ^ 4 pancakes 2nite?"

Quickly tapping the letters on her phone, she replied: "Yum." She'd never been to a pancake supper, but since it was a fundraiser for the Fire Victims Fund, she was certainly willing to participate. Pancakes were good anytime.

His reply came a few minutes later. "Meet u hi school 5:30?"

"OK." She set the phone on the table and went back to work, but the bell on the phone chimed again.

"XOXOX"

Hugs and kisses. Grinning, Emily set the

lists aside. "Well, that shoots my concentration." Relaxing for a minute, she let her mind drift back to their picnic on Sunday.

After they left the mesa, they drove around for a while, checking the cattle. She was amazed that he knew how many and even which ones were supposed to be in that pasture. He said each cow on the ranch had some unique characteristic that set it apart from the others. Evidently, everyone who worked with the cattle could tell the difference, though many of the cows looked the same to her.

After he was satisfied that all the stock in that area were accounted for and looked healthy, he found a picturesque spot along Jack's Creek to park the truck. They lazed on the creek bank beneath the shade of a weeping willow while he played his guitar.

He even gave her a short guitar lesson. It was mostly an excuse for her to sit in front of him so he could wrap his arms around her and show her how to position her fingers on the strings and strum. She abandoned the idea quickly. Those strings hurt her fingers. He admitted it took perseverance and gritting your teeth for a while until calluses built up on the fingertips.

When the sun set, he moved the pickup out into the middle of the pasture away from any tree or hill that might hamper their view. They snacked on the rest of the chicken and cake and indulged in a few chocolates.

He surprised her again by producing a thermos of hot, sweetened tea, which he took into the back of the pickup with them. Wrapped up together in the quilts and leaning back against the toolbox, they sipped tea from the same cup and waited for the stars to come out.

When the first twinkling light appeared, Chance took the cup from her hand, setting it and the thermos aside. "We should celebrate the appearance of each one with a kiss."

That worked delightfully well for a little while until the stars were popping out so fast that they bumped noses trying to keep up. Laughing, they had cuddled close, her head on his shoulder, his cheek lightly resting against her hair. They stared in awe at the splendor of the night sky as it can only be seen in Texas.

He used some shooting stars as an excuse to smooch a little more. When he took her back to the ranch house, he'd given her a lingering, heart-stopping kiss before he hopped out of the pickup and jogged around to open her door.

She would never think of stars, or kisses, the same way again. No man's touch had ever moved her, both physically and emotionally, the way Chance's did. They shared a closeness that came from honesty, respect, understanding, admiration, and a common faith. He never went beyond the bounds of propriety, but he stirred a longing in her heart that was new, exciting, and unsettling.

Although she'd never considered herself a coward — apart from enclosed dark places and being underground — this whole thing with Chance was a little scary. She couldn't allow herself to get in too deep. Close relationships, whether it be boyfriends or family, didn't work out well for her.

So when she'd received an email on Thursday from a former colleague about a job in Dallas, she jumped at the prospect. The new McGovern Historical Museum was in the final stages of organization. They wouldn't publicly announce the open positions until next week, but her friend passed on the contact info and told her to send them her resume ahead of time. She sent it off immediately. It was a wonderful opportunity to get in on the ground floor of a brand-new museum. The timing would be good too, since the start date wasn't until June.

Now, the waiting began, but she wouldn't sit around stewing about it. There would be dozens of applications for the assistant curator position for them to sort through, followed by interviews. She might make it to the final level of two or three candidates and still not be chosen for the job. It had happened before.

"Enough ruminating." Emily pushed back the chair and stretched out a kink in her back. Stacking up the lists, she put them away in her briefcase. Next, she turned off her laptop and put it in the case. She went around the house making certain all the lights were off and windows and doors closed.

Pausing in the hallway, she studied the portraits hanging there. The first was Doctor Kenneth Bradley and his wife, Margaret, on their wedding day in 1900. She was a breathtakingly beautiful nineteen-year-old with blonde hair pinned up in an elegant, puffy style. She had light eyes, probably pale blue. Since the photo was black and white, one couldn't be certain whether they were blue or green. Her long-sleeved, floor-length gown was covered with exquisite lace and had a long train. The lace veil was caught up at the top of her head in a pearl circlet and hung down her back.

He, too, was blond, but his eyes were darker than Margaret's. The doctor was attractive, though Emily didn't consider him handsome. Perhaps if he'd smiled, she would have thought otherwise. Generally people didn't begin smiling in pictures until the 1920s when faster film became available. Until then, all those somber faces were due mainly to the fact that nobody could hold a smile long enough to take the picture, which often required over a minute.

Still, in the Bradleys' wedding picture, there was a softness in their faces, a hint of happiness reflective of the day.

Emily moved down the hall. In the next photo, they were standing in front of their new house. It had been built in 1904, so she assumed the picture was taken then or shortly thereafter. Margaret had matured somewhat. She was still incredibly beautiful, but the lens captured an unmistakable sadness in her expression. Emily was taken aback by Kenneth's harsh countenance. Either he was a very unhappy man, or he had a bad case of indigestion.

The family photo celebrating Sally's arrival was markedly different. Though they still didn't smile, their joy was evident in the lightness of their expressions and the tender way that the doctor touched his wife's arm.

There were also numerous wonderful pastel drawings throughout the house, many of them portraits of Sally at various ages. All were signed "M.B." The housekeeper said that Margaret Bradley was an accomplished artist. She didn't think that described her talent well enough.

Emily decided to put some of the drawings in the main museum. They should be viewed by everyone, not merely those who decided to wander up to the grand Queen Anne on Third Street.

She loaded her laptop and briefcase in the van, locked the back door of the house, and set off in anticipation of pancakes and the company of a special, handsome man. And a bunch of other people.

Since she was a little early, she drove through downtown. Lindsey's dad had set up scaffolding in front of Maisie's antiques store that morning, and the talented artist had already drawn off the grid on the building. It would be fun to drive by each day and watch her progress.

Slowing as she passed the museum, Emily envisioned the sign that Lindsey had started painting for them. They would hang it across the false front. For now, it was set up in the artist's garage. Ed had asked about pressure washing the outside of the building to get rid of the soot, but Emily had nixed the idea. He was lining up some guys to help him scrub it down by hand next week. She hated to make the task harder, but they couldn't risk damaging the old bricks.

Driving the length of Main Street, she stopped across from where the cotton gin had stood. Much of the larger debris had been removed, but the crew still had some work ahead of them to finish the cleanup job. The gin had been fully insured because there was always a danger of a fire breaking out somewhere in the machinery or in the ginned bales. Being destroyed by a prairie fire probably had been at the bottom of their most likely hazard list.

She turned north, going through the section of town that had been hit by the fire. Two weeks earlier, block after block had been nothing but charred ruins. Now maybe a third of the rubble was gone, though even on those lots, the ground was still black. Some of the charred trees had been removed, but some of the taller ones still remained. The bottom half of the trunks and lower branches had burned, but the top branches had not. It was a strange sight. Still, some lots were cleared, so folks could start rebuilding if they had the means to do so.

Reaching the school, she found a place with two parking spaces side by side. After turning off the engine, she scanned the lot for Chance's pickup. Dub and Sue were already there, as well as Nate and Jenna and about seventy other cars. This pancake supper thing was a bigger deal than she'd imagined. Chance said various groups had done it over the years as a fund-raiser — churches, 4-H clubs, Scouts, Rotary Club, or some other organization. This one was sponsored by the Volunteer Fire Department, which meant Chance was involved. He'd been there earlier in the day helping set up tables and chairs and getting everything organized.

She spotted his truck as he turned off the street into the lot. He slowly cruised up and down a couple of rows until he saw her van. Flashing her a big grin, he pulled in beside her. She got out of her car and walked around to the driver's side of the pickup.

He opened the door, stepped out of the truck, and surprised her by pulling her close. "Hi, darlin'." He glanced around the parking lot, a mischievous sparkle lighting his eyes. "Coast is clear." He leaned down and gave her a slow, thorough kiss. Raising his head, he sighed softly. "Now I can make it through the evening."

It took Emily a moment to calm her heart and clear the haze from her brain. Coherent thought was up there somewhere — unless it had just been completely vaporized. Resting her hands on his chest, she stared up at him. "Shouldn't have done that."

"Why?" A light frown creased his brow.

"Short-circuited my brain."

Throwing back his head, he laughed and slowly released her. "Mine too. Good thing I'm cleaning up instead of cooking."

She stepped back and he followed, closing the truck door. Motioning to all the cars, she said, "I didn't realize there would be so many people here."

"There will likely be three or four times this many come and go before the evening is over. We usually get a couple hundred customers at a regular supper. Since this is for the fire victims, I expect a lot more than that. We didn't sell tickets like we usually do. It's strictly donation. Or not. We wanted folks to come even if they don't have a dime to spare. It's as much about getting together as it is about raising funds."

Before they joined the food line, they walked over to see the family, who had split up at two of the round tables to be sociable.

Sitting between Nate and Jenna, Zach diligently worked away on a pancake. He looked up and gave them a syrupy grin.

"Hi, buddy." Chance squatted down beside him. "Are the pancakes any good?"

"Uh-huh." The little boy nodded and picked up a piece of bacon. "Bacon too." He pointed the crispy piece of pork at the two empty seats beside Nate and Jenna. "You sit here."

"Okay. Thanks for saving us a place."

"There's sausage and ham too." Jenna wiped a syrup drip from her son's chin before it landed on his bright blue shirt. "Dad took one helping of each and four pancakes." She smiled at her father over at the next table. "Guess he couldn't make up his mind."

"Exactly. Besides, I've been cooking and smelling all that food, so I'm extra hungry," Dub said with a grin.

Chance stood, and Emily leaned down and planted a kiss on the top of Zach's head. As she straightened, Chance casually put his arm around her waist.

Sue's eyes danced with delight, and she nudged her husband. "Don't they make a purty couple?" She didn't speak particularly loud, but it appeared that everyone within a thirty-foot diameter heard her.

Or maybe some noticed that Chance was with a woman and told everybody around them. People craned their necks this way and that to see who he was with. Several who had heard Sue's comment nodded and smiled in agreement.

"He gave her a smooch out in the parkin' lot," said a grizzled old man in worn and patched overalls. His white hair and long beard accentuated the deep wrinkles in his tanned skin. "A good one too."

Heat flooded Emily's face. No doubt she was red as the proverbial beet.

"Now, Jinx, you aren't supposed to go spoutin' off about such things." Dub grinned at his son and winked at Emily. "You're embarrassing the lady."

"Sorry, miss, but it's 'bout time Chance got himself a gal. You're real good lookin' too. Wish I was thirty years younger. I'd give 'im a run for his money."

"You'd have to be forty years younger, Jinx," the man sitting next to him said.

"Or fifty," called someone at the next table.

"Don't pay these ol' coots any mind, darlin'." Chance tightened his arm minutely, but she didn't think anybody who was watching them — which was just about everyone in the cafeteria by now — missed that little display of possessive machismo. "They're just jealous."

"You got that right, son." Jinx leaned back and picked up his Styrofoam coffee cup. "You're the young lady who's settin' up the museum, aren't you?"

"Yes, sir." She subtly dug her elbow into Chance's hard side. The rascal just grinned at her. "I hope you'll visit it when we have everything set up."

"I'll do that. Might drop by sooner too. I got some old stuff gatherin' dust at my place that belongs in the museum."

"Now, Jinx," a man across the table said, "they aren't puttin' together a wax museum. They got no need of you standin' there like one of them figures in Madame What's-her-name's place."

As others joined in the teasing, which Jinx took in stride and returned with quick wit, Chance guided Emily around Zach's chair. "Let's make our getaway while we can."

A middle-aged woman with big poufy brunette hair smiled at her as they walked by. "You hang on to him, hon. That one's a catch."

A woman about Emily's age, sitting at the same table, sent a dagger-look at Chance, then caught Emily's eye. "He might be a catch, but he throws all of us back."

Chance's fingers flexed at her side, but he made sure she kept walking. As if she was going to stop and discuss him with a former date. When they got to the back end of the serving line, she asked, "Are you okay?"

"Fine." But he didn't look fine.

"So was she a one or two dater?" she murmured, watching two little boys jostle each other for a place in line.

"One. Actually more like a quarter of a date."

She glanced up, biting back a smile. "That bad, huh?"

He met her gaze, and a second later his lip twitched and a hint of amusement crept into his eyes. Turning his back to the rest of those in line, he said in a quiet falsetto, "I want to go someplace fancy, like the French restaurant in Fort Worth they talked about on that cookin' show I saw last week."

He changed back to his normal voice. "We're not going to Fort Worth on a date." He glanced over his shoulder and moved backward a few steps, returning to the falsetto with an added whine. "But I deserve a special night out. I was Miss Tumbleweed."

Emily giggled. "Miss Tumbleweed?"

"A festival attempt that only lasted a couple of years. It never got rolling."

255

Laughing, she pictured the big round, prickly weeds that sometimes tumbled across the highway or rolled along in the wind until they were trapped by barbed wire fences or the sides of buildings. "I can see why."

He switched to his imitation of the beauty queen. "And y'all have so much money, the price of a weekend in Fort Worth would be just a drop in a little ol' bucket. Just how rich are you, anyway?"

"A weekend? My, my, she did have high expectations."

"Oh yeah." He was back to his regular, deep musical tone. "I won't even tell you what she promised in exchange."

"I can imagine." Emily moved forward as he turned around to face the line.

"I hope not."

When she looked at him, her smile faded. He was serious. "That bad, huh?"

"Let's just say she'd learned some things while stripping in Vegas."

Emily's mouth fell open. "You went out with a stripper?" she whispered.

A dull flush spread up his neck and into his face. "I didn't know it until we were driving toward Sweetwater. I thought she was still nice Mary Smith who was a couple of years younger than me. When she said she'd gone to school in Las Vegas, I thought she meant the University of Nevada. It never crossed my mind that she meant exotic dancing school."

"Is there such a thing?" Emily tucked her arm through his because . . . well, because Miss Tumbleweed was staring holes in them.

He shrugged. "Guess I should have figured something had changed when she insisted I call her Jasmine."

Emily laughed and squeezed his arm. "At least she didn't change it to Candy."

He chuckled and gently drew her in front of him as they neared the front of the line. "I don't know. Maybe that would have been better. I might have put two and two together and saved myself some major embarrassment that night and for the next two weeks."

"Did she bad-mouth you?"

"Plenty. For some reason she didn't like me turning around halfway to Sweetwater and taking her home. But I was more humiliated because everybody in town learned I'd gone out with her. Seems I was the only dumb cluck around who didn't know what she'd been doing."

"I bet you were teased a lot, especially by Will."

"I was, but not so much by him. He

ribbed me a little when I told him what happened, but he didn't rub it in. He's slogged through the dating swamp as much as I have."

"Dating swamp. That's an interesting analogy." She watched a teenager as he piled his plate with pancakes and sausage. He'd come to the shelter with his parents the day after the fire, looking for food and clothes. Was he getting enough to eat? Was he back in school? Were they able to rebuild?

"Sometimes you get bit by mosquitoes. Other times you're attacked by alligators."

"What am I? A mosquito or an alligator?"

He leaned down next to her ear and whispered, "A beautiful, golden butterfly brushing your wings against my skin."

Emily sighed softly at his words, and sweet contentment filled her soul. She skimmed the crowd — rich, poor, old, young, and everything in between. In a tradition as old as time, they broke bread together, talked and listened, laughed and consoled, and wiped away an occasional tear.

They were the haves and have-nots. Those the disaster had bypassed and those who had lost everything. They were family, friends, community. They were Callahan Crossing.

She stepped up to the counter and smiled

at Will as he waited, ready to load up her plate. While Chance teased his brother about his fancy apron, she silently thanked the Lord for this town and these people, for their kind hearts and caring souls. She thanked him for the privilege of getting to know them, to care for them, especially Chance Callahan.

Pancakes and poetic prose. *Sweet.*

17

The three weeks following the pancake supper had raced by in a blur. Chance had never had several projects going at the same time, and he'd been as busy as a one-eyed cat watching three mice.

The insurance checks came through for four of his clients, and the building permits were approved for two. On the first house, the plumbing lines had been set in place and the slab foundation poured last week. His crew started on the framing when the cement was thoroughly dried. Chance would begin excavation on the second house tomorrow. It also was a slab foundation, so it was more backhoe work than anything and wouldn't take too long. Then he'd have another crew busy there.

The permit for the third house should come through by the end of the week. That was the last one he would try to work on right now. The other houses would have to wait until he could shift some of his crew to the job.

Emily had been busy too, spending long hours at the Bradley-Tucker House. They were getting the inventory done, though wading through the garages was taking longer than she'd hoped. After they put the ad in the paper, several people had offered other things for the museum, so his mom and Emily had been visiting folks and checking out potential items.

She'd also been designing displays on the computer. They were beginning to move some things into the museum, so she could start setting up the exhibits.

On Saturday evening, instead of going out, Emily brought over the fixings for a green salad and lasagna, along with some chocolate chip oatmeal cookies she'd baked earlier. At her insistence, Chance lazed in his recliner while she put together the lasagna. Enjoying the sound of her working in his kitchen, rummaging through drawers and cabinets as she looked for pans and a bowl, he indulged in a little daydreaming about hearing those sounds every day for the rest of his life.

After sharing a delicious meal, he politely escorted her to the living room and pointed to the recliner. "It's your turn to sit and relax. I'll do the dishes."

She grinned and settled in the chair, wiggling around a little to get comfortable. "Such chivalry. I'm so stuffed, I'll probably fall asleep."

"Snooze away, milady." Dropping a light kiss on the top of her head, he wandered back into the kitchen, estimating that it might take ten minutes to clean up. She had already washed most of the things she'd used preparing the meal.

He took his time transferring the leftover salad and lasagna into plastic containers and the buttered French bread into a plastic bag. He rinsed the dishes and put them in the dishwasher, then wiped down the table and countertops. Done in nine minutes flat.

Tiptoeing into the living room, he peeked around the lamp on the end table to see if she had fallen asleep.

Her eyes popped open, and she smiled at him. "Done already?"

"Yep." He held out a plate of cookies. "But I brought dessert. Do you want some ice cream too?"

"No, thanks. I'll do good to manage one cookie."

"Ah, more for me." He set the plate on the coffee table. When she folded down the recliner footrest, he held out his hand, helping her out of the chair. He grabbed a couple of cookies and plopped on the couch, pulling her down beside him. Laughing, she snuggled close.

"You want one of these?" When he held out a cookie, she shook her head, then rested it against his shoulder. He took a bite. "This is really good."

"Grandma Rose's recipe. She taught me how to make them when I was a kid."

"She said you were a good cook. Now I know why."

Emily nodded. "I learned from the best." They sat in comfortable silence for a few minutes. She brushed her fingertip around a purple diamond on his light gray shirtsleeve. "I'm going to Dallas on Thursday," she said quietly.

"To see your mom?"

"We're planning to have lunch on Friday. But that's not the main reason I'm going to Dallas." She straightened enough to look up at him. "I have a job interview on Friday for the assistant curator position at the McGovern Historical Museum."

Her eyes sparkled with excitement, and Chance's heart dropped into his boots. "A job interview." His voice came out hoarse. He cleared his throat. "I've never heard of the McGovern." Not that he paid much attention to the museums in Dallas. Or anywhere else.

"It hasn't opened yet. It's going to be one of the finest historical museums in the state. I'd be getting in on the ground floor."

He nodded, desperately trying to hide his disappointment. "It sounds like what you've been waiting for."

"It's a fantastic opportunity."

"You'll impress them."

"I hope so."

He hoped she did too, for her sake. But he couldn't be happy about it.

It was mid-March, almost two months since they first met, and she was still bent on chasing her career. He knew she cared for him. She simply didn't care enough to settle down with him in Callahan Crossing.

He might as well be chasing an eagle's shadow.

At noon on Tuesday, Chance went to Irene's Boot Stop to grab something to eat. He joined some of the regulars at a big square table in the back corner. Digging into his chicken fried steak, mashed potatoes, and cream gravy, he listened to the conversation.

"Spotted another FEMA trailer rolling in this morning," the bank president said. "I reckon that's about the last one."

"Must be," said an elderly farmer who was semiretired and a widower. He came to town for a meal and to shoot the breeze almost every day. "They've been hauling them in for the past three weeks. What I want to know is why it took 'em a full month after the fire to get started."

"Red tape. Forms to fill out, verify, and get approved." One of the men who worked at Hunter's Sporting Goods dipped a French fry in ketchup, waving it slightly in emphasis. "It all takes time."

"Too much time, to my way of thinking." The local insurance agent poured about three teaspoons of sugar into his glass of iced tea. "Some of my clients had their insurance checks last week, but they didn't have a trailer yet. Any of them come to see you, Chance?"

"I've been talking to several folks." Chance laid his fork on the plate and wiped a dab of gravy from his lip with a white paper napkin. "Trouble is if the house they lost was old, the insurance money won't come close to covering the cost of a new one."

"That's when they come see me," the banker said with a smile. "We can give most folks a loan." His smile faded. "Of course, there are always some who just can't qualify

265

no matter how hard we try to make it work."

"Don't they get money from the Fire Victims Fund? I heard it was about ten thousand for each family." The sporting goods guy took a bite of his hamburger.

"A little over eight thousand." The banker salted his plate of liver and onions. Chance cringed, both at the thought of eating liver and what all that cholesterol and salt would do to the middle-aged man's blood pressure.

"They're free to use it in whatever way they need," said Chance. "Some are trying to hang on to it to help rebuild, but that has to be hard when they need to replace even basic necessities. All the donations have helped, but they don't cover everything for everybody."

Jenna and Nate had opened up the new Mission a few weeks back, so people who needed to use the food bank had access to fresh things as well as canned and packaged goods. The building was big enough to house the clothing donations that continued to come in. His sister had rented another building to hold all the household donations, everything from furniture and appliances to linens and kitchenware. By moving all the supplies, they'd freed up the space in the churches that had been acting as distribution centers.

The farmer sadly shook his head. "It's going to take years to regain what we've lost."

"There was a reporter on TV last night who'd gone to Austin to interview an expert at the University of Texas." The banker cut off a bite of liver and scooped up some grilled onion along with it. "He said we couldn't ever recover. According to the reporter, experts at some other universities agreed."

"I think they're wrong." Chance took a drink of ice-cold Dr Pepper. "Cleanup of the town is about two-thirds completed, and the county, state, and prison crews are still hard at work. With the city council covering the cost of tearing down the dilapidated buildings, whether or not they were damaged in the fire, the town will look better than it did before. At least it will when things are rebuilt."

His mama had been mighty pleased with that decision. The Historical Society wouldn't be out any money getting rid of the old museum.

Irene stopped by with the coffeepot to refill a couple of cups. "I heard that several churches in West Texas and some from farther afield are still raising money specifically to build homes. They plan to send workers in to help build them too. 'Course, most churches can't handle building a house by themselves, so several are teaming together."

Chance smiled at Irene as she paused in her coffee refill rounds, then he looked back at the others. "I also know the people of Callahan Crossing. They won't sit by and wait for a helping hand, though they won't turn down help when it comes. In the meantime, they'll pick themselves up by their bootstraps as best they can and forge on."

"I hope you're right, son." The farmer laid his silverware on the empty plate. "I sure would hate to see this town dry up and blow away."

Irene laughed as she picked up the plate. "We're too ornery to let that happen."

After Chance returned to the office, he settled back in to work for a while, using his CAD software to modify a floor plan, and tried not to think about Emily running off to Dallas. He had to focus on his business and hope and pray she had a change of heart.

Half an hour later, he realized it had grown dark, more like dusk than the middle of the afternoon. He saved his work on the computer, walked over to the door, and stepped outside. A large, dark, low-lying cloud was almost over the town. The bird that had been serenading him from the tree outside his office had flown. The hot air was eerily still.

The cloud and sky turned a dark green, and the hair stood up on the back of his neck.

Tornado weather.

Chance jerked the door closed behind him and sprinted to his pickup. Emily was at the museum with those big windows all across the front. The storerooms each had an outside wall. The only safe place was the basement, and she'd never go down there alone.

"Keep her safe, Lord. Please, keep everybody safe." He jumped in the truck and started it, not taking the time to put on the seat belt. Shifting into reverse, he glanced up and down the empty street and backed out.

Everybody else had the good sense to stay inside and seek shelter. He gunned the engine, driving like a madman down the three blocks from his office to Main Street. He barely slowed for the stop sign on Main, whipped around the corner, and skidded to a halt halfway down the block beside Emily's van, barely noticing when the pickup bounced against the curb.

He turned off the ignition and grabbed a flashlight out of the glove compartment. Lightning streaked across the sinister green sky, and thunder instantly boomed. Suddenly, golf-ball-sized hail pounded the truck and the street. He bailed out, wincing as hail pummeled his head and back as he ran to the front door of the museum.

The second he opened the door and dashed in, the tornado siren at the fire station blasted. The long, steady wail brought back memories from the day of the fire, but Chance blocked them out. "Emily! Where are you?"

The bathroom door opened, and she stepped out, motioning for him to join her. "Over here. We'll be safe in here." Her wide eyes told him she wasn't as confident as she tried to sound.

"We have to go downstairs." He ran across the room to her side.

"No! Chance, I can't." The blood drained from her face, and she backed away. "You know I can't."

"We have to." He stuffed the flashlight in his pocket and grabbed her arm, dragging her out of the bathroom and toward the double doors of the storeroom. "It's the safest place."

"No, I can't go down there." She pulled against his grip and tried to jerk free. When that didn't work, she pounded on his chest with her free hand. "Let go!" Her voice grew shriller with each word. "Don't take me down there. Please, don't take me down there," she sobbed.

Chance stopped, glanced outside at the growing darkness and pounding hail. Gathering her in his arms, he held her close. "Shhh, darlin'. It will be all right. I'll be with you. I won't leave you down there."

She raised her head, tears pouring down her face, and pleaded, "Please, Chance, I can't."

Cupping her face with his hands, he gently searched her eyes. "You have to, Emily Rose. I won't risk losing you like this. Do this for me, please. I'm with you. I'll stay with you." He pulled the suddenly pathetically small flashlight from his pocket. "And I brought a light."

A loud roar sounded above the hammering of the hail.

"Emily, we have to go now."

Her nod was barely a movement, but it gave him permission to shove the flashlight into her hands and scoop her up in his arms. Somehow, she managed to flip the light switch on the wall as he ran down the stairs. When they reached the basement, the light from two puny bulbs softly illuminated the large space.

"Guess I need to replace some lightbulbs." He tried to keep his voice casual, but that was hard to do when he was terrified. Trembling, she clung to him, burying her face against his neck. When he reached the center of the large room, he eased her down to the floor beside a sturdy pillar. He sat down next to her and lifted her onto his lap, holding her close.

"See, it's not so bad."

"Not so bad," she repeated in a tiny, almost childlike voice.

Lord, have I done something terrible by making her come down here? His hand shook when he brushed her hair back out of her face. "You doin' all right, sweetheart?"

"Uh-huh," she whispered, the fingers of one hand digging into his shoulder. He was certain she didn't realize she was close to drawing blood with her fingernails. But he didn't mention it.

The lights flickered. Gasping, she buried her face even harder against him. He pried the flashlight from her hand and turned it on. A second later, the overhead lights went out.

"Chance . . ." He'd never heard a whispered wail before. His heart lodged in his throat. *Lord, please help her. Calm her fears. Free her from this living nightmare.*

"It's all right, Emily. I put fresh batteries in the flashlight just last week. And I haven't used it," he added quickly. "So it will last long enough." He set the flashlight on the floor, pointing the beam of light upward.

"What if the building collapses on us?"

"I don't think it will. They built these old ones to last. The windows are the biggest concern. Some bricks might fall and land upstairs, but I honestly don't think the whole wall would come down." He was worried about the roof, but he wasn't going to mention it. The way it was made, it would require a big tornado to rip it off.

"Those poor people in the trailers."

His Emily had such a compassionate heart. "Let's pray for them."

She nodded.

"Father God, we ask you to keep everyone safe, especially all those families in the trailers." Mobile homes rarely survived a tornado if they were hit. "Please, Lord, protect the people from harm and our town from more destruction. Show us your mercy, Father."

Emily shifted her head and whispered,

273

"Amen." Her voice was no longer muffled, and he didn't feel her hot breath against his throat anymore, but she hardly moved otherwise.

Chance listened to the noise above them. He hadn't heard the crash of breaking glass or the thud of falling bricks. "I think maybe the hail has stopped. The roar isn't as loud, either."

"The siren quit."

"It only blasts for five minutes."

"It was constant during the fire."

"True. But the standard here for tornados is five minutes. It's repeated again every ten minutes unless the danger is past." He checked his watch. "We'll give it twenty. If it doesn't go off again, we'll take a peek and see what's going on."

"Gonna be a long twenty minutes," she mumbled. But she wasn't shaking so badly.

"We could always pass the time smooching, as Jinx would say." He was only half kidding. It might be a good way to distract her.

"No smooching."

"Killjoy."

"Tough."

"Are your eyes open?" He shifted his back against the support pillar. The floor was getting hard.

"Yes."

"Are you looking around?"

"It's dark."

"Not right here." He smiled, thinking it had been a dumb question. How could he even smile when things above ground might be blown to smithereens? "I was wondering what you thought of this space. Will it be useful for the museum?"

He figured she knew he was just filling in the time. She eased her death grip on his shoulder and slowly raised her head. He almost shouted hallelujah.

Looking down, she said, "It has a concrete floor. I thought it would be dirt."

"A couple of the earliest buildings in town have dirt cellars, so that's what I expected too. Builders were using concrete even then. However, they weren't building many structures with real basements in this part of the country."

She leaned back slightly and touched the floor with her hand. "It doesn't feel damp. But they'll have to monitor it for a while before they put anything down here."

They, not we.

Chance's hope dipped another notch. "It'd be tricky getting anything big up and down the stairs. They were built to handle whiskey barrels, but nothing bigger."

She laid her head back on his shoulder, curling her hands against his chest. "I think I'll take a nap."

Like she had done when she was a child. "I'll just sit here and be quiet." And pray. For the safety of his family and folks in the area. He couldn't even call the ranch. He knew from the past that his cell phone didn't work down in the basement. He prayed for her emotional healing, and for himself. It was going to hurt awful bad when she said *adios* and trotted off to Dallas, San Antonio, or Timbuktu.

Five minutes later she asked, "Has it been twenty minutes yet?"

"Almost ten."

"Told you it was gonna be long."

"We could walk around down here. It would give you an idea of how big it is."

"In the dark? No thanks."

Chance shifted again. She was right. It was going to be a long twenty minutes. So he gave up at fifteen. It sounded as if the storm had passed by. He really wanted to see what had happened. And get up off that hard, cold, concrete floor.

"I think it's been long enough. Let's go see how things are."

She picked up the flashlight and scrambled to her feet. Thankfully, she waited for him, or he might have been feeling his way around in total blackness. When they reached the stairs, they walked up together.

The storeroom wall was still intact, and the door was still open. "So far, so good."

They walked into the main room on that side. Everything looked fine. It was raining, but the sky had lightened considerably. Relief swept through him. "It missed us."

"But what about the rest of the town? Or your family?" She looked at him with worried eyes.

"Let me check on the family, then we'll go see." He took his cell phone out of the case attached to his belt. There were three missed calls from his parents, one from Will, and one from Jenna. He called his folks, clicking on the speakerphone so Emily could be part of the conversation too.

His dad answered on the first ring. "About time you checked in, son. Are you and Emily all right?"

Chance smiled at his dad's assumption that he was with Emily. "Yes, sir. How about y'all?"

"We're fine. Had some quarter-sized hail, but it didn't last long. It looked mighty bad toward town. I spotted a funnel cloud dip down between here and there, but it looked like it went back up in the cloud without touching down."

"The warning sirens went off right when I got to the museum. Emily and I hid in the basement. I couldn't call you because my phone doesn't work down there. Before we went downstairs, I didn't see anything but green sky. It sure sounded like a tornado, but I don't see any damage from one so far. There's some hail damage to vehicles, and a couple of store windows across the street were knocked out. From what I can see, the museum weathered the storm just fine. We're going to scout things out. I'll call if there's a problem. Will you let Jenna and Will know we're okay?"

"They know. They're here with us now. I put you on speaker once I knew y'all were okay. They all came over when it started looking bad in case we needed to go to the storm cellar. I'd forgotten that building of yours had a basement. Good thinking."

"I figured it was the safest place in town to be." He glanced at Emily. She frowned, then nodded in agreement. "I'll call you with an update in a bit."

The instant he hung up, Emily grabbed her purse and headed for the door. "That's a relief."

"Yes, it is. I wasn't too worried because Dad is cautious about storms. He orders everybody into the storm cellar if things look dangerous." When she shivered, he laid his hand on her shoulder. "It's big, has electric lights and battery operated ones, and the exterminator comes out regularly. Not a bug or spider in sight. When we were kids, they used to keep a cot down there, so we could just curl up and go to sleep. Though I don't think we ever did. We were always too excited to sleep."

He cupped her chin and gently lifted her face so she would look at him. "How are you?"

"I still don't think I could go into the basement, or especially a storm cellar, alone. But I might be able to handle it if I'm with somebody else." She surprised him by throwing her arms around him and hugging him tight, although her big purse smacked him in the back. "Thank you."

He held her close and brushed a kiss across her forehead. "I don't want to lose you, Emily." When she pulled back and looked up at him with a worried frown, he decided he'd better lighten up. She clearly wasn't ready to hear what was in his heart. "If I let you get picked up by a tornado, it would just plain ruin my day."

She smiled, lowered her hands, and edged away. "It'd ruin mine too."

When they went out, she took the keys from her purse and locked the door. The rain had slacked off until it wasn't much more than a drizzle. She pointed to several small dents in his pickup and checked her van. It had suffered the same damage on the hood and roof. "It's not as bad as I'd anticipated."

Chance opened the pickup door for her. "Nothing that can't be fixed." He helped her into the truck and shut the door. The owner of the shoe repair shop across the street came out onto the sidewalk, examining the broken windows. "You okay?" Chance called.

"Fine. Not much damage except for the glass. How about y'all?"

"We're good. I'm going to drive around and check on things."

The older man waved and went back inside his shop.

Stopping for a minute to survey the street, Chance breathed a little easier. He prayed things were the same or better throughout town.

They drove up and down several streets but found no evidence of a tornado. A few people, including Jinx, walked out and stopped them to ask what they'd seen.

"Nothing but some hail damage," Chance

said. "Did you see a twister? We were in the museum and stayed away from the windows. But it sure sounded like a tornado."

Jinx slid his thumbs under the straps of his overalls. "Spotted a funnel cloud right over the gin. Or where the gin used to be. Don't know if it ever touched down. I dove in the bathtub right after I saw it."

"It looked all right when we drove by. We'll go on up toward the north side of town and check out that area." Chance shifted from park into drive.

"Let us know if anybody needs help." Jinx waved at Emily and backed away from the truck.

They drove around most of the town. Everyone they talked to said basically the same thing. They'd seen the funnel cloud, but it never touched the ground. The trailers had rocked in the straight-line wind but stayed fastened down.

When he turned back onto Main Street to take Emily to her car, they met Dalton coming the other way. There was no other traffic, so Chance stopped in the middle of the street. Dalton did the same.

Chance lowered his window. "Everything all right?"

"The Driscolls north of town lost the roof off their barn, but that's the only report I've heard so far. The weather service said the storm is moving on toward the northeast. They don't expect any more problems for us."

"That's good to hear. Talk to you later."

Dalton nodded, smiled at Emily, and drove on down the street.

Chance pulled up in front of the museum, easing against the curb this time. "I'm going back to the office to put things away before I head home. I'm not sure I even locked the door. Are you ready to call it a day?"

"I just have to pack up the laptop and turn off the lights. I think I'll go hang out with Jenna for a while. I need some Zach time."

Chance laughed and caught her hand, threading his fingers through hers. "Good idea. I might crash your party."

"Help yourself. That little guy has enough love to spread all the way around."

So did she. She just didn't know it yet.

18

"It's been a pleasure to meet you, Emily." On Friday afternoon, Sylvia Hanson, director of the McGovern Museum, walked her to the elevator. A good sign that the interview had gone well. "We have a dozen more applicants to talk to, but you have an impressive resume. You're equally impressive in person."

"Thank you, Ms. Hanson. The McGovern is going to be a wonderful museum. I hope I have the opportunity to be a part of it."

"I hope so too, but keep in mind that the final choice doesn't rest with me alone. The top applications will also be reviewed by members of the board."

"I understand. Thank you for your time, ma'am."

"I'll give you a call either way. We should have the list narrowed down by next week."

Emily thanked her again and shook her hand. As the museum director walked away,

Emily pressed the down elevator button. When the door opened, she stepped onto the empty elevator, selected the first floor, and waited sedately. The instant the door closed, she pumped her arm in the air. "Yes!" She danced around in a little circle, not easy in two-inch heels, and rejoiced at what undoubtedly had been the best interview of her career.

Emily had brought along a portfolio of her displays at the two small museums she'd set up. Ms. Hanson had raved about them and asked to keep the photos.

The director had also been interested in Callahan Crossing, how the people were doing and how bad things were. Some of it was normal curiosity about a tragedy, but it appeared that she sincerely cared.

She did, however, question why Emily was still in Callahan Crossing. A report on one of the Dallas TV stations indicated that the museum had been destroyed, and she assumed that Emily had gone back to San Antonio.

Emily explained about Chance donating a building and Mrs. Simpson donating the Bradley-Tucker House and its contents. Ms. Hanson was delighted as only someone who loved history and museums could be. But she also sympathized with the losses in the original building, assuming that all the documents had been destroyed, if not by the fire, then by the water.

That was when Emily explained how they had saved the records and pictures. Afraid she might come across as bragging — or being nuts — she hadn't planned on mentioning it. Judging by the moisture in Ms. Hanson's eyes as she told the tale, it obviously earned her some points.

For some reason, that bothered Emily. She wanted to be evaluated for the job by her qualifications and experience. Not by some crazy thing she'd done on the spur of the moment.

When she reached the van, she got in, leaned her head against the headrest, and breathed a huge sigh of relief. She'd cleared the first hurdle. Excitement swept through her. She had to tell Chance.

Digging through her purse for her cell phone, she found it squished into a corner. When she punched in his number, her heart tripped along at a staccato beat. Was that because she was excited about the job or about talking to a certain handsome cowboy? One she had yet to see on a horse.

Chance always checked the caller ID. "Hi, darlin'."

Oh, my. His voice sounded good. Warm

and tender. Almost . . . loving. "Hi. Are you busy?"

"Nope. Just sitting here twiddling my thumbs and hoping you'd call. Is your interview over?"

"Yes. It went well. I think. She seemed pleased with my qualifications and portfolio. And she asked about Callahan Crossing. She thinks you're absolutely wonderful to donate the building for the museum."

"Don't have anything else to do with it."

She figured he was thinking "Whoop-de-doo." Chance didn't care whether or not he impressed people. She was the same way in some situations but obviously not when it came to a big job.

"I knew you'd knock her socks off. I'm proud of you, Em."

She believed him, but she also detected a hint of sadness in his voice. "Thanks."

"You don't sound quite as excited as I'd expected. No girly squealing or anything."

She laughed and rolled down the van window for some air. "I did a little dance in the elevator."

He chuckled.

And she got goose bumps down her arms. "Wish I'd seen that."

"Probably just as well that you didn't. I've been wearing tennis shoes so much, I'm not up to dancing in two-inch heels."

"I am. Well, maybe not quite. I don't think my boots have that high a heel."

"I didn't know you were a dancer."

"I'm not much of one. But I don't mess up a Texas two-step too bad. Are you headed off to see your folks?"

"I'm going back to my grandparents'. Mom flew to New York this morning."

"I thought y'all were going out to lunch."

"We'd planned to. But her secretary called this morning and said she had a model who was clashing with the photographer. It's a major shoot, the cover of *Glamour,* so Mom took off to try and smooth things over. I don't know what Dad is doing. I didn't call him. I don't particularly want to see him." Not until she got this job. Then she could face him in triumph. "So I'm going to spend the evening with Grandpa and Grandma. Have a nice quiet visit."

"Are you coming home tomorrow?"

Home. Funny how right that sounded. When had she started thinking of Callahan Crossing as home and not San Antonio?

"I promised my grandparents I'd stay until Sunday and go to church with them. I'll leave for Callahan Crossing after lunch." Another reminder that she was away from the ranch and back in the city — where dinner was lunch and supper was dinner. "How are things there?"

"Pretty good. We started the second house. I think it will go up fast." He paused, then cleared his throat. "I miss you, Emily Rose. Zach gives good hugs, but they aren't the same as yours."

She got all teary eyed. "I miss you too." She was surprised by how much. "A lot." Glancing in the rearview mirror, she saw a car go slowly past for the third time. "I'd better go and let somebody have my parking space. The lot is full."

"Call me tonight after you visit with your grandparents."

"It might be late."

"That's all right. I'll probably be up. If I'm not, I won't mind you waking me up. Be careful in that big bad city."

"Don't worry. I'm a city girl, remember?"

"Yeah, I remember." He sounded depressed. "But I keep hoping to convert you."

"You may be rubbing off on me. The traffic is annoying the life out of me."

"Good. Hope you get stuck in an hour-long traffic jam."

"Chance!"

"Not really."

"Oh, dear, that poor woman is coming around for the fourth time. I have to go."

"Bye, darlin'. Be safe."

"You too." She ended the call quickly, blinked back a few tears as she fastened her seat belt, and started the car. The woman spotted her pulling out and waited to take the parking spot.

Emily left the lot and glanced at the clock on the dash. It was only 2:00. Although her grandparents were in their mid-seventies, they still led busy lives. Neither of them would be home until around 5:00, but the housekeeper would let her in if she returned before then.

She was too keyed up to sit around Preston Hollow and wait for them. The traffic might be a pain, but Dallas offered something dear little Callahan Crossing didn't. Shopping!

"Neiman Marcus, here I come."

After dinner that evening, Emily showed Grandma Iris the sleeveless floor-length formal gown she'd found at Neiman's. She needed something fancy to wear to the charity auction and gala. She held the hanger high enough to keep the hem of the dress off the floor and waited for her grandmother's comment. Iris had never been a model, but she had a great sense of style.

Her grandmother relaxed on the comfortable white and gold brocade love seat in the guest room and nodded her approval. "Violet is a wonderful color for you. The bateau neckline is nice. Elegant but modest and sedate. It just skims your figure."

"Yes, ma'am. It fits great. Not too tight or too loose. The little flare from the knee down makes it easy to walk." She particularly liked the high neckline in the front. It went right across her collarbones, so she wouldn't spend the evening worrying whether or not it was too revealing. The cutout back was another story. She turned the dress around. "Do you think the back will show too much skin?"

Grandma Iris laughed and propped her white-slipper-covered feet up on a small needlepoint footstool in front of the chair. "Not quite as sedate as I first thought. How low does it go?"

"About the middle of my back."

Iris waved her hand and shook her head. "That's nothing to worry about. It's fine, dear."

"Oh, good!" Emily relaxed and held the gown out to admire it again. "I fell in love with it as soon as I saw it." She hadn't liked the price but decided to splurge. She hadn't bought anything fancy or expensive in years. "It was the only one I tried on. I couldn't believe it when it fit perfectly."

"That, dear girl, is an amazing feat."

"It's never happened before. Usually, the dressing room is full of rejects." Emily hung the gown back in the closet. "I think this is one of God's little blessings." She smiled at her grandmother, knowing she would understand.

"Yes, indeed. Don't you just love it when he does that for us? I believe even your mother will be impressed."

"I hope so. I'd hate to disappoint her at her own event."

"Have you told her that you're coming?"

"No. I haven't had a chance to really talk to her. You know Mom, always on the run." Emily held up a bright yellow sweater with tiny white flowers embroidered along the crew neckline. "Isn't this cute?"

"Yes, it is. Did you find that at Neiman's too?"

"No. I only got the evening gown there. This was at a little shop in the mall. Macy's had some shoes that look nice with the dress. I have some similar ones in San Antonio, but I don't have time to go get them. There were good sales all over the place. I picked up a new purse, a blouse, and some more jeans."

"A fashion necessity for living on a ranch,"

her grandmother said dryly.

"They also come in handy when I'm digging through dusty storerooms or barns looking for treasures."

Emily could afford eleven hundred dollars for an evening gown, but she felt guilty spending so much when so many folks in Callahan Crossing were thankful to get secondhand clothes. So she'd spent most of the afternoon buying brand-new things for the Mission. Her van was stuffed full.

"Do you have a picture of the young man you've been dating?"

"Yes, ma'am." Emily rummaged through her purse for her cell phone. The new bag would work so much better. It had an outside pocket for the phone. Chance could quit teasing her about digging through her saddlebag whenever her phone rang.

She sat down on the love seat and clicked on the phone's picture gallery. "Here he is." She held the phone so her grandmother could see it easily.

"He's gorgeous." Iris studied Emily's face. "Are you two serious?"

Emily shook her head. "Just friends." Then why had her heart ached when she heard his voice that afternoon? Why had she cried and longed to be with him?

Her grandfather strolled into the room. "I

wondered where my ladies had gotten off to. Sorry about being tied up on that overseas call. Can't always take care of things when it's daytime here." He sat down on the foot of the guest bed, stretched out his long legs, and winked at his wife. "Now, what man is my wife calling gorgeous?"

"Chance Callahan."

"Ah." Grandpa Doyle nodded. "One of Dub's boys."

"Yes, sir. So you know Dub?"

"We've been acquainted for over twenty years. He's a good man. Met his boys a few years back at an oil meeting, but I can't remember the other one's name."

"Will. He's the oldest and helps Dub run the ranch."

"Is he married yet?"

"No, sir. But Dub and Sue's daughter, Jenna, got married on January 30."

"She was hitched to Jimmy Don Colby for a while, wasn't she?" Her grandfather glanced toward the open closet door. When he spotted her evening gown, his eyes lit up.

"Yes." Emily hadn't had an opportunity to tell him about her plans to attend the gala. But she figured he was putting two and two together.

"There was a lot of nasty gossip about him showing up at parties with another woman even before they split up." Her grandmother wrinkled her face in distaste.

"Do you know Jimmy Don?" Emily hoped he didn't run in the same circles as her mom. It would be a disaster if he showed up at the auction.

"No. Just know of him. As you're well aware, people in this town gossip."

"People gossip no matter the size of the town." Emily chuckled and scrolled through the photos until she found Zach's picture. "This is her little boy, Zach."

"Oh, isn't he sweet! What a beautiful child. Show your grandfather that adorable little boy."

When Emily hopped up and walked over to her show him the picture, Grandma Iris murmured, "You'll have beautiful children too, you know. And I'm not getting any younger."

Both of her grandmothers had been saying the same thing for five years. Emily sat down beside her grandfather and showed him the picture.

"Fine lookin' boy. I bet he's full of it."

"He goes nonstop and has a sweet disposition. Jenna says for the most part, his terrible twos haven't been too terrible. He's also smart as can be and adores his new daddy, Nate. Nate is a cowboy on the ranch and Chance's best friend. They're so happy it makes you smile just to look at them."

"She deserves it. If even half of what I heard is true, she went through a rough time with Jimmy Don. Show me the picture of Chance, so I can make sure I'm remembering the right son."

She clicked on Chance's picture.

"Yep, I was remembering the right man. They both resemble Dub." Her grandfather put his arm around her shoulders and hugged her lightly. "Let's go down to the family room where we can all be comfortable."

"All right." Emily laid the phone on the bedside table and accompanied them downstairs.

She fixed them all glasses of iced tea to see them through the evening. When they were situated comfortably, Grandpa Doyle rested his hands on the well-padded, tan leather recliner arms and smiled. "I want to hear all about what you've been up to in Callahan Crossing, and how the town is faring."

She started off relating how the townspeople had banded together, how they were helping each other. She mentioned the assistance that had come from all over the country and told them that the town was being cleaned up and rebuilding had begun.

Her grandparents kept asking gentle questions, and before she knew it she was telling them about the fire and confessed that she'd been in danger.

"I'm not sure I'd have gotten out in time if Chance hadn't stopped at the museum and helped. You know how obsessive I can be about historical documents." Her eyes misted over, taking her by surprise.

"So that's when you met him?" asked her grandmother quietly.

"Yes, ma'am. The fire was already roaring through the southwest side of town. It was afternoon, but the smoke was so thick I could barely see to drive. Every time I took a load out to the van, the flames were higher, closer. Chance came charging in there to tell me to get out of town. The Callahan men and some others were going up and down every street possible to make sure everyone got out." Sudden tears clogged her throat. "They risked their lives then and later when the winds died down enough to fight the fire."

Her grandmother took a box of tissues from beneath the table by her chair and came over to sit beside her on the sofa. She didn't say anything; she simply handed her the box.

Emily wiped her eyes and blew her nose. "Sorry. I haven't really talked about it to anybody." She shrugged and laughed self-consciously. "I spent a lot of time at the shelter listening to other people's stories. Guess I didn't realize I had some things bottled up inside too." If she did, what about Chance and all the others who had been right in the middle of the battle?

She cleared her throat and blew her nose one more time. "They weren't the only ones, of course. There were a lot of heroes that day. Callahan Crossing only has a volunteer fire department, and they made a valiant effort to stop the fire before it reached town. But even with dozens of other volunteer firefighters from around the county helping, they couldn't get ahead of it."

"Because of the wind." Grandpa Doyle took a drink of tea and set it back on a wooden coaster on the walnut end table. His expression was solemn, his eyes filled with compassion. Emily knew he'd fought some grass fires as well as some oil well fires in years past.

"That's right. Chance helped me get the rest of the boxes out to the van." She glanced up at her grandmother, who still sat beside her. "He carried two at a time with little effort. I'd been staggering with one."

"One look at his picture told me he was strong. He's a brave one too."

"Wouldn't expect any less from a Callahan," her grandfather said, but he didn't elaborate.

Emily thought the same thing could be said of a Denny, at least down to her grandfather's generation. Her father didn't fit the mold.

She shared how Chance and the others fought the fire and were leading in the recovery efforts. When the topic shifted to the museum and the Bradley-Tucker House, her tension eased. Her grandmother sensed it and moved back over to her recliner so she could look directly at Emily.

It was strange how she'd always been able to discuss almost anything with her grandparents on both sides of the family, yet she'd rarely had a relaxed conversation, much less a heart-to-heart talk, with her mom. And never with her father.

She didn't realize how often she mentioned Chance until she noticed them exchanging an amused, knowing glance.

"So Chance is a builder. I'd expect he's going to be busy as a coyote chasin' four rabbits."

Emily chuckled at the image her grand-father's comment brought to mind. "He is. He also works on the ranch, but he hasn't since I've been there. Still, when we went on a picnic on Valentine's Day, he seemed to know every cow in that pasture."

"You went on a picnic in the pasture." Her grandfather grinned at her grandmother. "Reminds me of some of the outings we used to have."

"Only there was usually an oil rig nearby." The sweet, nostalgic smile Iris sent her husband warmed Emily's heart.

I want memories like that. She already had some tucked away. But would they carry the same meaning forty years from now if those were the only ones she treasured in her heart? Her grandparents shared almost a lifetime of memories, good and bad. And they were still deeply in love, maybe more now than ever.

"Emily, dear, do you realize how your face lights up when you talk about Chance?" Grandma Iris had the expression of some-one imagining dozens of great-grandchildren running through her stately home, wreaking delightful havoc. "I believe y'all are more than just friends."

"Maybe. I think we could get serious, but I don't want to."

Liar. Emily froze. Where had that thought come from?

"Why not?" Grandpa Doyle straightened in his chair, lowering his feet to the floor. "He's a good Christian man, from a fine family."

"He's thoughtful, considerate, caring, and successful. He sounds perfect," her grandmother added.

"I don't know what I want. I've worked so hard on my career. I had a great interview today, and this job looks like a real possibility. Better than any I've ever had. It would be an amazing position for now and an excellent way to work my way up."

"Why is it so important for you to go to the top, Emily?" Grandpa Doyle asked quietly.

"I guess it's ingrained. I've always wanted to be the best at whatever I've done." She hesitated, trying to better formulate the answer. "And because I have to prove to Mom and Dad that I can. On the one hand, they expect — demand — that I succeed. Yet on the other, they believe I'll fail. I have to prove them wrong. Everyone in this family is a success." Even Grandma Iris. She'd been a full working partner in Denny Oil since the very beginning and was still active in the company. "I have to be too."

"There are all kinds of successes. In my book, a happy marriage rates above money and prestige." Her grandfather smiled and stood, winking at his wife. "Neither of those will keep you warm on a cold night."

Emily noticed that he was moving a little slower than he had the last time she saw him. When had that been? Six months ago? Far too long.

He walked over and held out his hand to her grandmother, helping her out of the chair. She, too, had a little difficulty getting up. When Iris stood, she tucked her arm through his.

"Don't worry about pleasing your parents, sugar," he said. "They're driven to succeed because they don't have anything else to keep them going or make them happy."

Arm in arm and heart in heart, they moved slowly across the Oriental rug until they were standing in front of her. "As for using all your education and training, you're doing that in Callahan Crossing. You're giving them a little light of hope, and that's important."

Her grandmother reached out and caressed her cheek. "Does Chance make you happy?"

"Yes, except for today when he said he

hoped I got stuck in an hour-long traffic jam."

"Why on earth would he wish that on you?" Frowning, her grandmother lowered her hand.

"He wants the traffic to irritate me so much that I'll convert to a country girl." She would freely admit that when it came to traffic, Callahan Crossing won hands down.

"The way you talk about him, the ranch and that little town, you already are." Grandma Iris laughed and rested her head against her husband's shoulder.

"Sugar, take some advice from an old man who's learned some lessons along the way. Ask the Lord if you're following the plans he has for you."

"I have, Grandpa. I asked him to open or shut the doors to the master's program, to direct my path. He opened them."

"Might be time to check in with him again. Sometimes he changes the route." He leaned down and kissed her on the forehead. "Jobs and careers come and go." Straightening, he patted his beloved's hand. "True love lasts forever. In the end it's all that really counts. Trust the Lord and follow your heart, Emily. What your mama and daddy expect you to do with your life ain't worth the spit on a postage stamp."

ALLEN PARK PUBLIC LIBRARY

19

Midafternoon on Saturday, Chance guided his horse around a stand of mesquite trees and down a steep hill in the most rugged pasture on the ranch. Spring was calving time, so he'd joined Will and Nate in checking on the stock where they couldn't take a pickup. They were moving them to a nearby pasture that hadn't been grazed and where it was easier to supplement their feed if necessary. Will, Nate, and the two hired hands had moved half of them earlier in the week.

Will said he'd saved moving the rest for the weekend because Chance needed to get away from the computer screen and out in the fresh air. He was right. Riding through terrain that required his focus was a good way to clear the cobwebs caused by lack of sleep and too much office work.

Despite Will's badgering to get off his backside and do some real work, it hadn't improved his mood all that much. That was his brother's main motivation for dragging him out of bed and pestering him until Chance got dressed and went with him.

He wouldn't be happy until Emily was back from Dallas, and that would only be temporary. She'd be moving on in a few months, and then he'd be in a permanent gloom.

A cow and calf grazed in the sparse grass at the bottom of the hill. The calf appeared to be about a week old and healthy. Mama watched him warily, but she didn't run. "Mornin', Miz Cow. This is just the appetizer. You need to mosey over to the buffet where the weekly special is still hay." He directed the horse around behind them. Easing forward, he prompted the cow and her calf to start moving. "We'll go nice and slow, take the long way around so your baby doesn't have to climb the hill."

The cow looked back at him and mooed in protest, but she went where he wanted with her calf trotting along at her side.

Too bad Emily wasn't as cooperative. He respected her desire to do well. He admired her accomplishments, knowledge, and the great way she worked with people. The one thing he didn't like — and that didn't even begin to express how he felt about it — was that she put her blasted career above every-thing else.

He navigated the animals through a tricky stretch of loose rock, cutting off the cow when she decided she'd take a side trip. Before long, they were on flat ground, near the corner of the pasture where Will and Nate were holding the rest of the herd.

"About time you showed up. We thought maybe you got tuckered out and decided to take a nap." Will gently nudged his horse with his knees and moved him forward. That spurred the cattle to start moving too.

"I'm not the one who got caught sleepin' on the job."

"That was in high school. I'd had a late night." Will squinted at him in the bright sunshine. "I've always wondered, did you spill the beans about my siesta?"

"Now, would I do that?" Chance grinned at Nate, who just shook his head and stayed out of the conversation.

"Does the sun come up in the morning?"

"Aw, now you've gone and hurt my feel-ings. You know I'd quit tattlin' on you by high school."

"No, you hadn't. You told Dad I put the dent in the pickup fender."

"Only because he thought it was my fault. I wasn't going to do your time." A cow decided to make a run for it, and Chance spurred his horse to catch her and bring her back into the herd.

When he returned, Will grinned at him like a possum eatin' persimmons. "You don't look all melancholy now. Told you a little honest work would cheer you up."

"I do honest work every day."

"Indoor, namby-pamby stuff." Will was trying to get a rise out of him. If he didn't watch it, he'd succeed.

Several cows picked that moment to get frisky, which was just as well. Nate took off to the right after a couple, and Chance went to the left to corral the same one that had tried to escape before. Will kept the rest of their little herd moving. By the time Chance returned, they'd reached a very dry area. Glad to put an end to the conversation, he pulled his bandana up over his nose and mouth.

After they had settled the cattle in the other pasture, they loaded their horses into the trailer and headed back toward the house. Chance sat in the backseat of the pickup, hoping his brother wouldn't start in on him again. He'd enjoyed being back in the saddle; it had been too long since he'd even gone for a pleasure ride. But he really wasn't in the mood for more razzing.

To his relief, Will kept his mouth shut. Nate, on the other hand, didn't. He glanced back at Chance with a thoughtful, concerned expression. "Have you talked to Emily since she had her interview?"

"She called right afterward. She thought it had gone well."

"Guess she was pretty excited."

"Yep. She really wants that job."

"A long-distance romance won't be easy. It would be worse if she was movin' clear across the country, but still, that four-hour drive is going to get old quick."

"I'll make the drive. For a while anyway."

Nate shifted around to look at him. On the ranch they didn't usually worry with seat belts. "For how long? You can't keep it up forever, even if you get married."

"Some people do."

"That would be a lousy way to live."

"Livin' without her would be worse." Chance stared out the window and tried to organize his thoughts. The short, new green grass and scattered yellow and white wildflowers barely registered. "Am I being selfish and unreasonable in wanting her to stay here? Maybe I'm wrong to expect her to give up her dream." And arrogant. There was that sin again. The one the Lord kept hitting him over the head with. Where was the rule that said his goals were more important than hers? "She's worked long and hard to get to this point."

"You have strong ties to Callahan Crossing. And commitments. With the rebuilding, you're more committed now than ever." When the pickup hit a big bump, Nate turned back around to face the road.

Will scowled at him in the rearview mirror. "Are you seriously thinking of packing up and heading to the big city?"

"It's crossed my mind." More than once since Thursday. The thought made him feel sick. "I have connections in Dallas. And San Antonio, for that matter. I could move my business. It would take time to get established, but I'm not hurtin' for money. She isn't, either."

"You can't just up and leave here." Will slowed down, bringing the pickup and trailer to a gentle stop. Shifting into park and turning off the ignition, he opened the truck door and got out. He impatiently motioned for Chance to join him.

Chance opened the door partway. "If you think you're going to beat some sense into me, you'll lose." They hadn't had a good knock-down, drag-out since high school, but there hadn't been a reason for one, either.

Will glared at him. "That's debatable. And a moot point. I'm not going to hit you. I just want to be where I can see your face when we talk. Trying to watch the road and you in the rearview mirror is killin' my neck."

Nodding, he climbed out. Nate came around the front of the pickup and leaned against the fender, crossing his arms. His casual appearance didn't fool Chance. He noted the careful way his old friend watched them. Nate was a war veteran. If there was a hint of tension or danger in the air, he was instantly alert.

Will smashed a dirt clod in the road. "Have y'all talked about this?"

"I've let her know that I don't want her to leave. And I've questioned her — okay, challenged her — about why working in a big museum is so all-fired important."

"How did she react?"

"She still plans to leave when the museum is set up. The only way she'll consider herself a success is if she lands a high-powered job. Being a success, as in having a high-paying, high-level job, has been drilled into her by her parents. They don't just expect it, I think they demand it. I honestly don't know if she really wants this job herself or if she just needs to prove to them that she can get it."

"That's the wrong reason for you to turn your life upside down." Will bent down and picked up a rock, throwing it like an outfielder who was trying to stop somebody from stealing home. He watched it hit the ground and bounce a couple of times before he looked at Chance. "You know I want you to be happy. You also know I don't want you to move away from here. The Callahans belong on this ranch. All of us. Everybody being here is what holds everything together."

"The place won't fall apart if I leave. I don't do much around here anymore anyway."

"Ain't that the truth," Will muttered and gave him a halfhearted smile. "Guess the only thing I can do is pray that God changes your mind since I can't."

"I haven't left yet. Even if I decide to move, it won't be for months. I have contracts to build four houses. Five whenever Dalton is ready for his." He shrugged and walked back to the pickup. "Who knows, she may not even want me."

Nate walked around to the passenger side front door and stopped, looking over the truck bed at him. "Have you told her that you love her?"

Chance stared at the ground for a second, trying to figure out a way to answer so he wouldn't be teased. When he looked up, his best friend was grinning.

"You haven't told her, have you?" Laughing, Nate shook his head. "And you gave me a bad time for moving slow."

Chance snorted and climbed in the truck. "I haven't been in love with her for fifteen years like you were with Jenna."

"It hasn't been fifteen years." Nate slid into the front seat and slammed the door as Will climbed in too. "Just fourteen."

"I've only known Emily seven weeks and four days."

"Which brings up another point," Will said, starting the engine.

"It's long enough," Chance interrupted before his brother could expound on him needing more time to get to know Emily.

His brother shifted into gear. "I hope you're right. Lord help you if you aren't."

Chance hung out at his folks' on Sunday afternoon with the rest of the family. He needed to spend more time with them. If he moved away, he wouldn't be able to visit as often. That brought an ache to his heart, but he told himself it was normal in most families. Kids grew up, got married, and

312

moved away. Maybe a few miles, maybe thousands.

But the Callahans weren't most families. Will was right about that too. They did better when they were all there. Not that his parents demanded it. But they welcomed the closeness and the unity. The family love.

Did Emily see that? Coming from a family so lacking in love, did she understand the special bond his family had?

He spent half the afternoon playing with Zach, helping him build a lopsided house out of Bristle Blocks, then galloping around on his hands and knees with his nephew on his back. He noticed Will and Nate exchange worried glances.

When he saw Jenna watching him with tears in her eyes, he knew Nate had told her what was going through his mind. He didn't care. He knew Jenna and Nate told each other most everything, though his brother-in-law had admitted to him one evening that there were things about the war that he wouldn't share with her. And that was probably just as well.

Later, when Chance went into the kitchen for some iced tea, his sister followed. "Nate said you're thinking about moving."

"I'm considering it, if it's the only way I can be with Emily. But I'm a long way from

313

that decision." He poured a glass of tea and took a long drink. Being a horsey was hard work.

She shrugged and refilled Zach's sippy cup with water. "Talkin' love usually comes before talkin' marriage. I think Emily could be happy here. I know she loves you."

Chance set the glass on the counter with a *thunk*. "Did she say that?"

"No. But I've seen how she looks at you. I don't think she even realizes it. Quit draggin' your feet, big brother. Raise this courtin' thing up a notch. Say the word."

He picked up his drink again and smiled at his sweet little sister. "What word is that?"

"L-o-v-e. It may not make the world go 'round, but it sure makes the trip more fun."

"I'll keep that in mind."

"Now, I'd better go put Zach down for a nap. He's worn out from riding the range."

"He's not the only one. I'm going to find a comfortable spot and see if I can doze a little." He put his arm around her shoulders and hugged her. "Thanks for caring, sis."

"You're always there for me. I just want to return the favor. I'll wake you up when Emily gets back."

"You won't have to. I'll know."

And he did, but it wasn't due to some romantic, love-related sixth sense. The minute she walked into the living room, a sleep-recharged Zach went barreling straight for her. "Emily!"

She scooped him up and hugged him, growling like a bear who sang soprano. Zach giggled and squeezed her neck one more time, then wiggled to get down.

Greeting everyone with a smile, she glanced around the room until her gaze locked with his. And Chance read her mind. *Zach gives good hugs, but they aren't the same as yours.* He may have said the words a few days ago, but sure as shootin' she was thinking them now.

His mom asked her about her trip, drawing her attention away from him.

Despite his heart racing like the "1812 Overture," Chance got up slowly and stretched out a kink in his back. He walked over to where Emily was politely telling his mother about her good visit with the grandparents. When he curled his hand around her arm, she looked up at him, her eyes shining with happiness. And maybe something more.

"Excuse us, Mom." Ignoring the wariness that sprang into Emily's eyes, he gently propelled her toward the kitchen.

"Chance! What are you doing?" she whispered.

"Escorting you outside so I can give you a proper welcome home."

"Oh."

When he opened the back door, she led the way out onto the porch. He briefly considered going to his house, but a hard rain shower that had started since she'd come home nixed the idea. They didn't have coats, and they'd be soaked by the time they got there.

He motioned toward the end of the porch where it wrapped around the house, away from windows and the curious eyes of siblings and parents. No matter how much he wanted to say the words, now wasn't the time. They'd have to go back in the house in a few minutes. Telling her he loved her wasn't something to blurt out and leave hanging in the air for a few hours.

So he did the next best thing. Rounding the corner, he pulled her into his arms and kissed her with everything in his heart — love and respect, loneliness and passion. Her response echoed some of those emotions but maybe not all. Affection, definitely. But lifetime-lasting love? Hard to tell.

He reluctantly ended the kiss and brushed a wispy lock of hair off her cheek. "You look wonderful."

She grinned and straightened his shirt collar where she had rumpled it when she put her hands around his neck. "I'm tired and probably look like it. It's a long drive. But thanks. You look pretty wonderful yourself." She searched his face, and her expression grew achingly tender as she trailed her fingertips along his jaw. "How are you?"

"A little sore. I worked cattle with Will and Nate yesterday. Since I hadn't ridden in a while, a few muscles are complaining."

"We should go riding when you get back to normal." Seeing his surprised expression, she chuckled. "Yes, I know how to ride. I had a horse all through junior and senior high. My grandparents kept her at their ranch south of Dallas. I tried to get down there as often as possible. When I went off to college, I told them to go ahead and sell her. She deserved to be with someone who could give her lots of attention, and I knew I'd only get back a few times a year. Grandpa found a good home for her with a young girl who lived on a ranch."

"Then it was a good solution. We have some good horses. You can take your pick. We also have some extra saddles for guests to use."

"Now all we have to do is figure out a time when we can both go." She glanced at the rain. "And when the weather cooperates."

He nodded. "We'll work it out. I missed you, Emily Rose. Somethin' fierce."

"I missed you too. A lot."

"Good."

"I haven't decided whether it's good or bad."

His heart sank, but he tried hard not to let it show. He smiled instead. "Reckon I'll have to work on clarifying that for you."

Before she could reply, or he could kiss her again, he heard the screen door slam and little feet pitter-pattering across the wooden porch. Chance grinned at the twinkle in Emily's eyes and stepped back. "He figured out how to open doors yesterday."

Zach peeked around the corner. "What are you doing?"

"We're talking."

Zach frowned as if he didn't quite believe them. He looked out at the rain. "Come play with me."

"In the house?"

He nodded. "Uh-huh."

Chance picked him up. "Did your grandma send you out here to get us?"

He nodded again. "It's cold outside."

"I don't know about that." Chance winked at Emily. "Depends on what you're doing."

"Shhh." Laughing, she started toward the

back door.

Carrying his nephew, Chance followed. His sweet Emily sure was cute when her face turned pink.

20

Emily had hoped to spend some time alone with Chance on Sunday evening, but there was a special service at church with a quartet from Austin. Dessert and fellowship followed, so by the time they got home, she could barely keep her eyes open.

Monday didn't work out any better. They were supposed to pour the slab foundation on Chance's second house, but the cement truck broke down on the way. He'd spent half the afternoon trying to get another delivery, but with the other construction going on in town, nobody had an available truck.

Then a potential client wanted to meet in the evening to discuss building the house of their dreams. They were late getting there and even later going home. Chance tried for two hours to convince them that their brilliant design, which they had done themselves, wasn't structurally possible. Finally, he'd given up, told them he couldn't help them, and they'd left in a huff. It was almost 10:00 when he got home.

On Tuesday, Emily worked at the Bradley-Tucker House by herself. Everyone else who had been helping sort and taking inventory had other obligations that day. One by one the day before, they'd stopped by her temporary office in the kitchen and explained why they would be gone. A couple of them, like Frannie, were just plan tired out and needed a break.

Emily enjoyed the peace and quiet. It gave her a good block of time to accomplish some work without interruptions every ten minutes. She was sitting at the kitchen table, entering more inventory into the computer, when her cell phone rang. Chance's name showed on the caller ID, and happiness spiraled through her. "Hi, handsome."

"Hi, darlin'."

"How's it going?"

"Not much better than yesterday. We got the foundation poured on number two, so that only put us behind one day. But the lumber company delivered the order for the first house to the second one. Nobody caught it before they unloaded. So now I'm waiting for them to come back and move it. I sure hope the rest of these projects don't go like this." He sounded tired, discouraged, and a little cranky.

"What time are you heading home?" She checked her watch.

"About 5:30, unless something else comes up."

"How about if I pick up some barbecue and salads and bring them over when you get home?"

"That would be great. Gotta run. There's a call coming in I have to take."

She said good-bye and quickly hung up. Poor guy. He was getting stressed out. She'd pick up some of his favorite things for dinner and give him a little tender loving care. Hopefully, that would make him feel better.

And her too. She'd been thinking about the advice her grandparents had given her on Friday night. They had just about everything anyone could want. Success, tons of money, a happy marriage, and restored relationships with Jesus. They'd made mistakes both in business and in their personal lives — spoiling her father, which led to a long-held rift between them, being the main personal one. But they'd persevered through the hard times because they had each other.

Emily cared for Chance more than she'd ever cared for any other man. Her feelings for him ran deep. But did she truly love him? Did she care enough for him to give up her dreams? To walk away from everything she'd worked toward for eight years?

She knew he had strong feelings for her, even though he'd never told her he loved her. Not in words anyway. If they got married and settled down at the ranch, would she be happy? Or would the excitement of new love soon dim, and she'd regret not achieving her goals? Would disappointment in unfulfilled dreams turn her into an unhappy, bitter woman? And make them miserable, possibly drive them to divorce? She'd seen it happen to others.

It didn't help that her father had left a message on her phone Sunday evening. He'd just heard about the McGovern Museum taking applications and had ordered her to get hers in right away. "Don't you fool around with that silly project in Callahan Crossing and miss this opportunity. Even though it'll probably turn out like all the rest. They'll hire someone else. But you won't have a shot unless you apply. You need to find a real job, Emily."

End of call. No "How are you? When are you coming to visit? I miss you." He'd never said anything like that to her. People didn't say caring things to someone they couldn't stand. Sometimes she thought her dad hated her, though she didn't know why.

For as long as she could remember, she'd tried her best to please him. Maybe just this once, if she could land the McGovern job, he'd be proud of her.

Rotating her stiff shoulders, she decided she'd better move around a little. She walked over to the window and stared out at the yard, admiring the sunny day. Bright green grass filled the yard after the rain on Sunday. Spring was a time of renewal and hope.

Did a new beginning await her this spring? In Dallas at the museum? Maybe here with Chance? Or would she go back to San Antonio to her nice house and . . . nothing else.

"Lord, I'm really confused and could sure use your help. I'm crazy about Chance, but I want that job in Dallas. I can't have both. He belongs here. I could never ask him to leave the ranch or Callahan Crossing. And maybe I'm totally off on his feelings. Does he love me? Or is he merely having a good time while I'm here?"

She knew the answer to that question two seconds after the words spewed out. He was serious. One-or-two-date-Chance-Callahan would never string her along.

"What should I do? I want to be in your

will, Lord. I thought I knew what that was, but now I'm not so sure anymore. I'd love the McGovern job. Living in Dallas again, not so much. I guess the easy way to know your will is to ask you to let me get that job in Dallas if that's where you want me. If you don't want me there, then slam the door shut." She pondered it for a minute and nodded as she made up her mind. "That's the way I'll know. If I get the job, I'll leave. If I don't, I'll see what happens here."

It was only 2:30, but she'd been sitting at the computer for most of the day. Besides, she was antsy.

She decided to go to the attic and look around. She hadn't gone up there the day Chance inspected the house because the lightbulbs had burned out. Though he'd had a high-powered flashlight, she didn't want to waste his time by asking him to shine the light here, there, and everywhere. Ed had replaced the bulbs early last week, but he hadn't taken the time to look around because they'd been focusing on all those boxes in the garages.

Climbing up the steep stairs from the second floor to the attic, she admired the beautiful cherry railings. In most houses, even fine old ones like this, the stairs to the attic were utilitarian instead of works of art.

She flipped the light switch in the hall and opened the attic door to find the big room brightly lit. Too bad they hadn't found any spare bulbs the day Chance was there. Using his big flashlight, he'd gone through the attic section by section. If he'd had all this light, he could have finished much faster.

On each side of a wide aisle, furniture and stacks of boxes, sometimes three rows deep, lined the walls. Or more accurately, the ceiling as it angled down from the peak of the roof until it met the floor.

Emily propped the door open with a cast iron cat doorstop to air the room out. She also checked the reception on her cell phone in case anyone called. Or if she needed help. It was an anytime-you're-alone precaution that had been drilled into her and the other students by one of her instructors. She didn't worry about someone hiding in a corner. The way things were wedged in here, the only thing that could hide was a mouse. But she understood her instructor's diligence. The woman had been hurt when a stack of heavy boxes toppled over on her. If she hadn't had her cell phone, there was no telling how long she would have lain there with a broken leg.

Tucking the phone back in her pocket,

Emily walked slowly down the aisle. "Where did you put the journals, Sally?" They'd seen no sign of them anywhere else. "Would you keep them where they were originally? Or hide them someplace?"

Stopping at a tall highboy, she carefully opened the drawers one by one. Clothes from the 1940s. She checked another dresser across from it. Hats, scarves, purses, and gloves circa 1930.

Going farther, she spotted an old trunk, and excitement zipped through her. If she were putting journals or diaries away, she'd hide them in a trunk. It creaked like sound effects from a bad movie when she lifted the lid. No journals, but there were some old newspapers and magazines from the late nineteenth century. Those were a find, but not the one she was after.

Slowly perusing boxes, opening drawers, and checking bookcases, Emily walked all the way to the other end of the attic. She found Doctor Bradley's receipt and accounting ledgers in a tall bookcase. Glass doors had helped protect them, though they were still coated with dust. An identical cabinet next to it contained old medical reference books.

In the inch space between the bookcases, a golden glimmer behind them caught her eye. Even without the books, it would take someone with Chance's strength to slide them out. So she decided to move the stack of medium-sized cardboard boxes beside one of the bookcases and try to squeeze in that way.

The first two boxes, labeled Christmas ornaments, were light and easy to shift aside. Reaching for the third box, she read a notation on the top and stopped. "Miss Olivia's Household Receipts" was written in faded but ornate penmanship.

"Who was Miss Olivia?" Intrigued, Emily freed the flap that held the others closed and spread them all open. The box was two-thirds full of notebooks, the kind used for diaries or journals.

Her heart racing with excitement, she noticed a piece of paper sticking out of the edge of one book. Opening it carefully, she found a sheet of fine stationery decorated with pink roses. The note, written in the same handwriting as the label on the box, stated, "Mrs. Olivia Johnson, affectionately known to all as Miss Olivia, was a druggist's widow who lived in the house next door to us on Third Street. She gave these to me in 1905 because I was interested in the history of the town. She had no family, and we had grown close. She died in 1906, and I sorely missed her wise counsel the first year after her passing. Indeed, I still do." It was signed Margaret Bradley, 1917.

Emily laid the note aside and opened the first page. It was dated 1885. Thumbing through the book, she found lists of items purchased, with prices and dates. Those alone were valuable. But on every page were notes about the weather, births and deaths, engagements, weddings, and other social events. Miss Olivia commented on church services and the latest fashions, on runaway buggies and a train wreck.

If this first journal was an example of what awaited them, Mrs. Olivia Johnson had left them a treasured history of Callahan Crossing.

Emily started to take the box downstairs, but the glimmer of gold behind the bookcases again drew her attention. "Might as well see what it is while I'm here, or I'll be wondering about it all night." She set the box of journals on a three-drawer chest across from her and moved the rest of the boxes out of the way.

Stepping into the opening, she eased behind the first bookcase, ducking her head to keep from hitting the ceiling. The prize she sought was a shiny black box about five inches high and a foot long, tucked as far back as possible between a rafter and the floor. Gilding around the edge of the top was what had attracted her attention.

Though she dropped to her knees, it was out of reach. Lying on her side, she scooted toward it and stretched as far as she could. She slid her hand in back of it and pulled it from the tight space, slowly working the gilded feet across the floor until she could move to her knees, then stand. Backing carefully from behind the bookcases, she carried it to the flat-topped trunk directly beneath one of the lights.

The wooden box had been stained black and heavily lacquered to make it resemble ebony. The top was covered in tortoiseshell and decorated with boulle, a scrollwork marquetry pattern inlaid with brass. The gilt around the top edges covered some other metal, probably bronze, which had been tooled to achieve a textured pattern. The small cabriole legs were of gilded bronze.

Ladies of centuries past used these small boxes to store sewing equipment, jewelry, or personal items. They came in all shapes, sizes, and materials. She had seen something similar only once. It was French and rare, dating from 1845–70.

The box was locked. That was not unusual

even if it had been used to hold scissors, needles, thimbles, and other sewing supplies. Those contents, however, would not have led the owner to hide it so carefully.

Emily squeezed back behind the bookcases. She hadn't noticed a key the first time, but she hadn't been specifically looking for one. After inspecting the area thoroughly, she concluded the key was hidden somewhere else. At least she hoped it was somewhere else.

She set the beautiful box on top of Miss Olivia's journals and closed the cardboard flaps as much as possible. Carrying them to the landing at the top of the staircase, she set them on the floor. She moved the heavy doorstop aside, turned off the attic lights, and shut the door. Cautiously carrying the treasures down the steep stairs, she took them into the kitchen.

Hot and thirsty, she stopped long enough to drink a glass of water before checking the first floor itemized lists on the computer. Hadn't Maybelle said something about finding some keys? She entered "key" as the search criteria, and the word was instantly highlighted on page two. *Seven keys — Doctor Bradley's desk.*

Was that all? She hit search again. *Four keys — small lady's desk in parlor.* "Bingo."

Hurrying down the hall to the parlor, she opened the shallow drawer in the desk and quickly dismissed two of the keys. One was obviously for the desk, and the other was much too large for the box. Either of the remaining two might fit. Clasping them in her closed fist, she rushed back to the kitchen and sat down at the table.

The first key wouldn't go in the lock, but the second slipped in easily. Taking a deep breath, she gently turned it. At the distinctive click of the lock opening, she let out a whoop. "Yes!"

She laid the key on the table and lifted the lid.

Two envelopes, a small journal, and a small heart-shaped gold locket lay on a black velvet cloth.

Emily took a deep breath and released it slowly. Were these the memories of a happy courtship? Or a lost love? She hesitated, reluctant to intrude into something so private and personal. Yet looking into the past and preserving history, both the good and the bad, was her job. Both Sally and her mother, Margaret, were gone. Because these things were hidden, not thrown away, their owner knew that someday, someone would find them and read them.

She opened the locket. Behind the glass, a

strand of dark brown hair sprinkled with gray curved around the base, forming a heart. The house was filled with old family photos and painted portraits. Both Doctor Bradley and Miss Sally's husband had been blond.

Lost love.

When she picked up the journal, her fingers brushed across something beneath the velvet. She moved it aside and found a picture frame, facedown. Lifting it from the box, she turned it over and gasped. It could be Chance fifteen or twenty years from now. It was not a photograph but a pastel portrait, painted by a talented artist — Margaret Bradley. Her initials were in the bottom right corner, just as they were on the portraits she had drawn of her family.

"Aidan Callahan." Emily's whisper sounded like a shout in the quiet house. The Callahan patriarch. Founder of the ranch and town. A man who didn't tolerate nonsense yet whose integrity and honor were renowned.

Tears misted her eyes. "Aidan, what did you do?"

Like his great-great-grandson, he was a striking man, with dark brown hair sprinkled with gray. In the three photographs of him at the ranch, one could easily see he was a force to be reckoned with. Even in a still image, he projected a stern, commanding presence.

Margaret's drawing portrayed him in a more approachable light. She captured a tenderness, even a twinkle in his eyes, that Emily suspected few people saw. Only those who were very close to him would be privy to this side of the man who had built a small empire.

Emily laid the picture on the table and ran her fingertip over the journal. Her gaze fell on the word *Maggie* scrawled boldly on the top envelope.

Hands trembling, she replaced the portrait in the box and covered it with the velvet cloth. She returned the locket, journal, and letters, closed the lid, and locked it. This was not something that belonged in a museum. Nor should it be seen by the prying eyes of the museum curator.

But what should she do with it? She couldn't throw it away. The logical answer was to give it to Dub and Sue, let them decide. Yet, just last night Dub had been sharing stories about his great-grandparents, tales of their long, happy life together. He told how Aidan helped establish the first church in Callahan Crossing, and how he had been an elder in that church off and on for forty years. Dub had been eight years old when Aidan died at ninety-four, so he remembered him well.

Emily was not the one to decide whether or not Dub should see the contents of that beautiful box. Nor did she want to put Sue in that position. From what she had seen, they didn't keep secrets from each other. But Sue might feel compelled to keep this from Dub if she thought it would hurt him.

Deciding to ask Chance how to handle it, she put the black box in the cardboard box, covered it with Miss Olivia's journals, and carried it out to her van. After closing up the house, she drove to the grocery store for the barbecue and salads.

A cold knot of worry settled in her stomach. Instead of an evening spent showering Chance with tender loving care, she was going to destroy his hero.

21

Chance studied Aidan's portrait, disappointment stinging him like the blast of ten thousand grains of sand during a sandstorm. Anger followed, directed at his great-great-grandfather — and at Emily for dumping the problem on him. Setting the picture on the coffee table, he rested against the back of the couch and pinned her with his gaze.

"Did you read the journal and letters?" The envelopes were addressed in his great-great-grandfather's bold scrawl.

"No. If it had been anyone besides Aidan, I probably would have. I'm a historian, after all. But knowing your family and caring for them the way I do, I couldn't pry into such a personal matter."

"So you brought them to me." Irritation roughened his voice, making her eyes widen. "Why?"

"I didn't know what to do with them. I can't put them in the museum, but I couldn't throw them away, either."

"Why not?"

"That's not a decision for me to make."

"Why did you have to show them to anybody?" Tossing them was the easiest solution, but he knew it wasn't what he would do. Not until after he looked at the journal and the letters. Now that he was aware of them, he had to know the truth, or it would gnaw on him like a dog chewing fleas.

"I don't know. It just seemed wrong for me to throw them out." She combed her fingers through her hair, shoving it back from her face. "The box and the things in it were precious to Margaret. Otherwise, she wouldn't have hidden them away in the attic. I suppose I should have given everything to Sue, but I was afraid that would put her in a difficult situation. I don't think your parents keep secrets from each other, and Dub has special memories of Aidan. Not just stories but memories of the man himself and the times they spent together. He saw how much everyone respected the Callahan patriarch, and that makes Aidan bigger than life in his eyes."

He was bigger than life in my eyes too, Chance thought. *Until now.* "Why didn't you call Mrs. Simpson? This was her great-grandmother's."

Emily closed her eyes, leaned her head against the back of the couch, and sighed. "Who knows how she would react if she got hold of this? She wasn't close to her grandmother. She doesn't care much about Callahan Crossing or the people here, either. Not in any kind of personal way. I've seen too many people tell tales about their ancestors at dinner parties, never considering that they might be maligning them or someone else who had been involved with them. Or that it might spread until it got around to someone who could be hurt by it. I didn't want to risk hurting your family."

"What about me, Emily? Just knowing about this hurts me."

"I know, and I'm so sorry. I really struggled with this. I hate hurting you, but I didn't know what else to do. I figured you could deal with it better than anyone else."

"Well, I don't like it. Not one bit." Generally, Chance was slow to anger, but this had him plenty riled.

He'd come home tired and irritated from dealing with stubborn, irresponsible people. The thought of spending a nice, relaxing evening with Emily had kept him from losing his temper when he had every right to give a few people what-for. With her curled up in his arms on the couch, he could have set all his problems aside for a while and simply enjoyed being with the woman he loved.

Instead he got shoved into another kind of trouble.

"You need to go so I can sort this mess out."

"All right." She carefully controlled her expression, which told him he'd probably hurt her feelings. Hopping up, she disappeared into the kitchen before he could drag his weary body off the couch and follow her.

He decided to let her go. He wasn't in the mood for a good-night kiss anyway.

And that was a mighty sorry state to be in.

After he heard the back door close, he left everything on the coffee table and walked into the kitchen without turning on the light. He peeked out the window but didn't see Emily between his house and the ranch house. Frowning, he started to go outside, then noticed the light come on in the bunkhouse.

Wise woman. She'd already learned that his mother could sense when she was upset and would start gently asking questions. His mom wasn't exactly nosy. She cared about people and had a way of getting them to unload their problems. The last thing he needed right now was for his mother to shift into pry-bar mode. Emily would be pouring out the story before she even knew it.

He didn't want to read through the diary. Ever. But he knew he would. He had to. If she'd waited another couple of days, after he'd had a few good days at work, maybe he would have handled it better. Or not.

Taking a fresh glass of water, Chance went back into the living room. He picked up the journal and the letters and settled in his recliner. Aidan's name was not on the envelopes, but Chance had seen his distinctive handwriting on other documents. Coupled with the portrait, he had no doubts that his great-great-grandfather had written them. He set the letters on the end table beside his chair.

"Lord, I wish I'd never seen this stuff, but I guess you want me to know about it for some reason. Give me understanding and wisdom."

Running his fingertip around the edge of the journal, he finally opened it.

Margaret Bradley. 1906
January 1. Another new year, but I have no hope this one will bring us the blessing

of a child. Since the last miscarriage in October, Kenneth fears for me to become pregnant again, though I am only twenty-five. He is truly concerned for me, but I don't believe that is the only reason he has grown distant. His disappointment in my inability to carry a child has expanded to most other areas of our lives.

We are such great actors in front of everyone else. We should go on the stage with our witty repartee and reserved but obvious affection for each other. Obvious but false.

Perhaps it is but the march of time that has dampened the flame of our love. Does all love grow cold when a marriage passes the five-year mark? Miss Olivia thinks not. I hope she is wrong. I do not wish to be the singular failure. It would be easier to bear if ours was but one of many.

January 5. Kenneth left two days ago on an extended trip to the East. For months he has focused more on the ranch and his business dealings than his medical practice. Perhaps he needs to since he built this grand house, and many of his patients cannot pay. He declared I was too delicate to make the arduous journey to New York. It is only an excuse. He cares naught for me. He is ashamed of me.

Miss Olivia tried to offer comfort, assuring me that he will soon grow lonely and hurry home, eager to regain the happiness we once shared. I hope she is right, but I have little faith in such a wish.

I thought I would welcome his absence — better not to have him here at all than to endure his frowns and criticism or alternately, hours of silence. Yet the house seems so empty, and I am lonely. Thank goodness I can spend time with my dear Olivia each day.

Chance paused and took a drink of water. It was easy to see how Margaret would be vulnerable to the attentions of another man. But why had Aidan pursued her? He had a reputation as an honorable man. What changed? Or had his uprightness been a charade and his sins well hidden?

He was ashamed the instant the thought crossed his mind. Aidan's integrity, strong faith, and Christian walk had shaped their family for four generations. He would not accept the possibility that his great-great-grandfather had lived a lie.

So far there was no mention of Aidan. Obviously, there had been something between them at some point, but maybe she had blown everything out of proportion, indulging in the fantasy of a lonely young woman.

He read several more entries, and the tone grew lighter. Margaret no longer talked about Kenneth and her loneliness. She and Miss Olivia, a dear elderly friend who lived next door, were busy organizing a project for the Ladies' Aid Society. That, along with her drawing and painting, seemed to occupy her days. She mentioned a dinner party she had attended and commented on the weather a few times. They had a warm spell, followed by a cold one, which was common for West Texas.

Then the journal entries changed.

January 15. Aidan Callahan stopped by this afternoon. How I was filled with trepidation when I saw him walk up the steps! The most powerful man in Callahan Crossing, whose stern visage and dark scowls make grown men quake. I thought perhaps something had happened to Kenneth, and he was the bearer of horrible news. Or that I had committed some unknown transgression, and he was there to chastise me in the name of the town.

He said Kenneth had asked him to check on me occasionally to see if all was well or if I needed anything. He was nothing but kind to me, as a father would be to a daughter. Though I daresay, I do not think he is old enough to be my father. He was ever so polite and stood on the porch the whole time. He is a handsome man, despite his rather stern manner. He promised to come by again when he is in town.

The next several comments talked about the Ladies' Aid project and a portrait of Miss Olivia that she was working on. She also received a short letter from her husband advising that he was traveling to Philadelphia, where he planned to remain for a month. From there he would go to Chicago for another few months. If he expressed any loving sentiment, she did not note it.

On the afternoon of the twentieth, Aidan came by again. That time he accepted some lemon cakes and a cup of tea — which made Chance raise an eyebrow. He had a hard time picturing Aidan with a delicate teacup in his hand. They spent a delightful hour in the parlor, discussing the Scriptures. Margaret found him to be as much of a Bible scholar as their minister, providing insights that she had never heard before.

January 30. Received a letter from Aidan, delivered by one of the cowboys. He has been tied up at the ranch but again tells me to send for him if I need anything. I am tempted to do so, but I fear loneliness would be a poor reason to summon him. His concern is endearing, but he seems only interested in my physical welfare — that I have enough coal for the fire, ice for the icebox, kerosene for the lamps, access to our funds at the bank to buy food, or whatever I require.

Does he not see that I need companionship? Conversation and laughter on a cold winter's eve? Tenderness and strong arms to hold me? Alas, I yearn for what I must not. I long for what I cannot have.

An entry a few days later stated that Aidan's wife, Clara, and their three children had gone to Boston for at least a month's visit to care for her ill mother. It was the perfect setup for trouble.

February 4th. Aidan came for dinner today after church. He was highly complimentary of the meal, especially the apple spice cake. Since he had two helpings of everything — ham, creamed potatoes and peas, canned peaches and fresh rolls from the bakery as well as my special cake — I believe he enjoyed it all. He stayed the

345

whole afternoon. What delight! He has such interesting tales of cattle drives and settling this country. He praised my piano playing, though I was nervous and missed a few notes. But when he started singing along with the music, I relaxed. His rich baritone wove golden chains of harmony and sweetness around my heart.

Chance shook his head and paused for another drink. He supposed Margaret's prose was typical of her era, but it was way too flowery for him.

Aidan allowed me to do a quick sketch of him, though I think he found it amusing. His countenance — gentle, with a twinkle in his beautiful green eyes and an indulgent smile — is so different from his normal visage. The image is indelibly imprinted upon my mind and heart. I will not require another sitting to use the pastels, though I may request it merely to study him.

I shall never grow tired of watching him or listening to his voice. I could spend every minute of every day in his company and never grow tired of him.

Sadly, I do not think he feels the same for me. He talked about his wife and children with great affection. He says he greatly misses them, though how can he when he spends most of his time at the ranch and they live in town?

Yet, when it came time for him to depart and I slipped my arm around his, he did not pull away. Indeed, he pressed my hand against his side, thrilling my heart. Judging from the look in his eye as he took his leave, he was not unaffected.

Chance laid the journal on his lap and leaned back in the recliner, turning on the massage unit to work on his low back for a few minutes.

Miss Sally had shown him portraits of Margaret Bradley when she was in her twenties. She appeared delicate, the kind of woman who naturally made a man feel protective of her. She was also very beautiful, far more lovely than Grandma Clara had been at her age. In 1906, Clara was forty-one; Margaret twenty-five.

He believed Aidan started off with good intentions, but he suspected Margaret was something of a seductress. So far, she certainly had used her feminine wiles and talents to entice him to spend time with her.

Still, Grandpa Aidan should have been wiser and seen what she was up to. Maybe he did, but having a beautiful young woman interested in him must have been flattering to a forty-six-year-old man. Chance supposed it went both ways. Having the most powerful man in several counties attracted to her must have done wonders for her self-esteem when she felt beaten down by her husband's disdain and lost affection.

It was certainly a lesson to keep in mind now and remember when he was older. Don't befriend an unhappily married woman. And never be in a position where they would be alone. He didn't think he'd ever heard a sermon on the subject. Might be a good topic to suggest to Pastor Brad. As long as he could do it without revealing how he came up with the idea.

Chance considered stopping there. He had the explanation about the portrait. He'd learned a lesson and gained something useful to protect him. But there was the locket and that strand of hair. According to Emily, women often kept locks of hair from those they held dear, even children. With that bit of gray mixed in with the brown, this was obviously not from a child. It matched the color of Aidan's hair in his portrait. He would only have given it to her because she meant a great deal to him.

If Chance quit now, he'd always wonder

what really happened. Wonder if he was assuming his great-great-grandfather had sinned when maybe he hadn't.

He eyed the two letters on the table. The answer might be there. Opening the first one, he scanned it quickly. This was the one Margaret had mentioned earlier when he was asking about her welfare. He picked up the second one but couldn't bring himself to read it yet. Maybe he was a sucker for punishment, but he needed to know the whole story.

Going back to the journal, he skimmed several days' worth of notes. Much of it concerned Miss Olivia. Margaret loved her very much and cherished her friendship. She also relied on her counsel, even if she didn't take it completely to heart.

Aidan stopped by a few more times, and Margaret talked to him about her problems with her husband. Though Aidan empathized, he encouraged her not to lose heart, to give Kenneth time to work through his grief about their inability to have a child. Chance doubted she said anything to him, but she vented in her journal about him taking Kenneth's side and not hers. Aidan also kept his distance. There were no further opportunities to slip her arm around his or to touch him in any other way. That greatly annoyed her.

Chance thought Aidan had tried hard to resist Margaret's tempting ways. "But you didn't do your best, Grandpa. Walking away and not coming back was the only safe way to fight it." He knew that from experience. More than one woman had tried to lure him into her bed, but he'd always managed to walk away. He wasn't any better than Aidan, but maybe he'd been a little wiser. Nor had he ever felt that strongly about anyone.

Until now.

If Emily decided to seduce him, he wasn't completely sure he could resist. It was a sobering thought. So much for his sanctimonious judgment of Grandpa Aidan.

He decided a break and a toasted peanut butter and jelly sandwich were in order. Walking into the kitchen, he looked out the window and checked the bunkhouse. It was dark. Emily must have gone back to the ranch house. He moved to the other window, confirming that the light in her bedroom was on. Was she mad at him? Or hurt by the way he'd treated her? Probably both.

He made the sandwich and paced around the kitchen as he chewed. Eating slowly, he wished he didn't have to go back and start reading again. It was too early to go to bed, not that it would do him any good anyway.

He'd keep thinking about Aidan and Margaret and worrying over what to do with that blasted box and its contents. Add needing to set things straight with Emily, and his slow cooker of a brain was bound to simmer all night. Too bad he couldn't toss some stew meat and veggies into the mix and cook tomorrow's dinner while he was at it.

"Lord, what's going on with me? Wearin' a hole in the floor ain't my style."

This thing with his great-great-grandpa bothered him plenty. Aidan Callahan was an icon, not only to his family but to just about everybody in the area. He'd come West with a herd of longhorns and made a fortune. He'd established the town, set up the bank and half a dozen businesses before anybody else bought a lot. When others did move in, they purchased land from him because he owned it all. He'd built the first church and the first school. Sent for the first doctor.

When the citizens wanted to erect a statue of him in the park, Aidan had scoffed at the idea and made his family promise they'd never allow such a thing. But he was a legendary hero who sat high on a pedestal anyway, in Chance's mind and most everybody else's.

Emily had knocked him off.

Which was why Chance was mad at her. No, he thought, that was only one reason. He was mad because she found the box in the first place. Because she'd spotted something behind those bookcases and couldn't stand it until she discovered what it was.

He rested his hands on the edge of the kitchen sink and hung his head. "Okay, that's dumb. She was just doing her job."

And that was the real problem. It wasn't because she'd found something that might destroy Aidan's reputation. Sure that bothered him, but what ate at him and had his heart and mind in turmoil had more to do with him and Emily than with Aidan and Margaret.

This was a hands-on, personal reminder of her talents as a historian and an indication of what a great curator she would be. She loved the search, the mysterious pulling together of bits and pieces to tell the story of people's lives. She wanted others to understand what it was like twenty or a hundred years ago — the challenges, sacrifices, innovations, and victories that laid the groundwork for what they had now. Yet, she had a keen wisdom about what stories belonged to everyone and what secrets needed to be kept.

She would be a fantastic curator.

He washed a smear of jelly from his finger and switched off the kitchen light. Resting his hand on the window frame, he stared at the glimmer around the closed curtain in her bedroom. The curtain was heavy, so he couldn't see anything except that fringe of light. He pictured her curled up on her bed, all bundled up in her heavy rose pink bathrobe and fuzzy pink slippers, her fingers flying on her laptop as she searched for jobs that would take her away from him. If she didn't get the job in Dallas.

"Father, don't let her go without me."

Don't make her want to leave.

Chance smiled ruefully. That still small voice in his mind was about as close as he'd ever come to getting a direct order from the Almighty to apologize.

He had some fences to mend, but he wanted to wait until he could fill her in on Aidan and Margaret's relationship. Maybe not too many details but the general scoop.

That meant he had to finish reading the story. Sighing, he went back to the living room, settled in the recliner, and picked up the diary.

On the afternoon of February 15, Miss Olivia died suddenly. Some ladies from the church and the undertaker tended to the body. Another lady stayed with Margaret for a while, then left her alone as she requested. Overwhelmed by the loss of her friend, she poured out her grief in the diary, desperate to send for Aidan but not daring to, afraid that people would find out.

Chance wondered how they'd kept his visits secret. Maybe they hadn't worried about it too much since he had always dropped by during the daytime. Chance supposed that being there in the evening or at night would have put a whole different slant on things. The clothesline chatter wouldn't have been any different back then.

Margaret didn't send for him, but he came anyway.

February 16. My dearest Aidan came to comfort me last night. When he heard about Miss Olivia, he knew the depth of my grief and rushed to my side. How much easier it was to bear the pain with his arms around me.

Chance groaned softly. He had a bad feeling about where this was going.

Aidan's strength sustained me; his tenderness comforted my aching heart. He held me throughout the night, his kisses and gentle loving brought joy to my withered soul and body.

But my beloved left me before the light of day, slipping away in the shadow of darkness. I rejoice in his love, yet I am heartbroken because he will never be mine. What I yearned for has happened, but the victory is bittersweet. I am his Maggie, a name he alone has called me. Yet, I am not truly his.

Before he went out the door, I asked him to choose between me and Clara. I will not be his mistress, though I would most willingly be his wife. He did not answer. He did not need to. The shame in his eyes said it for him.

There was only one more entry.

February 23. Kenneth arrives home today. May God forgive me of my sin and in his mercy never let my husband learn of my infidelity.

If I were wise, I would burn this account and the two letters from Aidan. I would throw away the lock of hair I so carefully trimmed while he slept. I would destroy the painting of him that came from my heart.

But I am not wise. I cannot let go of these precious memories and the deep love I hold for Aidan Callahan. I shall conceal these moments of my life and the yearnings of my soul in the beautiful box Miss Olivia left me. I will hide it away in a safe place where I can take it out from time to time and remember. As if I could ever forget.

Chance sat there, dumbfounded by his compassion for Margaret. She had led Aidan astray. He should despise her. But he didn't. He didn't much like her, but he didn't loathe her. She hadn't been a wicked woman who set out to have an affair or steal someone else's husband. She had been lonely and unhappy, beaten down by loss, criticism, and rejection. Aidan's concern and kindness must have been a balm to her wounded heart and soul. How could she not fall in love with him?

But he sympathized much more with Grandpa Aidan. Despite his strong morals and deeply held Christian convictions, Aidan had been caught in a web of seduction. He had been lured by his inclination to be a good friend, to give support and comfort to a young, beautiful, but troubled woman.

From the beginning there had been an undercurrent of sexual attraction. Margaret had felt it. Chance figured Aidan had too. That's why he'd stayed on the porch during the first visit. At times Aidan had tried to control it, even as Margaret tried to stir it up. Or so it seemed. But he couldn't stay away from her, and that was his downfall. He broke the most sacred of vows.

How that must have hurt him! To a man who put his principles right up there with his love for Christ, knowing he had sinned in such a way must have been devastating. Chance could imagine what he had felt like — distraught, burdened with guilt, shattered — because that was the way he would feel.

In the Psalms, David cried out to God, begging him not to hide his face. Had Aidan felt as if God had turned away from him that morning? Had he gone home and fallen on his face before the Lord, begging forgiveness and mercy?

He must have. He had stayed with Clara and his family, and from all accounts they had been happy. Still, he must have loved Maggie too. He had gone to comfort her that last night. Chance would never believe that he had arrived there with the intention of sleeping with her.

Chance closed the journal and set it on the table. He picked up Aidan's second letter and carefully eased the edge of the flap from beneath the body of the envelope. Drawing a deep breath, he took out the letter and unfolded the paper. It was dated February 16.

My dearest Maggie. I do not understand how I can love both you and Clara, but I do. If we were each not already married to someone else, it would be a privilege to have you as my wife. But that is not a choice we have. We are bound by vows before God, and I intend to honor that vow to Clara for the rest of my days.

I beg your forgiveness — and God's — for last night. I only meant to comfort you, not take advantage of your distress. I am deeply ashamed of my behavior, my lapse in morals. May God in his mercy forgive us of our sin. For it was sin, my dearest, in the eyes of God and the eyes of man. May our Lord heal the wounds I have caused you, which I fear are deep. May he lead us both back onto the path of righteousness.

Forgive me for abandoning you during your time of grief, but we cannot — we must not — see each other again. You will always hold a piece of my heart, Maggie. But there can be nothing more between us.

I have wired Kenneth, advising him of Miss Olivia's death, telling him that you need him here. He is returning as soon as he can make the train connections. He does love you, my dear. He, too, lost his way for a while, but if you will allow him, he will make amends. I pray you will make amends to him too, in the right way. Soften your heart toward him.

No good will come from Clara or Kenneth learning of our relationship and particularly our transgression. It would only hurt them deeply. Your heart is too kind and loving to want that.

May God have mercy on us all. Aidan

Chance folded the letter and slid it back in the envelope. He set it on the table, leaned back in the recliner, and wiped the tears from his cheeks with his shirtsleeve. Grandpa Aidan had sinned, but he had turned away from that sin and found forgiveness. There was no way to know if he ever confessed his infidelity to Clara. If he did, no one in the family ever knew about it. Or at least they never mentioned it.

Forgiveness after repentance was a promise that God always kept. He didn't have to show people in tangible ways that it was true. But in Aidan's case, he had. God continued to bless him with domestic happiness and material wealth. The ranch had provided for the family even when times were bad, and in 1923, oil was discovered on a portion of their land. The blessing continued from generation to generation.

Margaret had been forgiven and blessed too. Two years later, God had given them a daughter who was the light of their lives. Margaret and Kenneth had remained married for over forty years, and happily so, according to Miss Sally. He had also given them great material wealth.

Chance wasn't sure of all the reasons God had allowed Aidan and Margaret's story to come to light. He knew without a doubt that it was to go no further, except to briefly share it with Emily.

It had been a test to see how he would react, both to what happened so long ago and to Emily's involvement in discovering it. He had flunked on both counts. He'd judged Aidan and Margaret, condemning them before he knew the facts.

He'd quickly reversed course regarding Aidan, but it had taken him longer with Margaret. Easier to blame someone with whom he had no ties than someone with whom he did. God had shown him once again that he had a critical and holier-than-thou attitude. Righteous indignation really wasn't righteous unless the problem was dealt with in love. He'd been trying to work on that, but evidently he hadn't been too successful.

He'd also failed by being angry and cross with Emily. Definitely not the way to win her heart. He should have been thankful that she'd turned to him alone and sought his advice. Honored that she had trusted him not only with Aidan's secret but hers too.

Changing an attitude, particularly one he hadn't realized he had until recently, evidently would take time. But making amends, as Aidan so aptly put it, with Emily couldn't wait.

22

Emily checked the caller ID and answered her cell phone with cautious hope that Chance wasn't still mad at her. She didn't really blame him for being upset. But it had hurt.

"Hi, darlin'. I'm sorry I was a jerk earlier. Will you forgive me?"

It was amazing how those words took away the sting. "Of course. I know I dumped this problem on you, but I didn't know where else to turn. I'm sorry it hurt you."

"It's all right. After I sorted it all out, I decided having you turn to me was a compliment. I like knowing you trusted me to resolve it."

"Good." She sighed in relief. "Did you decide what to do with it?"

"I'm going to burn the journal and letters tomorrow."

"So it wasn't as I'd hoped, merely a young woman's fascination with an older, powerful man. But you don't have to give me the details," she added quickly.

"Actually, I think it might help to share the nutshell version. I know you won't say anything to anyone."

His trust told her how much he cared for her. Emily swallowed hard. "I appreciate that."

As he briefly told her what happened, she found herself sympathizing with both Aidan and Margaret. Aidan was an upright man who probably thought he could never be tempted in such a way. It was so unexpected, he was drawn in before he realized what was happening. She understood Margaret's situation because she knew how it was to have someone close who did not care for her, who was ashamed of her. In Emily's case, it was her father. It would be worse to have a husband's love grow cold, especially if she loved him.

When he finished the story, she considered how things had turned out. "So they received God's mercy. He kept Aidan and Clara's marriage sound and restored Margaret and Kenneth's."

"Yes. I don't think anyone else ever knew about their affair. I don't think anyone else should learn of it now."

"I agree." Emily pulled her pillow higher

behind her back. "But I have a lot more peace with you making that decision than I would if I'd done it. Thank you, Chance."

"You're welcome. You were right. It wasn't your call. I sure wish Margaret or Sally had tossed all the incriminating evidence decades ago."

"Do you think Sally knew about it?"

"Probably. She had a troubled expression once after she mentioned the journals. Looking back on it, I think she was wondering whether or not she was doing the right thing by leaving her mother's diary to posterity. I may be jumping to a big conclusion, but I remember it clearly because it struck me as being odd."

"What about the portrait and locket? What should we do with them?"

"I'll take the hair out of the locket and put the necklace back in the box. Then you can put them in the museum if you want. I guess I'll burn the picture too. If I keep it, someone in the family might see it and wonder where I got it."

"I'd like to have it." Emily grimaced, closing her eyes at her stupidity. How had that slipped out?

"Why?" His voice held a hint of caution.

In for a penny, in for a pound.

"Because you'll look like that in fifteen to

twenty years. I'd like to keep it to remind me of you." She stifled a groan. Had she really said that?

"Sweetheart, you won't need it to remind you of me. I plan on doing that personally every day — fifteen, twenty, fifty years from now."

Why did that sound so good? Emily's heart pounded so hard, she was sure he could hear it. *Get a grip. Don't lose sight of the plan and your goal.*

But was it really *her* goal? Drat the man. She'd never questioned what she'd set out to accomplish until she met Chance. She really needed to set him straight once and for all. Unfortunately, her brain and mouth had stopped working. A sassy comeback was beyond her.

When she didn't say anything, he sighed quietly. "Besides, I'd rather you have a picture of the real me. One where I'm young and full of vim and vigor."

Though she would cherish a picture, it was a very poor substitute for the man. When she answered, it came out all croaky. "I'd like that."

"Em, are you all right?"

She cleared her throat, but the frog seemed to have settled in for the night. Probably had something to do with the tears burning her eyes. "I need to go get something to drink." She glanced at the glass of water on the nightstand and felt a twinge of guilt. "Something bubbly."

"Emily Rose . . ."

Why had her name never sounded beautiful until he said it? At the tenderness in his voice, the tears rolled down her cheeks. "Yes?"

He hesitated, then took a deep, audible breath and released it slowly. "Sleep tight, darlin'. No worries about Aidan. About anything."

"All right. Good night."

"Night."

Emily shut off the phone and set it on the nightstand. Burying her face in a spare pillow, she wept for what she could not have. For what she would not let herself have.

Around 4:00 the next afternoon, Chance drove by the Bradley-Tucker House. Emily's van was the only vehicle still there. He parked his truck and walked up the back steps. After knocking on the door, he opened it and stuck his head inside. The kitchen was empty. He walked in, closing the door behind him.

"Emily . . . where are you?" he called.

"Back here. In the parlor."

He went down the hall, smiling when he saw her sitting on a settee in the ornately decorated room. "What's this? Did I actually catch you being lazy?"

"I'm thinking." She smiled up at him and patted the seat beside her. When he sat down, she continued. "I'm imagining what it would have been like, say around 1906, when someone came to call."

"They'd have tea and scalloped edged lemon cakes."

She sent him a quizzical glance. "You sound sure of that."

"It's what Margaret served Aidan the second time he came by."

"Lemon cakes. That probably means cookies." A light frown creased her brow. "I would have thought he was more of a coffee man. Tea doesn't fit."

Chance chuckled and draped his arm across the back of the settee. "That's what I figured too. I have the box and locket out in the pickup. Shall we return it to the attic?"

"Yes. I'm not going to put it where it was. That would make people wonder why it was so well hidden. I think a trunk is a better place."

"I'll go get it." He hurried out to the truck, retrieved the box, and carried it into the parlor. "It really is beautiful workmanship." Too bad every time he saw it, he'd think of what had been inside it. He took the key from his shirt pocket. "Guess you need this too. I locked it so the lid would stay closed."

"I'll put the key back in the lady's desk where it was." Emily tucked it away in the drawer. "Shall we go up to the attic?"

"Lead the way. I'll carry the box if you want."

She handed it to him with a smile. "Jinx came by this morning. He brought some Confederate Civil War memorabilia that belonged to one of his ancestors. A pistol, sword, and some pictures. He said he has a uniform and a Rebel flag in a trunk somewhere, but he'll have to dig it out."

"You'll be able to incorporate that into a display, won't you?" He walked beside her up the stairs, past the second floor landing and on up to the attic.

"I'm sure I can. It may not be very big, but then again, I've discovered that people have all sorts of things hidden away in sheds and barns. More Civil War items may show up." She flipped the light switch at the top of the stairs and opened the attic door. "Or attics."

"It's a lot easier to navigate up here with the lights on." He followed her down the middle aisle until she stopped beside a large trunk. He glanced around. Everything looked neat and tidy. "I thought you moved some boxes out of the way when you recovered this."

"I did. They're in that stack over there. I put everything back so nobody would ask why I'd moved them all in the first place." She opened the trunk and held out her hands for the box. He gave it to her, and she nestled it carefully amidst some lace tablecloths. She closed the trunk and straightened. "Do you want to look around?"

"Not this time. I'd like to go sit down and talk. Is anyone coming back today?"

"No one planned to. Why?"

He held the door for her and noticed the cast iron cat doorstop. "That's cool. My grandma used to have one of a dog. Wonder whatever happened to it?"

"Sue probably has it stashed away someplace. Do you know how many antiques and cool ranching stuff are in that room in the barn?"

He turned off the light, shut the door, and followed her downstairs. "Yes, ma'am. I moved some of it in there when Mom decided to turn our grandparents' house into a guesthouse. That's where Jenna and

Nate live now."

"And Zach." She flashed him a smile as they walked down the stairs side by side.

"Can't forget Zach. He's sure crazy about you."

"I love him to pieces. But who wouldn't? He's such a sweetheart." They reached the first floor. She pointed toward Miss Sally's sitting room. "Do you want to go in here? Those are the most comfortable chairs in the house."

"I'd like to sit beside you. I might try to steal a kiss." He pretended to leer at her, which only made her laugh.

"Then it's the parlor. There are a couple of settees in there."

Chance stopped in the parlor doorway and glanced around the room. The piano sat in one corner. Had it been right there when Margaret played for Aidan and he sang? Had his great-great-grandfather sat in that side chair while she served him cookies and tea? Or had he been closer, on the settee beside her? He was going to have problems with this place.

"Those don't look too comfortable. Why don't we pack it up here and drive over to the park. It's warm out today. We can sit in the pickup where it's comfortable and nobody will come barging in."

She searched his face. "I have the impression this talk is serious."

"It is." And the second most important one of his life. The most important one would be when he asked her to marry him. Today, he was only going to try to firm up the foundation.

He found a good spot underneath a large oak tree with new leaves. It was private, hidden away from the picnic and play area, with a view of the creek. Two of the ducks that called the city park home swam lazily up and down the slow-moving stream.

Emily looked around, then turned to him with a hint of suspicion in her eyes. "I bet you've brought girls here before. Probably in the dark."

He laughed, silently thanking her for putting him a little more at ease. "Not since high school. I'll 'fess up. I didn't go by my one or two date rule when I was in school. I went with one girl for six months. Another for four. But most of the time, the relationships rarely lasted past a month. Either the girl would decide someone else was more interesting, or she'd start getting too serious."

"So you were just out to have fun."

"Exactly. And I never pulled any punches

about that. Every one of them knew it from the get-go." He turned in the seat so he could see her easier. "But I didn't bring you here to talk about my wild high school days."

"What do you want to talk about?" She watched him closely.

"You. Me. Us." He searched her face for any sign of distress or happiness. For the first time since he'd known her, she could have been playing poker. "I love you, Emily Rose. I fell in love with you the night of the fire when I walked into the shelter. You looked up at me with those incredible blue-bonnet eyes and such a tender smile . . . I knew you were the woman for me. Beautiful, brave, compassionate. You had me on the line that afternoon at the museum, but you set the hook at the shelter."

"Chance, there's no such thing as love at first sight," she said gently.

"I disagree. I loved you then, and I love you now. But this isn't an official proposal." Confusion clouded her expression. "That'll come when the time is right. I want to marry you, Emily, but I don't want you to feel pressured. I don't want you to feel like you have to say yes or no right now — to marriage or to love. I just want you to know that I'm willing to do whatever it takes for us to be together. Even if that means moving to Dallas — or wherever — because you've landed the job of your dreams."

She shook her head, a deep frown wrinkling her brow. "I can't ask you to do that. You hate the city. You belong here with your family. I've never known any family who cared so much for each other and who got along so well. And the town needs you. To build houses, to give encouragement, to protect them."

"I belong with you, sweetheart. If and when you decide you love me and want me. Living in the city will take some getting used to, but that would be easier than living without you."

"I'm so confused. I don't know how I feel. I'm crazy about you, and I missed you terribly when I was in Dallas. But is that really love? Forever kind of love?"

He smiled, trying to hide his disappointment. Even though he didn't want to pressure her, he'd hoped she would fall into his arms and tell him she was madly in love with him and always would be.

"It sounds like it to me, and I hope it is. But you're the only one who can sort that out. We'll take our time and see where this goes. Just keep in mind that you don't have to choose between me or a great career move. You've worked long and hard toward your goal. You're amazing at what you do, and you deserve the best job out there. I'll support you and cheer you all the way."

Tears filled her eyes. *Uh-oh. That can't be good.*

"You would do that for me? You'd leave everything you love for me?"

"Yes, I would," he said quietly. "Because I love you more. I spent a lot of time thinking and praying while you were in Dallas. If the Lord wants us to be together, and I believe he does, why should my goals and dreams be any more important than yours? Sure, I'd rather stay here. But maybe God has something just as good for me somewhere else. Better, as long you're with me. I'll never know unless I'm willing to change."

When she scooted toward him, he moved too, and met her halfway. They wrapped their arms around each other and held on tight to dreams, possibilities, and hope.

He never wanted to let her go. He should have proposed then and there. Swept her off to Vegas and married her before she changed her mind. If she'd said yes.

His shirt felt wet beneath her face. "Darlin', don't cry. Don't be sad."

"I'm not. Well, yes, I am." She loosened her hold and straightened enough to look up at him, wiping her cheeks with her fingers. "I feel awful because I can't give you an honest answer one way or the other. But I'm deeply touched too. Nobody has ever cared for me the way you do, Chance. Not even my grandparents, though I know they love me."

He shifted on the seat and dug a clean handkerchief out of his back pocket, handing it to her. "People show love in different ways. Take Zach, for example. If he likes somebody, he's full of enthusiasm. All out, no holding back."

"He likes everyone."

"Not quite. There are a couple of kids at church he doesn't care for. I don't, either. They're obnoxious brats. So when he's in the nursery, he tries to avoid them."

"And you know this how?"

"I've helped out in there a few times when they were shorthanded. I babysit Zach occasionally, so I'm not a complete novice. But I'm better at playin' than changing diapers. You do want kids, don't you? You're good with them. Zach thinks you're the pick of the litter."

"Oh, he does, does he?" A smile lifted the corners of her mouth as she stuffed his handkerchief in her pocket.

He didn't know whether she planned on

crying some more or washing it. He didn't ask.

"He's a sweetheart. Like his uncle."

Chance liked that. She called him "sweetheart." Sort of. "Thanks."

"I meant Will."

"Oh no, I'm not going to let you get away with that." Figuring he needed to lighten things up, Chance tried to tickle her.

Laughing, she twisted away and slid back across the seat. Resting one hand on the door handle, she held up the other. "Behave or I'll bail."

"It's a long walk back to your van." He waved his fingers, making her giggle, before he moved back into the driver's seat. "Want a burger?"

"Sure." Instead of buckling up the seat belt, she slid back over next to him. "Thank you for understanding and being patient. I've been doing a lot of thinking and praying too. I've asked the Lord to guide me, to show me what his plans are for me. I've done it before, back in college. But as Grandpa Doyle suggested, it's time I checked in with the Lord again about this."

She cradled his jaw with her hand and leaned up to give him the sweetest kiss he'd ever had. "You are by far the dearest, most wonderful man I've ever known."

Chance got a little choked up, and not just because of her words. If that wasn't forever love glowing in her eyes, he'd eat his hat.

23

On Saturday night, they decided to go bowling in Abilene with Dalton and Lindsey, Nate and Jenna, and Will. Will protested that he was a fifth wheel, but it wasn't hard to convince him to come along. He enjoyed the game and didn't want to let the prospect of beating his brother pass him by.

Nate said he was a little rusty, but the Callahan men and Dalton had bowled in a league the year before. Since Lindsey and Jenna hadn't been bowling since high school, they didn't expect to do very well. Emily was the only one who'd never attempted it. In high school, her friends had considered it beneath them. In college, she'd been so busy with other things that she never thought about it.

Though she enjoyed being with her friends, she wished her first foray into the sport had been only with Chance. She was going to embarrass herself. And him.

After she put on the special shoes, Chance helped her choose a ball. "These are the light ones, but they're still heavy. When you pick it up, use your left hand to help support the weight." He showed her how to put her fingers and thumb in the holes, and Emily carefully lifted the red ball from the rack.

"Yikes! It is heavy." She looked up at him with a frown. "I'm supposed to swing this thing around?"

"Not around." He rested his hand on her shoulder. "Back and forth. I'll show you how. You'll catch on pretty quick."

"I don't know about this. I don't want to make everybody wait on me. What if I drop it and dent the floor? Or hit somebody? Or drop it on my toe? Chance, I don't want to break my toe." *Take a breath and calm down. You sound like a dork.* A frightened dork. Which she was.

His arm tightened around her, holding her against his side. "Relax, darlin'," he murmured softly. "It's just you, me, and Will. The others have their own lane. You can take all the time you want. It won't hurt the floor if you drop it. Everybody stays out of everybody else's way, and I've never known anybody who broke their toe."

"That doesn't mean it hasn't happened."

"Well, it won't happen to you. Come sit

379

down over here and watch how we do it. When it's your turn, I'll give you some instruction. You're not a weak-kneed wimp."

"Wanna bet?" She was so scared her knees did feel wobbly.

He leaned down and murmured in her ear, "You're only supposed to get weak-kneed when I kiss you." He brushed a kiss on her temple.

Emily almost dropped the ball. "Stop that!"

When he chuckled, she glared at him. He winked and shrugged, grinning unrepentantly. "Reckon it works."

"Grrr."

"That's my girl." Laughing, he pointed her toward their lane, which was on the end. Their friends were right next to them. Will was taking some practice swings or throws or whatever they were called. He made it look easy. But she knew it wasn't.

Jenna's ball started out in the middle of the lane. Halfway down, it slanted off to the right and bounced into the channel beside the lane. She laughed and moseyed back to her seat. Nate gave her a quick kiss in consolation.

"Maybe I should miss all the time." Jenna batted her eyelashes at her husband.

"Kisses for gutter balls and strikes only.

Otherwise, they're liable to throw us out of here for neckin'." Nate draped his arm across her shoulders.

Chance showed Emily where to put her ball and where to sit until it was her turn. He threw his ball a few times for practice, wiping out all of the pins on the last one. "I think that strike should count."

"Dream on, bro." Will bumped his shoulder. "You ready to start?"

"Yep. Go ahead."

Will knocked down all but one pin right off the bat. Or out of the gate. Or . . . whatever. As he waited for the pins to reset and his ball to return, Lindsey took her turn in the lane next to them. She only knocked down three pins. Laughing, she walked back to the others and waited for her ball to come back.

Emily felt a little better knowing that Jenna and Lindsey hadn't done well but didn't seem to mind. They were having fun. She could too, if she'd relax and not worry about it. Enjoy being with Chance and her friends.

A little red warning flag popped up in her mind — she hadn't included Chance in the friend category. But she didn't have the time or inclination right then to analyze it. Besides, he was her date, so he naturally fell into a different column. The more-than-a-friend category? Or the much-more-than-a-friend category?

Focus, Emily. She needed to watch how the others moved. How many steps to take, how far back to swing the ball, and at what point to release it.

Chance was next. Power and grace. He was in excellent shape, either from work or putting his treadmill and weight set to good use. Watching his fluid motion and the muscles ripple across his back, Emily sighed softly.

Sitting next to her, Will made a little sound in his throat.

As her face turned pink, Emily glanced at him, expecting a wisecrack. Instead of a teasing grin, his expression was thoughtful, perhaps even a little wistful. "He's a good man, Emily. And a lucky one. I hope one of these days a woman will look at me like that."

Her face grew hotter, but she wasn't going to belittle his feelings — or hers. "She's out there. You just haven't met her yet." Emily noted that Chance got a strike and clapped.

"Wish she'd hurry up and wander by. Too bad you don't have a sister. How about a cousin?"

Emily laughed at his grin. "Nope. Both my parents were only children. Sorry."

Chance joined them, frowning slightly. "What are you sorry about?"

"That I don't have a cousin to introduce to Will." Emily stood. "Guess I'm next." She wiped her sweaty palms on her jeans. "Promise not to laugh."

"Promise."

They waited for Lindsey to throw again and take out a few more pins.

"We won't count the first couple of throws since you didn't get any practice earlier." Chance glanced at Will, who nodded. "Do you have an idea what to do?"

"I think so. An idea, anyway. I've been watching everybody." She refrained from adding "especially you." "I swing it back like this, right?" Without the ball, she demonstrated what she thought was the proper procedure.

"Perfect."

"I doubt that, but thanks for the compliment. The tricky part is going to be taking the right steps and letting go at the right time."

"Without going over the line." Will gave her a cheeky grin.

"You be quiet." Chance fake-frowned at his brother.

"Who's gonna make me?" Will grinned and stood up, puffing out his chest.

Emily laughed. It wasn't the first time she'd seen the two of them act like little boys.

"Y'all behave or I'll sic Jenna on you." Nate winked at his wife, who put up her fists and danced around like a boxer in the ring. "She'll tie your ears in a bowknot."

"Sounds painful." Will's eyes twinkled as he smiled affectionately at his sister.

"You can be her guinea pig." Chance motioned for his brother to sit down. "Shut up and let Emily bowl. Go on, darlin'. Ignore this rowdy bunch. Let's figure out where you should start."

They paced out the right distance before Chance handed her the ball, and she slipped her fingers and thumb into the holes. "Line up the big toe on your left foot with that big dot on the floor. Keep your arm relaxed and swing the ball easy, let the ball's weight do the work."

Emily lined up in the lane as he'd instructed and breathed deeply. As she took her steps, she swung the ball back, brought it forward, and released it. It hit the floor with a thud and slowly rolled about twenty feet down the lane before dropping into the gutter.

Groaning, she covered her face with her hands, turned, and walked back to Chance. He put his arms around her and held her close. "That's good for your first try."

Red-faced, she looked up at him and said sarcastically, "Right."

"It is. You didn't drop it behind you or fail to release it and go flying down the lane with the ball. I've seen both happen."

"You're kidding."

"Nope. Of course, it was on a bloopers show, but they're supposed to be real. Now, turn around and watch Dalton."

When she faced the lanes, Chance slid his arms loosely around her, resting his hands at her waist, and gently pulled her back against his chest. It felt good in an exciting way, but it was also comforting, as if his calm strength was drawing some of the stress right out of her.

"Watch where he releases the ball in the swing. It's a little sooner than when you let go. See, it's closer to the floor at that point. Think about rolling it instead of throwing it. The force to make it roll basically comes from the forward movement of your body."

"That makes sense. I'll just pretend I'm rolling the ball to Zach."

"That's right, only with a little more oomph than with him. Don't worry about aiming. Just roll it." He leaned down and kissed her cheek. "Try again."

"You really need to stop kissing me. It ruins my concentration."

"I think that's a compliment."

"Interpret it however you want, but quit doing it. The manager is watching us."

"Don't worry about him. He won't say anything. He wants Will and me to join the league again." Chance straightened and waved at the manager. He waved back, shaking his head and chuckling as he turned away. "Now, go get 'em, tiger."

Emily started the swing and the steps, concentrating on rolling the ball. This time it didn't bounce when she released it, and it zipped down with more power. Holding her breath, she watched it go straight down the lane, smack into the first pin, and knock eight of them down.

"Yes!" Jumping up and down, she ran back to Chance. He grabbed her at the waist, picked her up off the ground, and spun around while her friends cheered. When he set her back on the floor, he gave her a big hug.

"Think we should count that one?"

"You'd better." Laughing, she grabbed her Dr Pepper — Chance was converting her — and gulped a big swallow while Jenna had her turn.

Emily threw a gutter ball next, and several times during the evening. But it didn't matter. She also made a strike and knocked down lots of pins now and then. When they were finished, Will had barely beat Chance, who declared that he'd let his big brother win so he wouldn't get an inferiority complex. Dalton had the top score in the other group, with Nate coming in second as expected. Along with Emily, Jenna and Lindsey had quit keeping score halfway through the evening.

Afterward, when Jenna suggested they go to Cold Stone Creamery for ice cream, Emily squealed in delight. Chance stared at her in amusement. Since he had a sister, he'd evidently experienced girlish enthusiasm on occasion. Unlike her father, he didn't seem to mind.

When they arrived at the strip mall and bailed out of the pickups, Jenna switched places with Nate so she could walk beside her. Chance was on Emily's other side, possessively holding her hand. That was becoming a pleasant, comfortable habit. Maybe it was dangerous, but right then she didn't care. She intended to enjoy every minute of the evening.

Emily turned her attention to Jenna. "This

is a great idea. I'm such a regular customer at the Creamery near my house in San Antonio that they start working on my order when they see me come through the door."

"So you always have the same thing?" Jenna asked, her expression filled with disbelief.

"Yep. Stuck in a rut."

"Then you have to try something different tonight."

"I can never decide what to mix in." Emily could only remember a partial list of the fruit, nuts, candies, and who knew what else that was available. "There are too many choices."

"Come on, live a little. You didn't know how to bowl, either, but you did all right. As good as Lindsey and me, anyway."

"Do you always have something different?"

"Every time. Though I admit there is usually some chocolate in there somewhere."

"Is there anything else?" Emily laughed and looked up at Chance. "What kind do you like?"

"Vanilla. No mix-ins," he said in a monotone.

Emily stopped and studied his deadpan expression. She didn't believe for one second that he could go in there with all that wonderful ice cream and other goodies and order plain old vanilla.

"You can't be serious."

Nate chuckled as he and Jenna halted. "He's slipped into Sergeant Monday mode. It's okay, he'll come around in a few minutes."

"Dum-de-dum-dum." Will sang the opening lines to the *Dragnet* theme song.

"Don't you mean Sergeant Friday?" Emily asked, looking from Nate back to Chance.

"No, ma'am," said Chance in that same even-toned voice. "Just the facts, ma'am."

"Don't you have the facts mixed up?" Emily played along, pulling her shoulders up to make her back ramrod straight and assuming what she hoped was a tough cop stance.

A glint of laughter danced in Chance's eyes, but he kept the straight face. "No, ma'am. Sergeant Monday is my name."

Emily slowly circled him, tapping her fingers together. Grinning, the others watched. "So tell me, Sergeant *Monday,* do you actually prefer plain vanilla ice cream? Not even a few sprinkles?"

Chance kept his back straight and head forward, though he glanced down to meet her gaze. "Sprinkles are for kids, ma'am."

She switched tactics. Moving to his side,

she poked his hard bicep with her index finger. Laying her hand on his shoulder, she said in a honeyed, exaggerated Southern accent, "Shugah, nobody would evah mistake you for a kid."

Will hooted, Jenna giggled, and Nate laughed out loud. Dalton put his arm around Lindsey and leaned down to make a quiet comment, evoking a shared grin. Chance's lip twitched, but he managed to keep a straight face.

Emily walked around behind him, trailing her fingertips lightly across one shoulder, the nape of his neck, and the other shoulder.

"Aw, that's sneaky." Will shook his head.

When she was in front of Chance again, she toyed with the edge of his shirt collar. "You need to live a little, shugah. Walk on the wild side. Break out of that vanilla mold. Try cotton candy, bubble gum, or maybe green apple gummy bear."

That did it. "Gross! No thanks." Putting his arm around her, Chance nudged her toward the shop.

"So did you take drama?" Absently noting that everybody else was following them, Emily put her arm around his waist as he shortened his stride to match hers.

"Some."

"Don't let him off that easy," said Dalton.

"He had the lead in half the plays they did in high school."

"Among other things, he played a pirate, a cop, and even did a little Shakespeare," Jenna added. "Forsooth, what light in yonder window breaks . . . or something like that. I should remember it since I helped him practice his lines."

"So was the Monday character part of a spoof on *Dragnet*?" she asked, looking up at him.

"Yes. Another student wrote the play. It was pretty good." He smiled smugly. "And the lead actor was great."

"Meaning you." Emily tickled his side.

"Of course." He released her and dodged her fingers.

"I think Emily has taken some acting classes too," Lindsey said. "You're good."

"I did. All through high school and a couple of classes in college. I had the lead in a few plays, but more often I was a secondary character. I started out in first grade." She lifted her chin proudly. "I played a lady pilgrim at the first Thanksgiving dinner."

They reached the ice cream store, and Will opened the door, holding it as everyone trooped in.

"Y'all would make a great couple to head

up the cast at our community theater." Lindsey walked backward as she talked, and Dalton quickly moved a chair before she tripped over it.

"I didn't know Callahan Crossing had a theater." Emily glanced at Chance. He appeared as puzzled as she was.

"We don't, but we could start one." Lindsey bubbled with excitement. "Jenna took drama too, and I could paint all the scenery."

"I'd help build the sets," Dalton offered. "Chance would have to do double duty. Build and act."

"I could be the director." Will made a cutting motion across his throat. "Cut!"

"You never took a drama class." Chance shook his head.

"No, but I'm good at ordering people around."

"That's an understatement." Nate grinned at his boss and friend.

"Seriously, y'all, I think we should do it. There are several buildings that might work. I bet we could get a lot of people involved."

Emily kept quiet as the group tossed ideas around and ordered their ice cream. She wouldn't be there to take part in a community theater. Or see the town rise from the ashes. Or to know whether or not the museum and Bradley-Tucker House brought people into town.

Lord willing, by the time they were beyond the talking stage about the theater, she'd be working at the McGovern in Dallas. She'd received a call on Thursday that they were down to choosing between her and two others. The board had decided to go over the applications and talk to the director to make their decision. She wouldn't have to go back for another interview.

Chance had been happy for her and proud, bragging about her to the family. They had congratulated her, but she sensed some worry too. Which was perfectly normal, since he had told them how he felt about her and that he might be moving. Dub and Sue probably wanted to send her packing, but they were too nice to throw her out.

Oddly, she wasn't as excited about the job as she'd expected to be. Even knowing that Chance was willing to go with her hadn't helped. Or maybe that was part of the problem. He was willing, but she didn't think he should. He talked about moving his company to a smaller town near Dallas and even seemed enthused about it. But she was afraid he was trying to convince himself as much as her.

Tonight, the thought of moving away, even to a new, fascinating job, filled her with sorrow. It would be easier with Chance there. And it wouldn't. She would feel terribly guilty about taking him away from Callahan Crossing and the people that he loved.

Nor was he the only one who would miss the Callahans and Nate. And Zach! She'd miss Dalton and Lindsey and all the folks in the Historical Society. If she got the job — and it was still a big if — she wouldn't start until June. She could set up the Callahan Crossing Museum before she left. But she would no longer be a part of it. Or of Callahan Crossing.

Emily shook off her melancholy thoughts. None of that might happen, and as Grandma Rose was fond of saying, she shouldn't borrow trouble. This was not a night to dwell on troubling things.

She didn't think she'd ever had such a good time with friends as she had this evening. Bowling was not her sport. But that hadn't mattered. She didn't feel like a loser. She'd enjoyed the company of friends who were dear to her.

And I'm with the man I love.

Emily gasped softly, relieved that Nate's laughter at Jenna's order drowned out the subtle, telling sound. That thought had been definite and final. No wishy-washy wobbling about whether or not she loved him. Why had she had such a hard time recognizing it and accepting it?

There was still the problem of what to do if she got the job, but she'd deal with that another time. The quest to prove to her father that she was worth something didn't seem quite as crucial as it always had. For a little while, she would forget about goals, expectations, and a father who might never be proud of her. Or care for her.

Tonight she would thank God for life by living it in his joy. Tonight was for stepping out of her comfort zone and taking nothing for granted.

Snuggling against Chance's side when he put his arm around her, she smiled at the clerk. "I'd like mango ice cream with straw-berries and macadamia nuts. And two bites of devil's food cake on the top."

"Hey, you got out of the rut." Chance gave her a quick, little squeeze.

"Just followin' my own advice, shugah. Livin' on the wild side." She looked into his eyes and softly added, "And lovin' my man."

He went still, searching her face, seeking her heart. She nodded ever so slightly, and he drew in a slow, deep breath. Tucking her hair behind her ear, he leaned down and whispered, "Do you mean that?"

"With all my heart." Heat suddenly flared in his eyes, and she caught her breath. Her knees went weak, and he sensed it, tightening his arm around her waist.

Her heart racing, she looked away. Good thing Will had come with them. If they'd been alone, they'd be in a heap of trouble.

24

On Sunday afternoon, at Sue's suggestion, Emily took a couple of Miss Olivia's journals over to show Chance. She quickly realized that she'd been set up. When she walked through the back door, he removed the journals from her hand, laid them on the kitchen table, and handed her the end of a piece of thick brown twine. The rest of the string disappeared beyond the doorway of the kitchen.

"What's this?" She grinned at the pure mischief in his eyes.

"A treasure hunt. Just follow the string."

"Do you want me to roll it up?"

"Naw, that's too much work. Just wad it up as you go." He looked like a kid on Christmas morning waiting to run downstairs to see what was under the tree.

She followed the twine out of the kitchen and down the hall to his workout room. It wrapped around the handrails on the treadmill, went over to the weight set, and looped around a barbell. It took her a few minutes to unwind it and go back out the door. It led down the hall to his office, wrapped around his chair three times, went in one side of a closed drawer, and out the other.

"Do I open the drawer?"

"Yep."

Opening the drawer carefully, she found an old ranch record book. She tossed the twine on the desk, reverently removed the book from the drawer, and opened it. It was dated 1886. "You talked Dub into loaning it to the museum?"

"Yes, ma'am. And it wasn't easy, either. This is one of the better ones because it isn't only a record of expenses, but it's a diary of the year too."

Emily looked through it randomly, finding weather information, cattle bought and sold, supplies purchased, notes about visitors and cattle buyers. There were even a few notations recording national events. "This is wonderful. Thank you." She laid it on the desk and gave him a lingering kiss. "I'll thank Dub later."

"But not in the same way," he teased. "Or Mom and I will both be after you. Now, pick up the twine again and keep going."

"There's more?"

"Yes, ma'am."

She followed it to his bedroom, where it meandered around a pair of boots, across a straight-backed chair, into the closet where it draped over the rod between some empty hangers, and went back out again. "I should have rolled this up. It's a big wad of string."

"Hang on." He took a pocketknife off his dresser and opened it. She stretched the twine taut so he could cut it. "Throw the rest of it on the bed. I'll clean it up later."

Emily resumed the treasure hunt. The string was wrapped around the door handle to the guest bedroom, but it didn't go in the room. She unwound it and followed it in a straight line to the living room.

It ended taped to the fireplace mantel beneath a small, ornately carved silver container. Rectangular with a lid, it would have sat on a lady's dressing table a century earlier to hold hairpins. "It's beautiful. Where did you get it?"

"It was Grandma Clara's," he said quietly, picking it up. "She kept her wedding ring in it. According to family legend, she was too practical to get another ring when they got married and used her engagement ring."

He looked down at the silver container. "Clara left this to Grandma Irene, my dad's mother. She liked the box but not the ring.

It wasn't fashionable in her day. But she kept the box on her dresser because it was pretty, and it reminded her of Clara."

Emily's pulse kicked into high gear. A man didn't talk about engagement or wedding rings unless he had something in mind. His hands were shaking slightly. His hands never shook — except when they had been hiding from the tornado. And that didn't count.

She was about to receive a marriage proposal from a man she loved and adored. *Calm down, let him do this his way.* That wasn't easy to do when she was itching to see the ring — and his face when she accepted his fantabulous offer.

"Grandma Irene gave it to Mom, and she's kept it on her dresser for years. Saving it for the right person." Chance lifted the lid on the box and took out the ring. Emily couldn't see it, partly because his big, beautiful, work-worn hand was in the way and partly because her eyes were all misty.

He set the box on the mantel, took her left hand in his, and dropped to one knee. "Emily Rose, will you marry me?"

"Yes." Without hesitation, without worry. Everything would turn out all right. She felt it in the very core of her soul. "Oh yes!"

He slipped the ring on her finger. A large, faceted ruby, circled by six slightly smaller diamonds on a rose gold band.

"Chance, it's beautiful. Absolutely incredible." She held it out in front of her, tears of happiness pooling in her eyes as he stood. "It's perfect." She threw her arms around his neck and hugged him.

"I thought you might like it."

"And it even fits. That's amazing."

"Not really." He settled his hands at her waist. "Jenna drew a template of one of your rings last week. She'd noticed that it was one you wore on your left hand, which is good because I never considered that your hands might be a little different size. I took the template and the ring to the jewelry store, and they sized it."

"Last week. You were pretty sure of yourself, weren't you?"

"Not completely, but I was determined and wanted to be prepared." He shrugged. "It's a Callahan trait. Let's seal this deal."

"With a handshake?" she asked, suddenly feeling impish and giddy. Resting her hands on his shoulders, she wiggled her fingers, catching the light in the diamonds.

"No way. Come here, soon-to-be Mrs. Callahan." He lowered his head and touched his lips to hers — giving, taking, and filling her heart with promises of a wonderful life together.

When he raised his head, she sighed happily and leaned her forehead against his chin. "Mom is going to want a big society wedding."

"Tough."

She giggled and looked up at him. "My sentiments exactly. Want to elope?"

"I've thought about it. Mom and Jenna would kill us. Let's sit down and figure it out."

Emily took his hand and led the way. They plopped down on the couch, and he put his arm around her, tucking her in close. She held out her hand, staring at the ring, and he laughed.

"How long does this last?"

"What? Admiring my beautiful ring? I don't know. I've never been engaged before. But I expect a lifetime."

Emily finished the preliminary work on the ranching exhibit at the museum on Wednesday. Besides saddles and other horse tack, they had a wall displaying ranching pictures from the 1880s through the 1930s. Another wall held branding irons from many of the ranches in the area and some horns from a longhorn that measured almost eight feet wide.

The Callahan Ranch record book would

be added when the display case was finished. She had transcribed its contents onto the computer and printed out a copy. That gave people access to the information without handling the book. It pleased Dub so much that he surprised both her and Sue by deciding to donate the ranch chuck wagon, which had been in use since 1885.

He tried to make light of it, though he knew both of them were thrilled. "We only use it once every year or two anyway, and it'll need some major work if we keep hauling it around the ranch." Sue had hugged the stuffing out of him and whispered something in his ear that made him grin. When Emily gave him a hug, he leaned down and said quietly, "Consider it a wedding present. Not the only one, but I figure it's a good way to show you that I'm glad you'll be part of the family."

All the Callahans enthusiastically shared his sentiment and had taken time individually over the past four days to tell her so. No one mentioned the possibility of them moving away, though she knew it was on their minds. Chance said it was their way of showing respect and support for whatever decision he and Emily made. She hoped he was right.

She also hoped Dub and Chance could

figure out a way to get the wagon inside the building without too much trouble. Going through the door at the loading dock wouldn't be a problem. The storeroom doors, though they were double, might be an issue. Her sweet fiancé said he would dismantle part of the wall if necessary and put in a larger door in case someone else donated something big.

On Thursday morning, Emily started seriously reading through Miss Olivia's journals. She'd browsed through a few of them over the past week whenever she had a minute, or when Sue wasn't looking at them.

She planned to spend two hours a day recording Miss Olivia's history of the town on her computer. The remainder of her work time would mainly be at the museum setting up exhibits. The Historical Society had finished the inventory at the Bradley-Tucker House. Now it was up to Emily to decide what to use in the museum. There were more than enough items to have some revolving displays as well as permanent ones.

At some point, it would be worthwhile to transcribe every word of the journals, including the very thorough lists of purchases. For now, she mainly recorded events and comments, adding brief notations when Olivia picked up something special such as seasonal fruits and vegetables. When she got to 1886, it would be interesting to compare Olivia's observations with those in Aidan's record book.

She glanced at her watch and decided to try to catch her mom and wish her happy birthday before her schedule filled up. There hadn't been a good time since Sunday to call her parents and tell them about her engagement.

No, she thought with a sigh. That wasn't really true. She hadn't wanted to listen to their rants and raves, so she'd put it off. If only they could be as happy for her as all of her grandparents were. It was so typical of her life. She'd called Grandma Rose and Grandpa and Grandma Denny right away to share her good news, but she kept putting off contacting her parents.

Since her mother's birthday was on April 1, she might think it was an April Fool's joke if Emily said anything about the engagement. But telling her mom on her birthday was the one guaranteed way to talk only to her and not to her dad. She'd let her mother break the news to her father.

Taking her cell phone, she stood and walked over to the bunkhouse window.

Spring had arrived in full force with new green leaves on some of the trees, except the mesquites. Wildflowers were springing up here and there. The lovely pink flowers on the two redbud trees in Dub and Sue's backyard were mostly gone. But the Texas mountain laurel shrubs were in full bloom. Medium green, shiny leaves provided a nice backdrop to the beautiful deep purple flower clusters.

Emily waited as her mother's secretary put her call through and her mother answered.

"Happy birthday, Mom."

"Why, thank you, Emily. What a nice surprise, as were the Yellow Rose Chocolates. Those are wonderful. I've already had six and hid the rest in my desk."

Emily chuckled, wondering how long it had been since she'd shared a laugh with her mother. "I thought you'd like them. Chance gave me some for Valentine's Day, and I thought I'd gone to chocolate heaven."

"Is Chance a cowboy there at the ranch?" Disapproval crept into her mother's voice.

Emily tried to ignore it and keep her tone light. "Chance Callahan, Dub and Sue's son. He's a rancher, Mom. There's a difference. He's also a successful builder, with his own company."

"Building houses in the toolies. How grand."

"Even people in the toolies need new homes. Especially now."

"How are things after the fire? Are folks beginning to recover?"

"Slowly. They've received almost a million dollars worth of donations, some of it in money and some in goods. We're hearing of people in churches around the state, even some other states, who plan to come in and help build houses.

"Chance is already building two houses for folks who had insurance. He has contracts for two more but is waiting for the permit on one. The other one will have to wait a month or so until he can shift some of his crew. He spent some time at first helping with the cleanup, then turned his attention to building."

"So is this Chance good-looking?" Depend on her mother to get to the important stuff — at least what she deemed important.

"Amazingly so. Six one, muscular, dark brown hair, and green eyes. He'll turn heads at your charity auction and gala."

"You're coming?" Her mother's voice rose an octave in surprise.

Emily grinned to herself. "If I'm invited. I hear it's a buffet, so you won't have to order more food." Although the way Chance ate, it might not hurt. "Supporting the homeless shelter is a worthy cause, and I'd like to help." She paused, hoping her mother would be receptive. "And I'd like to see you. I miss you, Mom."

"I'd like to see you too. But bringing your cowboy . . . do you think that's wise?"

Emily had expected the question. "I think you'll be pleasantly surprised. He can hold his own even with your friends." She thought she even managed to say it without contempt in her voice.

"It's a black-tie affair."

"I know. I'll take care of it. I promise he won't spit chewing tobacco in the punch bowl."

"Don't even joke about such a thing."

"He doesn't chew tobacco. Or smoke. Or even drink, for that matter. He's a good Christian man."

"He won't get all bent out of shape because there's alcohol, will he?" Poor Mom. One minute she was afraid Chance would do something uncouth, and the next she was worried he'd start preaching.

"No, ma'am. He knows what to expect. His family owns the largest ranch in this area, plus they have oil. Grandpa Doyle has known his father for years."

Her mom sniffed as if something stunk. "Doyle knows a lot of people. Many of them would be a disaster at my party."

"I promise, he'll be fine."

"What about you? I'll never forgive you if you cause a scene."

Emily took a deep breath, releasing it slowly, biting back the retort on the tip of her tongue. "Have I ever caused a scene?"

"Well, no. Not that I can recall. But you have a way of letting people know of your displeasure without saying much."

"Just the way you taught me. I'm working on not being so critical. I might slip up, but bear with me, I'm trying. I'll be on my best behavior." It would help to have Chance with her. She didn't want to look like a brat in front of him.

"What brought this on?"

"God pointed out to me that I was being judgmental and that it was wrong. So I'm trying to change."

"As simple as that?"

Emily laughed. "It isn't simple. It's hard. But I want to be a better person. I want our relationship to be better, to be based on mutual respect. Focusing on the good we see in each other and not the things we disagree on will help that."

"But you still think me being in the

fashion industry is frivolous."

Did she?

"No, actually, I don't. I dislike the emphasis people put on being fashionable, but I enjoy finding new styles when I go to the store. I know that all the shows and ads may have helped make the clothes I like available. So when I've put you down in the past, I've been hypocritical. You love what you do, and you're good at it. I've been wrong to criticize your career. You take care of the people you represent and those in your office. You also use your position as a platform to help a lot of people. And that makes me proud of you."

It was true, though she hadn't realized it until she spoke the words. "I'm different since the fire. Looking back on that day, I realize I was in more danger than I thought at the time." She hadn't told her mother about stubbornly trying to rescue things from the museum. If her parents knew, they would never let her hear the end of it. "I've also discovered that I'm a compassionate person."

"You always have been, Emily." Her mother's voice had softened minutely. "That's why you had trouble with your peers in school. You felt sorry for the person who didn't belong, the one who was on the outside of the group. You always wanted to include them, and it only brought you trouble."

"Maybe that was part of it. But mainly I just didn't like the people you and Dad wanted me to hang out with. Most of them were self-centered jerks."

"True, but there were a few good ones."

Had she heard right? Emily could only remember her mother criticizing someone in the group one time. Her mother was too concerned about offending any of the influential people within their sphere of acquaintance to risk anything negative getting back to them. "Mom, are you all right?"

"Just having an introspective day. Isn't that what you're supposed to do when you turn fifty? Look back at your life?"

"I don't know. I'm not fifty."

Her mother laughed, but it sounded hollow, almost sad. "That's good. If you were, I'd be seventy-four."

"And the most beautiful seventy-four-year-old ever." She waited for a comment, but none came. Emily concluded she'd been distracted by something. That happened often when they talked, especially when she was at work.

"Your father is trading me in on a new model," her mother said quietly. "Literally."

25

"What!" Emily almost dropped the phone. She walked to the closest table, pulled out a chair with a shaky hand, and sat down.

"A twenty-four-year-old from my agency. Cover and runway," she added, which told Emily the woman was following in her mother's shoes in more ways than one.

"She's younger than me." Emily was momentarily stunned, then decided she shouldn't be. Her father had always had an eye for pretty ladies, particularly those in their twenties. An incident from her early childhood had caused her to suspect that he hadn't stopped with looking at them.

"I've known he was seeing her for some time, but we finally talked about it this morning. He's filing for divorce."

"He told you on your birthday." Her father was a harsh, self-centered man, but this was over the top even for him. "That's Dad. Such a sweet, sentimental guy."

Closing her eyes, Emily tried to calm the rage that swept through her. She had never liked him. She didn't think she'd ever loved him, certainly not in the way that Jenna and her brothers loved Dub. That had been bad enough. But this felt like hate, and it made her sick to her stomach. *Please God, help me not to feel this way about him.* She needed to forgive him for all the hurt, but she hadn't been able to.

"I confronted him." Her mother sighed. "I wanted it out in the open and over with. I'm relieved. I didn't realize what a heavy weight our marriage had become. We've never loved each other, though at the beginning we were greatly attracted to each other. Still, it was more of a business arrangement than anything. He wanted a beautiful wife, and I wanted a rich husband who moved in elite circles."

"Why? You already had money and a great modeling career."

"I needed security. I'd gotten used to moving within the moneyed set. I didn't want to lose that. I've been a benefit to him over the years, as he has to me. But as my daddy used to say, it's time to fish or cut bait. Clark is moving out today. And in with her, I expect. I wish her luck. She'll need it."

"Are you keeping the house?"

"For now. He doesn't want it, and I'd just as soon sell it. But that will happen later. Our attorneys can hash all that out in due time."

Her mother sounded too happy. Emily wondered if she was trying to hide her true feelings. "Are you okay? Do you want me to come stay a few days?"

"There's no need. I appreciate your concern, but I'm really doing fine. I'm going to be free of him, Emily. You can't know how good that feels." The chair creaked. "Then again, perhaps you do. I've expected this for years. As long as he doesn't get mean and ornery, we should be able to resolve everything amicably."

"Moving in the same circles afterward could be a little dicey."

"People in our world do it all the time. There is no reason your father and I can't stay within the larger circle and remain civil to each other. I expect he'll come to the gala. I told him it wasn't necessary, but he thinks he should make an appearance. Make a grand show of support for the cause so he looks good."

"You'll both put up a good front, but people will know about the divorce by then."

"It won't matter. We're a cynical bunch.

People know about his affair already. That's how I found out. However, attending the party might be hard on you."

"I can handle it. I want to be there to support you now more than ever."

"Thank you, dear. Are you and your rancher staying with Doyle and Iris?" It was a natural assumption. Emily hadn't stayed with her parents when she visited Dallas since she'd finished college.

"That's the plan. I assume that you'll be swamped with last-minute details for the auction."

"As always. But if you can stay in town a while on Sunday, I'd like for you and Chance to come over for lunch."

"We'll do that. Have you talked to Grandma Rose?"

"She called a bit ago to wish me happy birthday." Her mother sighed. "I didn't have the courage to tell her about the divorce. She'll be upset."

"Probably. Though she might surprise you. She never has liked Dad."

"I'm well aware of that."

"She misses you."

"She washed her hands of me years ago."

"If that were true, she wouldn't have called you on your birthday. It won't be easy to patch things up between you two, but I hope you'll try. She's not getting any younger."

"Is she ill?" There was a note of worry in her mother's voice.

"Not that I know of. I saw her a couple of months ago, and she seemed fine. But the way things are between you two hurts her."

"I know you think she walks on water, but she's hurt me plenty too."

Emily rubbed her forehead, where a king-sized headache was setting in. "I know. I just want y'all to make peace with each other."

"Like you're trying to do with me," her mom said, surprisingly without sarcasm.

"Yes." She wanted the kind of relationship Dub and Sue had with their kids, but she didn't think blurting that out would help. "I don't want to spend the rest of my life constantly being at odds with you."

"Nor I you. I'm willing to try, Emily."

"That's all I'm asking." Her head pounded, but her heart felt lighter. On that score anyway. "Do you want me to tell Grandma Rose?"

"I guess you'd better. Otherwise, she'll get wind of it somehow. But wait a few days."

"So you won't get chewed out on your birthday." Emily didn't envy her mom. Rose was liable to give her what-for.

"And I need some time to regroup before I do battle with her."

"I don't blame you. Do Grandpa and Grandma Denny know?"

"Yes. Iris called earlier. She was concerned about me. They're angry with Clark. It's a shame such kind people have an overbearing, egotistical, self-centered son. Although these days, they freely admit they're much to blame. They gave him everything he ever wanted, right down to setting him up in his medical practice."

"So he expects to have his way in everything."

"I soon learned that challenging him wasn't an option. He never retaliated physically, but as you know, he has other ways of making life difficult. It was easier to give in or support him, even though I didn't always agree."

Emily heard a soft thump, like a drawer shutting. Was her mom digging into the candy again? "Did you stop him from locking me in the basement?"

"Yes."

Any other time, the quiet sound of chewing in her ear would have made Emily laugh. Instead, knowing her mother had stood up for her brought tears to her eyes. She'd always wondered if Miranda had intervened or if her father had changed his mind after she'd been left there overnight. The sound of her fastidious mother licking her fingers brought a smile despite the tears rolling down her cheeks. Emily cleared the lump from her throat. "Thank you."

"I threatened to leave him and take you with me. Obviously, keeping me as his wife meant more to him then. I hadn't been aware of how you were being treated. I'm ashamed that I was too busy to notice. I'm sorry, Emily."

"It's all right, Mom." Not really, but she wasn't going to heap more guilt on her mother. "I think Nanny and Dad went out of their way to hide it from you. They took me down the back stairs if you were home."

"But why didn't you cry or scream? Surely I would have heard you." It sounded as if her mother was tapping a pen on the desk.

"After the first couple of times, I learned that if I made any noise, I had to stay down there longer."

The tapping stopped. "How often did it happen?"

"I don't know. It seemed like a lot, but that may be a childishly distorted view. I'm guessing every month or two, starting a few days after my fourth birthday."

Her mother gasped. "That often? How do

you know it started then?"

"Nanny knocked that pretty music box Dad gave me off my dressing table and it broke." An image flashed through her mind of her father kissing the nanny and bumping the table. She'd never mentioned it to her mother, even after she got older. "They blamed me."

"They?" Her mom's voice was instantly sharp, alert.

Emily cringed. She hadn't meant to let that slip. *Lord, I hope I'm doing the right thing.* "I was supposed to be watching *Sesame Street* in my playroom, but I wanted Teddy to come watch too. When I walked into my bedroom to get my bear, Dad was kissing her and they bumped the table. I saw the music box fall off and started crying.

"I'm not sure how everything happened after that. I just remember Dad yelling at me, telling me what a naughty little girl I was and that I had to be punished. He carried me down to the basement and put me in the storeroom. He said if I ever told anybody about him being there with Nanny, he'd send me to live with mean trolls in a forest far away."

Emily had never heard her mother swear — but she did now. She held the phone away from her ear for a good thirty seconds while Miranda vented.

"I suspected they were up to something, especially when he got so riled because I fired her. But what makes me hot as Hannah's hairbrush is that he told me you had only been punished like that a few times. I should have known he was lying. I should have left him then." She huffed out a breath. "I suppose it's too late to have him arrested for child endangerment."

Emily laughed. She didn't know how it was possible under the circumstances, but her mother's comment cracked her up. "I could put my hair in pigtails and dress like a little kid if you think it would help."

Her mother chuckled. "Probably not. We can't nail his hide to the wall for that, but I've decided I won't make this process easy for him. He's going to pay dearly for the mental anguish he's caused us."

Emily was tempted to point out that her mother had caused her mental anguish too, but that wouldn't help matters. "Don't turn it into World War III. That won't be good for anybody."

"Perhaps not, but winning a few battles to show him he can't walk on me will be extremely satisfying. Now, I should go. I have a meeting in ten minutes. It will be good to see you when you come to Dallas.

Oh, I forgot to ask. How is your project coming along?"

"It's going well. Amazingly well." She quickly filled her in on Chance donating a building and about the Bradley-Tucker House. "We've finished cataloging everything, and I've started setting up exhibits at the museum."

"Will you be there longer than originally planned?"

"Yes. Until the first of June." Unless she and Chance stayed there after they got married.

"Have you heard about the new McGovern Museum here in Dallas?"

"Yes, ma'am. I interviewed for the assistant curator position a couple of weeks ago. I'm in the final three, but I don't know when they'll make a decision."

"So that's why you were in Dallas. I'm sorry I couldn't do lunch."

"It's okay. Your secretary explained that you had an emergency."

"What a mess. I don't want to even think about it. I hope you get the new job. It's ridiculous for you to keep working on these small-town, inconsequential projects. Since you're determined to do this museum thing, you need to be involved in something worth your time and education."

Emily bit back an angry retort. "Callahan Crossing's museum is worthwhile to the people who live here, and it will be to those who visit." Thankfully, her irritation didn't come across in her voice. "The town and the museum may be small, but they have a rich history that's worth preserving. I'm not wasting my time or my education. And it adds to my resume."

She was also having the most wonderful time of her life.

"Your resume will stand out much more if you're an assistant at the McGovern."

"True." Emily didn't want to get into the same old argument.

"I hope it works out for you."

"Thank you."

"I've been thinking about how lovely it is on the Riviera this time of year. All those handsome, tanned young men . . ."

"Mom!"

"Don't be such a prude, Emily. I'm free now. Not legally but in every other way. If I want to have dinner with a handsome man, I will."

Emily wasn't so sure her mother would stop at dinner, but she didn't dare say anything about it. They didn't share the same beliefs. Nothing would stir her mother's ire quicker than if she thought Emily was preaching at her. "Just make him old enough to be my father, or at least close to it. I'll have to see a psychiatrist if both my parents date people my age."

"I'll keep that in mind," her mother said dryly. "*Ciao,* dear."

"Bye, Mom." Emily hung up and laid the phone on the table. "I'm a coward." Miranda was practically dancing with joy, which had Emily mildly unnerved. Still, she was afraid telling her mother about the engagement would be overload.

Looking down at her ring, she blew out a deep breath. "Guess she'll learn I'm getting married when I wave this lovely ring in her face."

26

That evening, Chance was channel surfing on the muted TV when he heard a knock at the back door, followed by it opening and Emily calling his name.

"I'm in the living room." He hopped up and walked into the kitchen as she came in.

"Hi, darlin'. I thought you were going to the Ladies' Night Out at church."

"I begged off with a headache."

He studied her white, drawn face and decided more than a headache was bothering her. "What's wrong, sweetheart?"

"My parents are getting a divorce."

"Aw, Emily. I'm sorry to hear that." He drew her into his arms and held her close for a minute. "Let's go sit in the living room. Do you want something to drink?"

She lowered her hands to her sides. "Do you have any hot chocolate?"

Not what he'd choose on a warm spring day, but if that's what she wanted, that's what she'd get. "If a mix is okay."

"Sure. Just go heavy on the chocolate."

"When did you find out about your folks?" He retrieved the milk from the refrigerator and the can of hot chocolate mix from the pantry.

"This morning when I called Mom." She stuffed her hands into her jean pockets.

Taking a mug from the cabinet, he spooned a generous amount of the mix into it. "Isn't today her birthday?"

"Yes. She'd heard he was having an affair and confronted him about it."

Chance grimaced as he added milk to the mug. "Not a great way to celebrate a birthday."

Emily watched as he put the mug into the microwave to heat. "I think it is for her. She sounded slightly subdued when we first started talking. Said she was having a bit of an introspective day. But after she told me they were splitting up, she sounded brighter, happier."

"Maybe she was worried about telling you." The microwave beeped and he removed the mug. He stirred the hot chocolate until all the lumps disappeared. "Want marshmallows?" She shook her head. "A shot of whipped cream?"

That earned him a small, but real, smile.

"That would be nice."

He took the can of cream from the fridge and squirted a big thick white swirl on top of the chocolate. "You're liable to have a moo-stash."

"Is that what Zach calls it?"

He nodded and handed her the cup. "Only he stretches out the moo part. Do you want a spoon?"

"No, thanks. The cream will fall flat in a few minutes anyway."

Chance grabbed a paper napkin from a drawer, handed it to her, and motioned toward the living room. He could always offer to lick off her milk moustache, but that wouldn't be very polite even on a normal day. Fun, but not GC — gentlemanly correct — a phrase he had just made up, but one he thought his mother would like. Emily was feeling low tonight and probably vulnerable. He needed to be extra careful that offering comfort didn't lead to anything else. Wisdom courtesy of a lesson learned by Grandpa Aidan.

She sat down on the couch, and he joined her, clicking off the television. Taking a sip of the hot chocolate, she wound up with a white dab on the tip of her nose. "Maybe the whipped cream wasn't such a good idea."

"Sorry." He watched her swipe it off with the napkin. There had to be some good in a man who could craft such a perfect nose. Maybe being a fine plastic surgeon was his only redeeming quality. "So your mom's okay with the divorce. What about your dad?"

"I don't know. He's moving out. Mom said he's probably going to move in with his girlfriend, so I assume he's happy. I suppose I should call him, but my feelings or opinions have never mattered to him. And I don't think I could talk to him calmly. I want to scream at him for being such a jerk." She took another sip of cocoa, managing not to coat her nose this time.

"That's understandable. Not only is he in the wrong, but he's hurting other people. Maybe not your mother so much but you."

She pushed her tennis shoes off with her toes and propped her green-sock-covered feet up on the coffee table. "That's what I can't figure out. I shouldn't care. I don't think I've ever loved him. I know I've never liked him. It's wrong and sad, but I don't want to ever see him again."

"Right now." He put his feet on the coffee table too. Big white socks next to green ones. Nice and homey. "You'll change your mind after things have settled down."

"I don't think so. After staying with Dub and Sue, it's only worse. Y'all love each other and get along so well. Your dad is such a good man, and he has a wonderful relationship with all of you, including Nate. Even before this last news, I was jealous of what y'all have."

Chance drank some iced tea, pondering whether or not to share a few family secrets. In reality, they weren't really all that secret from anyone who had known them for a long time. And she was going to be a member of the family. "Dad wasn't always the loving, patient man he is today. When we were growing up, he was more like a tyrant, and he had a quick temper."

"You're kidding." Setting her mug on the table, she shifted around until she faced him, curling her legs up on the couch. "That's hard to imagine."

"He's mellowed the last fifteen years. When we were younger, we knew he loved us, but the least little thing could make him angry as a teased rattlesnake. He was a controller too. Nate recently told me that during high school, Dad caught him watchin' Jenna with his heart in his eyes. She's always been Dad's princess, and he was determined she was going to marry somebody important. He flat out told Nate

428

that he wasn't good enough for her."

"And Nate believed him?"

"We'd all been friends since we were little, but he was working here at the time. Coming from the boss, who was also her dad, maybe had more impact. He was just a kid, and in awe of my old man. In awe of Jenna too, I think, despite being close. He also considered her the Callahan princess and figured he could never give her the kind of life she deserved."

"But they're so happy. Everybody can see that they're perfect for each other."

"Now. They might not have been back then. I'm a firm believer that love can overcome just about any obstacle, but I expect they both needed to do some growing up before they could make a go of marriage. It's a shame they had to experience a lot of heartache before they found each other again."

She picked up her cup. "What changed your dad?"

"The Lord mostly. And Pastor Brad. Last fall, when Nate was going through a rough time due to PTSD — post-traumatic stress disorder — us kids learned that Dad had it too, from Viet Nam. The folks had known he had a problem for years, though for a long time they didn't know what it was.

They worked through things mostly on their own with God's help.

"Later, they asked others to pray for them and went to Pastor Brad for counseling. The pastor has special training to work with people with PTSD, but he uses prayer and seeks the Lord's guidance too. God has used it all, plus some direct healing, to make Dad the man he is today."

"I never would have guessed anything like that had gone on." She was quiet for a few minutes, her expression thoughtful as she drank her hot chocolate. "I don't think my father is capable of truly caring about anyone else."

"What about his patients?"

"Not the rich women who come to him to look younger. That's all about money and pride, but he takes some cases for free. People who've been in accidents or have deformities."

"So he's not all bad."

"I suppose not. But I've never seen that goodness when it comes to family. Maybe that's what happens when a marriage is based on business and lust. By the time I was in middle school, I figured out I was born six months after the wedding. I weighed seven pounds, so nobody could claim I was a preemie.

ALLEN PARK PUBLIC LIBRARY

"I've tried all my life to please my dad, but he's never told me he was proud of me. Not once. He's never praised me for doing something well, no matter what I achieved. I've never been pretty enough, smart enough, anything enough."

"Maybe he felt forced into marriage and wrongly blames you."

She nodded, curling both hands around the mug. "I think he does. Mom told me once that before they got married he wanted her to have an abortion, but she refused. He thinks she did it to trap him, but she didn't. She would have kept me even if they hadn't gotten married."

"Who's the girlfriend?" He wished Emily would turn back around and scoot over next to him.

"A model with Mom's agency."

Chance winced and shook his head. "That's low."

"It gets worse. She's twenty-four. Two years younger than me."

He stared at her. "You're kidding."

"Afraid not."

"That's reason enough right there to be mad at him." And hurt. "It has to be embarrassing."

"It is. Plus she's done covers and runway, which means she's gorgeous."

ALLEN PARK PUBLIC LIBRARY

And once again, Emily wouldn't measure up in her father's eyes. Chance supposed it didn't matter much right now that he thought she was the most wonderful woman in the world. He reached over and took the mug from her hands, setting it on the table. "Come here."

When she unwound her legs and slid over next to him, he put his arm around her shoulders and pulled her close. "The only reason for you to be embarrassed is because your father is making a fool of himself. I may be a country boy, but I've been around the high and mighty some. When it comes right down to it, they aren't much different than anybody else when a man pulls a stunt like your dad has.

"They may be polite to his face and act like he hasn't done anything wrong, but they'll be talkin' plenty behind his back. The women will scorn him for what he's done to your mother and you and ridicule him for robbing the cradle. The men will congratulate him on his conquest, then mock him because he got taken in by a gold digger.

"You're a strong woman, Emily." He lightly caressed her arm. "And you have the Lord to help you through this. I know you're praying for wisdom and guidance, and I'll do the same for you. It may be a while before you can talk to your dad one-on-one, but you'll go to that gala with your head held high. You'll be so beautiful and gracious that people will be in awe. If Clark shows up with his girlfriend, or insults you in some other way, I'll deck him."

She giggled and shifted her position, sliding her arms around his waist. "That would certainly stir things up, especially if you broke his nose. Who'd he get to fix it?"

"He'd probably try to do it himself. I wouldn't really hit him, even if I wanted to."

"I know. But I appreciate the thought." She looked up at him. "Does that make me bloodthirsty?"

"I think it makes you human."

"But not very Christlike," she said with a sigh, resting her head on his shoulder, her hair brushing his jaw.

"Suppose not. Are you going to visit your mother? Have some of that girl time you were talking about on the picnic?"

"She wants us to have lunch with her on Sunday after the party. Then she's going to spend some time on the French Riviera. I wouldn't put it past her to bring a handsome man home with her. She's a beautiful woman. All she has to do is smile, and men of all ages trip all over themselves to do her bidding. Of course, she might take one look at you and decide you're the one she wants."

Chance chuckled and felt her hand flutter against his chest. "Won't do her any good. The only woman I'm interested in is about to be kissed."

Emily lifted her head and looked up at him, her eyes alight with love. "She is?"

"I intend to do a thorough job of it too."

And he did — within GC constraints, of course.

27

Ten days later as Emily dressed for the gala, she was still thinking about the day she'd heard about her parents' divorce. More specifically, she was remembering that evening when she'd gone to see Chance.

Hurting, angry, and needy, she'd turned to him for solace. And he had given it. The man had a way with comfort food. Macaroni and cheese or scrambled egg sandwiches for Jenna. Hot chocolate with whipped cream for her, despite it being sixty degrees outside.

More importantly, he had listened to her words and seen into her heart. He'd been angry on her behalf, ready to defend her against the one man who could wound her like no other. He had offered insight and words of wisdom, encouraged her when she felt beaten down, and brightened the darkness of a difficult day.

When he put his arms around her and

kissed her gently, the sorrows and frustrations of the day, the hurts of a lifetime, vanished in a sweetness unlike anything she'd ever known. Her heart sang with joy and ached with longing for this man, for his strength and gentleness, for his steadiness and passion.

That night a new passion had flared between them the instant his lips touched hers. They both kept control, although it wasn't easy. In years past, she would have yielded to her desire, especially one so powerful.

But as Chance had once reminded her, she was a new creature in Christ. One who struggled with all sorts of issues, but who earnestly sought to live the way God wanted her to. Still, it was a good thing they'd decided on a very short engagement and were planning the wedding for the first day of May.

Her mother would probably faint when Emily told her she was getting married in three weeks. She hoped her mom could clear her schedule and be there. The date was set, and Emily wasn't going to change it.

They'd reserved Grace Community Church in Callahan Crossing, and Jenna and Lindsey had agreed to stand up with her. Along with Sue, they'd gone to Abilene a couple of times looking for dresses. On the second trip, Emily found the perfect wedding gown, and the others found what they wanted too.

With all the wedding interruptions, Emily hadn't accomplished as much as she needed to at the museum. She told Sue and the Historical Society board that she would refund them the money they had paid her and finish the job for free. Whether she did that driving home from Dallas on weekends or settled in as the newest permanent citizen of Callahan Crossing remained to be seen.

She had not heard anything more about the position at the McGovern. It didn't worry her because she was too busy enjoying life.

That was a sobering, thought-provoking situation. She had never been happier, and not only because of Chance and their love. For the first time, she felt as if she belonged — to a family who loved her unconditionally, to a church small enough to recognize every face, to a town that welcomed her as one of their own.

The part of her that had worked so long toward her goal still hoped she would be offered the job at the McGovern. But she no longer needed to prove to her father that she was worth something. She really didn't care what he thought.

After she put on the dangling diamond butterfly earrings her grandmother had loaned her, she walked across the large guest room, one of six, and studied her reflection in the long mirror. She had pulled her hair back in a chignon at the base of her neck. The simple style complemented the classic shape of her violet gown. Her only jewelry was the diamond earrings and her engagement ring. She looked good and felt confident. With Chance by her side, she could conquer the world.

And even her parents, she thought wryly.

Some people, her mother included, thrived in this kind of life. Emily didn't. She could put up with the glamour and glitz on occasion, and possibly even enjoy the evening, especially when Chance was with her. If she moved up in the museum world, attendance at these functions would be mandatory. That was one more thing in favor of small-town life.

Picking up her small rhinestone bag, she moved toward the doorway. "It's really not such a hard choice at all, is it, Lord?" she murmured.

Chance was waiting for her when she walked into her grandparents' living room.

He whistled softly. "You look incredible." Turning to her grandfather, whose face glowed with approval, he said, "Isn't she the most beautiful woman you've ever seen?"

Grandpa Doyle chuckled and glanced at her grandmother. "Now, son, don't put me on the spot like that. She's lovely, but so is my wife."

Chance grinned and winked at Grandma Iris. "Yes, sir. Both of them are incredible."

Grandma laughed and hooked her arm through her husband's, something Emily noticed she did more and more. "I was a looker when I was Emily's age, but she takes the prize these days. Spin around once, dear."

Meeting her grandmother's twinkling eyes, Emily turned around slowly. When she faced Chance again, the dear man looked dumbstruck. Finally he found his voice and eloquently proclaimed, "Wow."

Emily laughed and her grandmother practically cackled. "Is that all you can say, boy?" Grandma Iris asked, nudging Emily's grandpa with her elbow. "Good thing he's already proposed. He'd be too tongue-tied to do it now."

Chance's face turned a ruddy red, but he grinned and went along with their teasing. "I'm stickin' to you like glue tonight, sweetheart, 'cause you're gonna need a bodyguard."

"And you're just the man to do it." Grandpa Doyle slapped Chance on the back. "I'm mighty glad our Emily found you."

"So am I, sir. So am I."

Emily watched in amusement as Chance studied the architecture of the Pavilion Ballroom in the prestigious Rosewood Mansion on Turtle Creek. He glanced at her and smiled. "Do I look like a gawkin' country bumpkin?"

"You, sir, look absolutely gorgeous." She hadn't been surprised to see him in a western-style tuxedo and black cowboy boots. The black coat, black vest, and crisp white shirt with a black crossover tie suited him perfectly. The only other man in the room dressed in a similar fashion was her grandfather, which pleased her immensely. Confident and fiercely independent. That described them both. "Personally, I'm glad you're more interested in the arched windows than all of these low-cut gowns."

"Darlin', I only see one woman in this room, and that's you. Everybody else fades away in comparison."

"Such flattery." She curled her hand

around his. "I'm lovin' it."

"It's not flattery." He looked down at the floor. "Great tile. This is quite the place. Interesting how they've combined modern design elements with the original Italian Renaissance style. It's hard to imagine that it was a private home for years."

A couple who looked vaguely familiar walked by, smiled, and said hello. They had the same expression on their faces that she probably had on hers — *I think I'm supposed to know you, but I don't have a clue who you are.* She was glad they didn't stop. That had happened three times in the five minutes they'd been in the ballroom.

"Do you see anything on the live auction list that you want to bid on?" She held the sheet of paper where they could both study it.

"That trip to St. Thomas would make a great honeymoon. I've never been there. Have you?"

"No. Let's bid on it. We might wind up spending more than if we simply booked a trip on our own, but that's all right." When he put his arm around her, she leaned lightly against him. "It's also first on the list so we can make our getaway after that if we want to."

"You don't see anything else that you're

interested in?"

"Not really. Sports memorabilia doesn't do anything for me. I don't need a new shotgun."

He chuckled close to her ear. "But they're a matching His and Hers set. We'd look cute totin' them together."

"You want a shotgun, you buy one. I don't want one."

"I'm still going to teach you to shoot."

"But I don't need a fancy gun for that. None of the jewelry is my style. All the restaurant packages are here in Dallas. Too far to drive just for dinner. Though we might bid on some of the sports tickets or packages."

He eased the list from her hand, drawing her attention. "What do you mean it's too far to drive for dinner? It won't be if we're living here."

"The Lord and I had another little talk earlier. I would have told you sooner, but I couldn't talk in the car with the grandparents. And since we've been in here, we kept getting almost interrupted."

"So talk fast."

"I don't belong here, Chance. Callahan Crossing is my home now."

"What about the museum job?" He nodded politely to a middle-aged woman who ogled him as she walked slowly by.

Emily wanted to tell her to close her mouth or she'd catch flies, but she'd promised to behave. "I hope I'm offered the job, just for the pleasure of knowing I was chosen. That's prideful, I suppose, but it would be nice to have my abilities recognized. Still, I won't take it. It might be interesting, but I'll be happier being the unpaid curator at the Callahan Crossing Museum.

"In retrospect, I realize I was trying to please my parents, particularly my dad, more than I was me. The way things are now, to borrow one of Grandma Rose's sayings, I don't give a hoot nor a holler what my dad thinks."

"I could kiss you right now." He smiled as big as a politician in a runoff.

"Better not. Mom alert. She's heading our way. She's the blonde in the green strapless gown with the beading on the front." She looked even more beautiful than the last time Emily had seen her. This time, however, with admiration and love glowing in Chance's eyes when he smiled down at her, Emily felt on equal footing with her mother.

"I would have known her anyway. There's a striking family resemblance. How old did you say she is?" Chance asked with a hint of disbelief. He lowered his arm and shifted slightly, putting a little space between them.

"Fifty last week." She barely looked forty. "She works out religiously and takes good care of herself, but she's the best example of my dad's skill."

"Who'll she see now?"

"Good question." Emily smiled and lifted her head slightly under her mother's scrutiny. "Hi, Mom." She kissed the air beside her mother's cheek. And Miranda did the same. Couldn't mess up the makeup or wrinkle a gown with a hug.

"Hello, Emily. You look lovely tonight, dear."

Emily caught her breath at the unexpected compliment. She waited a second for a *but* . . . When it didn't come, she did a mental reboot. "Thank you. So do you, as always."

"So, this is your cowboy." Her mother gave Chance an appraising once-over. Nodding her approval, she smiled her most enticing smile. "Very nice. If you want to go into advertising, let me know. You'd make a lot more money than you do herding cows."

Emily barely kept from rolling her eyes. "Chance, this is my mother, Miranda Denny. Mom, this is Chance Callahan."

Her mother held out her hand, and

444

Chance shook it. "Nice to meet you, ma'am. You're as beautiful as Emily said you were."

Her mother's eyes sparkled. "I like a man who knows how to compliment a woman and make it sound sincere."

"I don't say things I don't mean, ma'am." He gave her his most charming smile.

Her mother stared, and Emily barely held back a laugh.

"I absolutely must sign you with my agency."

"No, thanks." He flashed that smile again, with a spark of mischief added. "I like herdin' cows, and I don't need the money. I have plenty." He put his arm around Emily's shoulders. "My fiancée has a bunch too."

Well, that takes care of that, Emily thought ruefully. So much for worrying about how to break the news to her mother.

Miranda's eyes grew round. She looked at Emily and back at him. "Your wh-what?"

"Fiancée."

Emily dutifully held out her hand to show her the ring. "Isn't it beautiful? It was his great-great-grandmother's. She was married to Aidan, who established the sixty-thousand-acre ranch the Callahans still own." She leaned closer to her mother and

445

said quietly, "Don't worry, Mom. He's rich."

Her mother frowned up at Chance. "You are?"

"Cattle, oil, land, buildings." He smiled lazily. "Typical Texan."

"I know a lot of typical Texans who don't have a row to hoe," her mother snapped. "Emily, what about all your education and your career?"

"I'll do some things here and there. I'm really happy in Callahan Crossing." Despite the curious stares of those around them, Emily wasn't going to back down. "Mom, I love him. And he loves me," she said softly.

"Just like a man, expecting you to give up your life's goals for his."

"He volunteered to move here, but I said no."

"He did?" Her mother studied him for a moment, then focused on Emily. "How could you say no to that?"

"I've discovered I'm a country girl at heart. I love the town, the people, the ranch." She shrugged and smiled at her mother. "You had to go from the country to the big city to find happiness. I had to do it the other way around."

"Who says I found happiness?" her mother said under her breath. She tapped her foot, her gaze flickering back and forth between them. Emily could practically see the wheels turning in her mind. "Do you really love my daughter?"

"Yes, ma'am. With all my heart."

People were beginning to murmur and shift around, trying to see what was going on. Emily smiled to herself. Dallas or Callahan Crossing, folks were the same all over. Nosy.

"All right. We'll start making wedding plans tomorrow over lunch."

"We've already made wedding plans, Mom," Emily said gently. This might be harder than breaking the news about the engagement. "May 1 at our church in Callahan Crossing. Nice and simple." Surprising tears misted her eyes. "I really, really hope you'll be there."

"But I have to plan the wed—" Her mother stopped, glanced down at the floor, and looked back up again with a watery smile. "I'll be there."

Chance quickly handed her his handkerchief, and she dabbed her eyes, being careful not to smear the mascara.

"Thank you, Mom." Emily hugged her gently.

"The dress, dear, don't wrinkle the dress." But her mother hugged her back and handed her the handkerchief. "Looks like you need this now." Her eyes shifted toward the doorway, and she grimaced. "Drat. It's time to deal with the devil. Here comes your father."

Emily blotted her eyes and stuffed the handkerchief in her purse as she looked up at Chance. "Hope you don't sneeze."

"I brought a spare."

She laughed and hooked her arm through his. "I should have known." Her grandmother and grandfather casually moved behind them. They chatted with someone but were really moving closer to lend their support.

Before her father reached them, Sylvia Hanson, the director of the McGovern Museum, came hurrying over. "Emily, how nice to see you here. And how fortuitous. I can give you the good news now instead of calling you on Monday."

Emily's father stepped into their little group. He nodded a greeting to Emily, glanced curiously at Chance, and turned to Ms. Hanson. "What good news?"

Ms. Hanson shot him a quick glance and returned her attention to Emily. "Emily, we'd like to offer you the position as assistant curator at the McGovern. The three finalists all had similar qualifications, though personally I liked yours a bit better than the others. What put you on top, however, was your interview. You were by far the most articulate and personable of the whole group. And how poised and beautiful you look tonight. You'll be a tremendous asset to the McGovern."

She was the best! A thrill zipped through her.

"Finally," her father said, with more than a hint of sarcasm.

Her mother beamed her a smile of obvious pride, bringing healing right along with it.

"It's about time you used all that education for something besides digging through a bunch of old worthless junk in Podunkville." Wearing his usual disapproving expression, her father shook his head. "Who cares if century-ago cowboys chased a bunch of longhorns around on the prairie, set up a few worthless ranches, and built a dozen pathetic little towns?"

"I do!" Emily, Chance, and Ms. Hanson all answered in unison.

Still smiling politely for the benefit of the crowd, Miranda muttered, "Shut up, Clark."

"Why should I?"

Did the man have any idea how childish he sounded?

449

Before Emily could correct her father, Ms. Hanson turned on him like a mama bear protecting her cubs. "Because you obviously don't know what you're talking about, Dr. Denny. So please do be quiet."

As her father sputtered, Emily felt Chance's hand lightly press against her side. He leaned down close to her ear. "You can still change your mind, darlin'."

Though she felt the tiniest twinge of regret at forgoing the job, she smiled and shook her head. "Thank you for the opportunity, Ms. Hanson, but I'll pass on your kind offer." She shifted a little closer to Chance, a movement the other woman didn't miss. "My plans have changed."

Ms. Hanson's gaze flickered to Emily's engagement ring, to Chance, and back to her. An approving smile slowly spread across her face. "I see."

"Well, I don't," her father blustered. "You can't refuse the only good job offer you've had. I won't allow it."

Emily desperately wished she had a sock she could stuff in his mouth. Almost everyone in the room — around three hundred people — shifted this way and that to see what the commotion was all about. Wondering if a handkerchief would do just as well, she was about to open her purse when

Chance moved to her father's side.

Smiling cordially, he put his hand on her dad's shoulder and gripped it hard. "It's not up to you, sir," he said congenially.

Her dad flinched beneath Chance's powerful hand. Her sweetie hadn't lugged all that lumber or wrestled all those cows for nothing.

"Who are you?" Her father's voice was strained.

Steely resolve replaced Chance's smile. "Chance Callahan. The man who is going to marry your daughter."

"What? She's not —" Her father flinched again as Chance's fingers dug in deeper.

"Now, sir, you'll apologize to Emily for embarrassing her in front of all these people."

Her father tried to pull away, but Chance held on tight. "You should include your wife in that apology."

He shook his head, glaring first at her mother, then her.

Anger flashed across Chance's face, and Emily caught her breath.

"Dr. Denny," Chance said quietly. "You're trying my patience. If I break your nose, who will you get to fix it?"

That did it. The color drained from her father's face.

Since Emily had made the same comment the night she told him about her parents' divorce, she bit back a laugh. She knew he'd never hit her father, but her dad didn't.

"Sorry, Emily, Miranda," he mumbled. As apologies went, it wasn't much, but it was likely the first time he'd ever said the word. It was good enough.

Chance looked at her, and she nodded. "Dr. Denny, I suggest you leave right away. And exit quietly, please." He lowered his hand to his side.

Her father adjusted his coat, and ignoring all of them, started toward the exit. A beautiful young woman stepped from behind the crowd and joined him.

"Why, that cad! He did bring her." The room was silent as they neared the door, and Miranda hollered, "See you in court."

Emily buried her face against Chance's chest. So much for not causing a scene. He put his arms around her and held her gently.

Someone clapped, and within seconds, the whole room thundered with applause. When Emily came out of hiding, her mother winked at her and strolled to the stage with the poise and style of all her years of runway.

Reaching the podium, Miranda smiled at the crowd. "That should keep y'all talking for a few days." After the laughter died down, her smile faded too. "I apologize for our little family drama. I do have some good news to share before you return to the buffet and go back to talking politics and football . . . or about next week's parties. I expect some of you remember my daughter, Emily." Several people nodded, though Emily only recognized a few of them. "I'm pleased to announce her engagement to Chance Callahan of Callahan Crossing."

After polite applause, most folks got back to whatever they were doing before the Denny fiasco. However, within five minutes, over two dozen couples surrounded Emily and Chance to offer their congratulations. She recognized a handful as acquaintances of her parents. A few were people she had gone to school with. But the majority either knew Chance and hadn't spotted him earlier, or they knew Dub. They were ranchers, oilmen, bankers, politicians, and other movers and shakers.

Her mother worked her way back through the crowd to her side. "How does he know all of these people?"

"He's a Callahan."

Grace Community Church was packed as Chance watched his beautiful bride walk down the aisle escorted by Grandpa Doyle. Her soft white gown had a modestly scooped neckline and tiny little sleeves. Venice lace appliqués trimmed the bodice and around the lower half of the skirt. The back of the skirt formed a short train. He didn't remember the name of the material, but it was soft and draped prettily. She wore her hair pinned up in curls on top of her head. Instead of a veil, a ribbon of bluebonnets circled the pile of curls. She carried a single yellow rose.

Jenna and Lindsey were already at the front of the church, wearing knee-length dresses in bright blue. Will and Nate stood on the groom's side. Chance considered them both his best men. Zach stood in front of Jenna, his expression solemn until he spotted the bride. "Emily!"

Jenna grabbed him before he raced down the aisle to meet his new aunt. Not that he knew what an aunt was. He just loved Emily.

Her mom and grandparents were there. Miranda and Grandma Rose were mending their fences, despite Emily's mother inviting a debonair Frenchman from the Riviera to escort her to the wedding.

Her father had ignored the whole thing. Chance had worried that it hurt Emily, but she seemed relieved because he wasn't there. Chance prayed that God would heal the wounds to her heart — and change Clark — so that reconciliation might happen someday.

He thought of the cartoons he had drawn right after the fire, the ones he had framed and hung in his home office. His heart pounded with excitement and nervousness, and he still had stars in his eyes.

Emily reached his side, and her grandfather placed her hand in his with a murmured, "God bless you."

Here they were, beautiful bride and lovestruck groom standing before the preacher.

Man meets woman. Man loves woman. Man marries woman.

When God had a plan and two hearts sought his will, it really was that simple.

ABOUT THE AUTHOR

Sharon Gillenwater was born and raised in West Texas, and loves to write about her native state. The author of several novels, she is a member of the American Christian Fiction Writers. When she's not writing, she and her husband enjoy spending time with their son, daughter-in-law, and adorable grandchildren.

The employees of Thorndike Press hope you have enjoyed this Large Print book. All our Thorndike, Wheeler, and Kennebec Large Print titles are designed for easy reading, and all our books are made to last. Other Thorndike Press Large Print books are available at your library, through selected bookstores, or directly from us.

For information about titles, please call:
  (800) 223-1244

or visit our Web site at:
  http://gale.cengage.com/thorndike

To share your comments, please write:
  Publisher
  Thorndike Press
  295 Kennedy Memorial Drive
  Waterville, ME 04901